ADVANCE PRAISE FOR AMAH AND THE SILK-WINGED PIGEONS

"Jocelyn Cullity's *Amah and the Silk-Winged Pigeons* highlights the lost history of the women descended from African slaves who fought so valiantly to save Lucknow during the famous 1857 resistance to English rule. Cullity—whose English family lived in India for five generations—infuses the grand narrative sweep of her story with poetic elegance, and succeeds in adjusting our lens on the past to illuminate a crucial part of Indian history."
—PRAJWAL PARAJULY, *The Gurkha's Daughter* and *Land Where I Flee*

"This book goes straight into the category of good historical fiction that brings the past vividly alive. Inspired by her own family's history, Jocelyn Cullity brings style and flair to an episode of the Great Uprising in India. Beautifully written and deeply researched, this debut novel will hold and intrigue its readers. Warmly recommended."
—ROSIE LLEWELLYN-JONES, *Engaging Scoundrels, True Tales of Old Lucknow*

"I admire the lucid, fluent prose and shimmering atmosphere of this novel, which in many ways recalls the best of E.M. Forster. Cullity's setting is redolent of Indian life, its tastes and smells, its colors and textures. She handles the themes of empire and cultural conflict with huge tact and clarity. Her storytelling is

first-rate. Jocelyn Cullity is a fresh voice, and *Amah and the Silk-Winged Pigeons* is a memorable achievement."
—JAY PARINI, *The Last Station*

"*Amah and the Silk-Winged Pigeons*, based on real people and events, is a novel prodigiously researched, in which the research is so thoroughly composted into character that we lose ourselves in the rich settings and these imagined lives. A wonderful read."
—JANET BURROWAY, *Writing Fiction: A Guide to Narrative Craft*

"Jocelyn Cullity's literary novel aims to address the absence of women's voices at a key historical moment in India. Focusing on Indian women's perspectives— through the eyes of a *begam*, a slave, and a group of courtesans —during the 1857 resistance to English rule in Lucknow, this book is a must-read."
—SALEEM KIDWAI, Islamic Studies Scholar; Co-Editor, *Same-Sex Love in India: Readings from Literature and History*

"Though I have read many historical accounts of this conflict, Jocelyn Cullity's novel is the first that immersed me in its reality, making me feel what it was like to live through those events; the level of realism and excitement were such that there were times I looked anxiously over my shoulder to see if the British soldiers were coming."
—CHINNA OOMMEN, former Senior Research Officer, National Council for Education, Research and Training (India), former Headmistress, The School, Chennai, India

Amah and the
Silk-Winged Pigeons

Long live
the BBC! :)
Jocelyn

a novel by
JOCELYN CULLITY

inanna poetry & fiction series

INANNA PUBLICATIONS AND EDUCATION INC.
TORONTO, CANADA

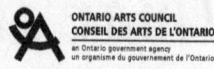

We gratefully acknowledge the support of the Canada Council for the Arts and the Ontario Arts Council for our publishing program. We also acknowledge the financial support of the Government of Canada.

Cover design: Val Fullard

Amah and the Silk-Winged Pigeons is a work of fiction. All the characters portrayed in this book are fictitious and any resemblance to persons living or dead is purely coincidental.

Note from the publisher: Care has been taken to trace the ownership of copyright material used in this book. The author and the publisher welcome any information enabling them to rectify any references or credits in subsequent editions.

Library and Archives Canada Cataloguing in Publication

Cullity, Jocelyn, author
    Amah and the silk-winged pigeons / a novel by Jocelyn Cullity.

(Inanna poetry & fiction series)
Issued in print and electronic formats.
ISBN 978-1-77133-437-2 (softcover).-- ISBN 978-1-77133-438-9 (epub).--
ISBN 978-1-77133-439-6 (Kindle).-- ISBN 978-1-77133-440-2 (pdf)

       I. Title. II. Series: Inanna poetry and fiction series

PS8605.U428A81 2017   C813'.6   C2017-905371-X
                                                  C2017-905372-8

Printed and bound in Canada

Inanna Publications and Education Inc.
210 Founders College, York University
4700 Keele Street, Toronto, Ontario, Canada M3J 1P3
Telephone: (416) 736-5356 Fax: (416) 736-5765
Email: inanna.publications@inanna.ca   Website: www.inanna.ca

For the women of Lucknow,
then and now.

Contents

...The city is in a state of tranquility .... Everything bids fair for the quiet introduction of our rule.
—Sir James Outram,
Chief Commissioner of Lucknow,
to Governor General Dalhousie, Calcutta, 1856

There was a time when showers of pearls were trodden underfoot / Now I feel the cruel sun above and pebbles underfoot.
—His Majesty, Wajid 'Ali Shah

Pea-fowls, partridges, and pandies rose together, but the latter gave the best sport.
—Colonel George Bouchier, C.B.

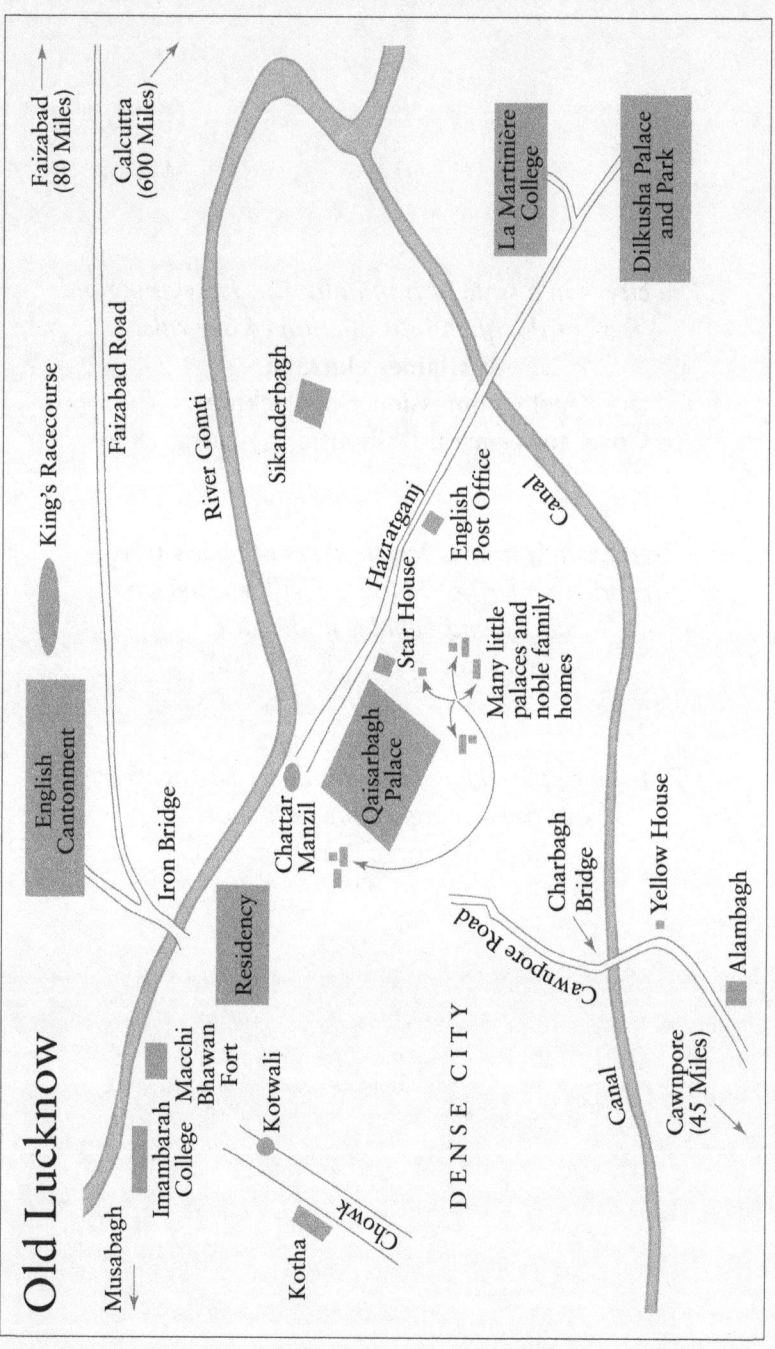

Old Lucknow

Faizabad → (80 Miles)

Calcutta ↗ (600 Miles)

King's Racecourse

Faizabad Road

River Gomti

English Cantonment

Iron Bridge

Musabagh ←

Imambarah College

Macchi Bhawan Fort

Residency

Kotwali

Chowk

Kotha

DENSE CITY

Chattar Manzil

Qaisarbagh Palace

Star House

Many little palaces and noble family homes

Sikanderbagh

Hazratganj

English Post Office

La Martinière College

Canal

Dilkusha Palace and Park

Cawnpore Road

Charbagh Bridge

Yellow House

Alambagh

Canal

Cawnpore → (45 Miles)

List of Characters

———⋄•••⋄———

Abhi — a wheat and barley merchant who lives in Lucknow

'Ali Shah — a *taluqdar* (village land-owner)

Amah — royal bodyguard and member of the Rose Platoon; of Ethiopian Muslim descent

Amah's grandmother — Muslim slave from Ethiopia purchased by the royal family in Lucknow; deceased

Amah's mother — of Ethiopian Muslim descent; married a Muslim man from Lucknow (deceased) and also had a son (deceased)

Begam Hazrat Mahal (Begam Sahiba) — divorced wife of King Wajid 'Ali Shah; of Ethiopian Muslim descent

Birjis — son of Begam Hazrat Mahal and Wajid 'Ali Shah

Fatima — Amah's cousin; of Ethiopian Muslim descent

Geeta — shopkeeper in the courtesans' shop

Gulbadan — Muslim woman who is the head of the *kotha*

Gulbadan's brother — a peasant

Hasan — Laila's son and Amah's cousin; of Ethiopian Muslim descent

Jai Lal Singh — courtier at Qaisarbagh Palace and army commander

Jang Bahadur Sahib — ruler of Nepal

Judea — a jeweller

Kasim — Amah's old cousin; of Ethiopian Muslim descent

Kavanagh — Irish soldier who works for the English East India Company

King Wajid 'Ali Shah — Muslim (Shi'a) King of Awadh; deposed by the English East India Company
The *Kotwal* — Lucknow's chief police officer
Laila — Amah's aunt; of Ethiopian Muslim descent
Lal — one of the Queen Mother's favourite advisors
Malamud — a young Tamil Hindu man from Madras
Nawab Mirza and Sharif-un-nissa — son and daughter of Wajid 'Ali Shah's brother by a slave girl
Mohammed — newspaper vendor
Mrs. Gunning — Englishwoman who lives in the cantonment
Nana Sahib — leader in Cawnpore
Neill, Brigadier General James — Scottish militant Christian who works for the English East India Company
Omar — Hasan's friend; a villager from Awadh who fought the English in Delhi
Pavan — poor Hindu man from Cawnpore area
Queen Mother — His Majesty Wajid 'Ali Shah's mother, Queen Mother of Awadh
Queen Victoria — Queen of England for sixty-four years; adopted the title, Empress of India, in 1876
Rasheed and Akbar — messengers between Lucknow and Calcutta
Red Man — nickname for John Graham, an officer in the English East India Company
Sai — Gulbadan's Muslim nephew who works at the *kotha* and milks goats around Lucknow, including in the English cantonment
Shahzadi — Begam Sahiba's pet tiger
Sir Henry Lawrence — Chief Commissioner of Awadh

GLOSSARY

achkan: a knee-length coat worn by men
adab: informal greeting used by Muslim men
angarkha: upper garment worn by men
ayah: a child's nurse
bhang: a form of marijuana; hashish
begam: a married Muslim woman of high rank
beedi: a cheap, Indian cigarette made with tobacco and wrapped
  in a leaf
burqa: a loose garment worn over other clothes that covers the
  body from head to foot; worn in public by Muslim women
  to maintain seclusion
cantonment: a permanent British military station in India
chai-wallah: a person who makes and serves tea
chapati: unleavened flatbread
cheroot: a thin cigar
chikan: type of embroidery produced in Lucknow
Chowk: busy shopping street; marketplace
coir: fiber from a coconut's outer husk used to make rope
cossid: a spy
dhobi: a washerman or washerwoman
dhoti: worn by male Hindus, a garment tied around the waist
  and covering most of the legs
duppata: a long, light mantle draped across the shoulders or
  over the head
durbar: an official public reception

faqir: in this case, a Muslim mendicant

ghat: steps leading down to a river

ghee: clarified butter

habshi halwa: dark-brown, sweet confection; a type of halva

Habshi: based on the Arabic word for Abbysinia; term used to describe African slaves, mercenaries, and merchants who came to India

Huzoor: a highly respectful term used for someone like a monarch or a ruler

imambarah: a building or room used by Shi'as for ceremonies

Ishqnama: His Majesty Wajid 'Ali Shah's illustrated autobiography

jinn: supernatural creatures or spirits found in Arabian and Muslim mythology

jinni: individual member of the *jinn*

kebab: a round patty similar to a meatball made with finely ground meat and spices, and fried

katar: type of dagger

Kathak: a form of classical dance with fast, fine footwork

kismet: fate

kotha: a place where courtesans lived, trained, performed

Kotwal: chief police officer [combined with town mayor]

kotwali: police station

kurta: upper garment worn by women and men

lakh: Indian unit equal to 100,000

laudanum: the English took opium in the form of laudanum, a popular remedy

lungi: a cotton loincloth worn by men

mandeel: a simple turban of gold and silk thread

mashallah: term used to express admiration or appreciation

memsahib: form of address for a white foreign woman of high social status, particularly the wife of a British official

naan: type of leavened, oven-baked bread

namaste: a respectful greeting used by Hindus

nawab: specifically meaning deputy; someone deputising in

the emperor's name

Om Vakratundaya Hum: mantra lyric in the Ganesh prayer to remove obstacles; Hindu

paan: betel leaves wrapped around pieces of betel nut, lime, spices, sometimes tobacco and made into a small packet to chew

palanquin: a covered passenger conveyance for one person used for short journeys, carried on two poles by four to eight men

pandy / pandies: a derogatory term used by the British for Indian soldiers who resisted English orders

paratha: thick, unleavened bread made with milk and fried in clarified butter, used on special occasions

puja: prayer, act of worship

pulau: rice and meat dish prepared elaborately, using a lot of meat, and coloured and flavored with saffron, among other spices

punkah-wallah: servant who manually moves a large fan for cooling

puris: unleavened, deep-fried bread, often eaten as a snack

raga: a pattern of notes in Indian music

Rasayana: a medical component; a tonic produced particularly to rejuvenate, to increase lifespan, strength, and the intellect

roti: a flat, round, unleavened bread

rupee: a unit of money used in India

sahib: polite form of address for a man

sahiba: polite form of address for a woman

salaam: peace; formal greeting used by Muslim men; usually *salaam aleikam,* "peace be upon you"

seer: about two pounds in weight

shami kebab: a kebab made with minced lamb, lentils and spices

sheedis: African community living in India

shir mals: popular / elite choice of light, scented bread

tabla: a pair of small drums

taluqdar: a village land-owner

tamasha: a celebration

tasleem: greeting used by Muslim women
Yahu: name for God
Yunani: as in Yunani medicine; the Greek system of medicine
  that produced famously skilled physicians in Lucknow

PRELUDE

MID-NINETEENTH CENTURY: the Kingdom of Awadh lay between Calcutta and Delhi in North-Eastern India. Awadh's capital city, Lucknow, was India's seat of the arts and also its granary. Like rulers before him, King Wajid 'Ali Shah attracted engineers and architects from Europe to help build Lucknow alongside equally skilled local professionals. From all over the world, he brought poets, musicians, dancers, artists, and East-African slaves, offering everyone an opportunity for prosperity.

The English East India Company—a lucrative, powerful business based in London—had traded in India for over two hundred years, including in Lucknow, and stealthily, steadily the Company took charge of towns in their quest for India's rich resources. In February 1856, the Company presented King Wajid 'Ali Shah with a treaty that gave the English authority over Lucknow, but he refused to sign. The Company annexed his Kingdom anyway, deposing him. The King's mother left for England to meet with Queen Victoria, mother to mother, with the request to return Lucknow to her family. The King left Lucknow for Calcutta to plead his case with English officials.

Before 1857—what became known as the Red Year—Lucknow had little experience with violence or war.

I. BEFORE

1.

———•◦•◦•———

MARCH 14, 1856

AMAH FIRST REALIZES how much she loves the city of Lucknow in the same month she first fears losing it. March in 1856 is unusually dusty and anxious. The Gomti river, cutting east and west through the city, does not swell with boisterous bathers. Smoke from funeral pyres hangs suspended in the air. The ashes, taken out to the middle of the river by boatsmen, glitter black and gold before they vanish in the water. Cool dawns brim with the sharp edges of things to come.

Thousands of Englishmen want to take over Lucknow, and Amah stands alone in the crowded market, observing the English East India Company's auction. The noise of frightened animals fills the sky. The Englishmen have emptied stables and menageries all over the city, and now they are selling off horses, elephants, camels, cheetahs, and silk-winged pigeons to foreign merchants. Amah's favourite horse is among them, a brown Waler from Australia—a gift from the King to show his admiration for her riding skills. Years of training and careful breeding are being purposely erased like pencil with rubber. Like they hope to erase His Majesty.

Amah pushes through the crowd to the line-up of horses. An Englishman with red hair and a dimpled chin bars her way. She smells whisky on his breath, hears hatred in his English words. He puts his hand across her rifle, and stops her from going forward. She reaches out to stroke her mare despite him. The auctioneer mops his face with a handkerchief, slams down his hammer, and nods toward an Indian merchant, a foreigner from far away. The Englishman's hand stays firm against Amah.

"The horses have sold, African slave boy," the man says.

Boy—she understands the word, what they often call out to men in the streets. Boy. Her hair is cut short. She wears a red jacket and rose-coloured silk trousers. The man doesn't recognize her as a young woman, but she does not care to correct him. "These horses are royal horses," she says in Urdu. "And this is my horse."

She can see the man has understood her, but he replies in English. "They belong to the King, and we've deposed him," he says. "It's time to get rid of them, boy."

She does not understand. She reaches for her mare's reins but the Company man stops her with his pistol. "I said she's already sold. You're trespassing. Get back now."

The foreign Indian merchant comes forward. He won't meet Amah's eyes. He takes her mare's reins, but he also waits while she holds out to her horse a piece of sugar, spun orange and shaped like a small carrot. She pats the animal's warm flank, as if everything is all right. Then she leaves the auction to find Begam Sahiba, her friend and the King's ex-wife.

* * *

When Amah reaches Qaisarbagh Palace where she lives, she cuts through it to get to Begam Sahiba's house on the other side of the vast property. In the front hall, old Kasim, Amah's cousin, an Ethiopian palace guard like herself, asks if it's true—he's heard rumours. "Yes," she says. "They're getting rid of all of them. They've taken my horse. Where's yours, Kasim? Have you seen your horse?"

"She's here, inside."

"Keep her safe," Amah calls. She runs out of the hall, past the statue of Neptune and the water tanks shaped like fish, through the Queen Mother's billowy rooms filled with Hindu accountants and engineers, Shi'a scholars, Sunni paymasters, Jain sculptors, and Jewish musicians, around the Fairy House where His Majesty's dancers rehearse, under apartments of his lounging wives, and across the gardens that stretch out like small, green oceans. From the city somewhere, an English band practices "The Girl I Left Behind Me." Nothing ever stops the persistent blasts of English horns that have played for one thousand nights and make Amah's head ache. She slips out a door in the far wall of the palace and into the canopied street that leads to Begam Sahiba's home.

Amah finds her friend in her garden. Her title remains Begam Hazrat Mahal, though everyone at the palace affectionately and respectfully calls her Begam Sahiba. Her marriage to the King only lasted long enough to produce a child, her soft-lipped, kite-flying son, Birjis, who has inherited her green eyes. Begam Sahiba lives with the child in her own home. With an annual income, she runs her own affairs.

"*Tasleem*. I am here," Amah calls, bowing her head.

Begam Sahiba feeds her four black swans, brushing their long necks with her fingers. A pink headscarf covers her hair. "*Tasleem*. I've been waiting for you, Amah," she says. "Tell me. What's happened?"

"The trainers say all of the royal animals will be auctioned. From all over Lucknow. Seven thousand, they estimate."

"Impossible," Begam Sahiba says.

"This English officer went to the trainers yesterday with an order from Residency Hill. He said His Majesty's trainers must assist in the removal of the animals from the city. The trainers waited, hoping someone would come from the palace to put a stop to them, but no one came, and so this morning the removal began. Auction notices are posted as far as Nepal, Delhi, Calcutta. Merchants have arrived from those places to take advantage of the sale prices. The silk-winged pigeons His Majesty purchased for twenty-five thousand *rupees* each just sold for five hundred. My horse sold for three hundred. They're emptying our stables."

Begam Sahiba listens and does not blink. She's slim, smaller than Amah. "They are cutting up love," she says. "Are the tigers there? And the quails?"

"Not that I saw."

"We must shelter what animals we can. I'll go to the meadow to get Sita before it's too late. Tigers will perish in their hands. You fetch the quails."

* * *

Dusk and butterflies waver. Amah takes the grey mare that belongs to her old cousin, Kasim, to get to Sikanderbagh—a grand mosque and summer house with pink walls located a mile away where they keep their quails. She rides beside the river Gomti where kingfishers whoop, people pray, and vendors sell fish. On the far side of the river, light from the English cantonment winks in the distance along with the strains of a waltz. On her side of the river, groves of old mango trees shift from orange-green to blue-grey in the evening light. She rides past homes with windows open wide for the breeze. Inside, storytellers seated on flower-patterned carpets prepare to wash away the sound of hammers, the sight of auction posters slapped on walls, the lingering fecal smell in the empty stables, the taste of ignored pleas from soft-spoken attendants. Well into the evening, tales from *Julius Caesar, One Thousand and One Night*s, and *Hamlet* will help remove the tales of the day, the dust clouds from the hooves of English horses. All over Lucknow, Hindus, Muslims, Christians, Jains, and Jews listen to stories about beauty and war, love and deception.

At Sikanderbagh, Amah tethers the grey mare and crosses the courtyard to a side room where they house the blue-breasted quails. They usually sing like a chorus of little flutes. But the quail cages are gone, except for one that is broken, its brass wire door bent. Feathers, crushed eggshells, and droppings litter the floor. No flute sounds anywhere, no covey of quails, no contented coos.

She picks up the cage, then finds a broom and prays for the souls of birds as she sweeps the silence clean. She prays for pretty blue-breasted quails, for green, silk-winged pigeons who long to come home to their cots, and for the little pink pigeons who peep into the room now from a window to watch her—pink-winged pigeons small enough to fly through a child's bangles and to be protected by Lucknow's trees.

When she walks back across the courtyard, she sees Abhi, a wheat and barley merchant, squatting in a shadow beside Sikanderbagh's well.

"What are you doing?" she asks, approaching him.

The man doesn't get up. He does not greet Amah with any sort of respect. He gestures in the direction of the side room, shrugs his shoulders. "Look at the mess that's been made." Abhi's teeth are stained red from chewing betel nut. He wears a gold-and-silver stitched cap and silk clothes. Everyone knows he married a wealthy, older lady to add to his income, a fact that is the subject of jokes.

"You must have been at the auction," Amah says.

"Yes, everyone was there. One big *tamasha*."

"One big *tamasha*. The English are having a good time." She studies the man with red-stained teeth. He likes to smoke cheroots with the English. Abhi. An 'Ali Baba and his English thieves.

"Looks like bad luck, palace guard," Abhi says. "African woman who only courts rifles."

"Bad luck for whom?" she asks.

The man smiles.

Amah raises her gun and his face changes. He contemplates her red jacket, her rose-coloured trousers. "Amah the African. African Amazon. The English have a good name for you," he says, breaking into a smile.

Amah shrugs and turns to her grey mare. "Company men

are like parrots," she says. "Unfaithful, and green with envy. Watch how close you fly to them."

* * *

Scarlet-headed cranes flap their slate wings and glide into the night. At Begam Sahiba's house, the gardeners have been called from their evening meal to build a bamboo cage half the length of the garden, away from the four black swans who huddle under the low branches of a bushy neem tree.

The garden is flooded with lamplight. Begam Sahiba watches an animal trainer feed mutton to a baby tiger in the new bamboo cage. From under the neem tree, the black swans also watch. Begam Sahiba's face is a dark cloud but when she sees Amah, she brightens.

"*Tasleem*," Amah says, bowing her head. "No quails. And Sita?"

"*Tasleem*," Begam Sahiba says. "Sita is gone. And the English know how wrong they are because they didn't dare stop us when we opened the cage to take her cub." She shows Amah her arm, bare under her light shawl. A deep scratch glistens with aloe. "It took some doing, but I carried the wriggling baby home myself. Go inside and see her. She's Shahzadi. Call her Shahzadi."

Inside the bamboo cage, Shahzadi is quiet, all white face and legs in the lamplight. Her wet nose nudges Amah's arm. The fur on Shahzadi's chest is encrusted from gorging her mother's milk.

"Amah, we need to make a record of what the English are doing," Begam Sahiba says. "Work with me to make a record."

Amah hesitates. "His Majesty wants us to protect his storerooms until he returns."

"Is your cousin Kasim still in charge? He would agree that there are plenty of people to watch the storerooms. Things are moving fast. Faster than it will take for the Queen Mother to arrive in London, or for the King's petitions to be read in

Calcutta. Someone must document what's going on. Is there anyone at the palace making plans to counter what they are doing?"

"The auction surprised us."

"Work with me, Amah. Someone has to record what they are doing. Be my eyes and ears on the streets."

Amah thinks about her friend's request. There are many East-Africans in the Habshiyan Risala, the African Cavalry Regiment, who receive prizes, rifles, and titles because of His Majesty's respect for their military skills. Amah belongs to the Rose Platoon of female African soldiers—His Majesty's personal bodyguards. They are each to receive ten *rupees* per month for protecting the royal household's valuables while the King is away. His Majesty surely would not want her to think about doing anything else. And his mother, in England to meet with Queen Victoria over the false treaty, would not approve of Begam Sahiba doing anything at all. Amah looks at Shahzadi, thinks about the empty stables. "But what if making a record of what they are doing is not enough? There was no agreement and yet our animals are gone. Just like that."

"We will do things the right way, proceed with justice, regardless of how the English choose to do things. It's extraordinary. Baffling, even. But we will remain courteous, Amah, while we properly document the wrong-doing."

Begam Sahiba comes from a poor family outside Lucknow. Her father, an Ethiopian slave, married an Indian village woman. His Majesty paid to have Begam Sahiba train with some of Lucknow's royal courtesans at the palace. Begam Sahiba became a Lucknow citizen, a Lakhnavi. She's older than Amah by just a few years, and Amah grew up listening to her rehearse new poems. The young women used to sit together at night-long Kathak dances, observed kite competitions, and cock fights. They lay in Lucknow's bamboo grove studying white egrets, and before the divorce they watched *Macbeth* in

His Majesty's gardens. Nowadays, like Amah, Begam Sahiba is content to be alone. Despite any hard feelings Begam Sahiba still might harbour about the divorce, both women have shared in Lucknow's royal graces. And because both women's families have come from Ethiopia, they are not unlike sisters. Surely, Amah thinks, it's natural that she might work closely with Begam Sahiba now. Together they can protect Lucknow.

Amah tilts her head in consent. Begam Sahiba smiles, and touches Amah's arm. "We will change our fate, change our kismet," Begam Sahiba says. "Now, Amah, I'm going to lie down."

Amah stays, listening to the baby tiger whimper in her sleep. "Little motherless child," she says. She goes to Begam Sahiba's kitchen and brings back a dish of warm milk and honey for Shahzadi. "Dream a thousand sweet dreams," she whispers to the cub.

***

Lit lanterns dot the gardens and terraces at Qaisarbagh Palace. In the front hall, Amah removes her shoes, bathes her feet, and dries them with a soft cloth before she walks across the cool marble floors inlaid with mosaic, past stucco mermaids and gurgling water tanks, to the palace kitchens—a vast, noisy hall on the grounds. Among the dozens of cooks, boys watch over boiling pots, preparing overnight what the cooks will need tomorrow. She breathes in the sweet fragrance of recently-baked *shir mals*, light and scented bread, and the pungent steam of herbs. One of the cooks stops chopping ginger and passes Amah her supper. "Your favourite dish, Amah," he announces, and she knows he's heard about the sale of her horse. A plate of sweet saffron rice with *shami* kebabs made with lamb and hot spices sits on the food tray. The cook has surrounded the plate with paper flowers. She thanks him deeply and leaves.

She's sitting under the stars eating the lamb kebabs when

Laila, her aunt, a thin, nervous woman, comes to sit with her.

"Go and see your mother," she says. "She wants to leave. She wants to travel to Calcutta to stay with His Majesty. She wants you to accompany her."

"His Majesty will be back," Amah says. "It's best to stay here, Auntie. He does not expect us all to leave home."

"Go and see her," Aunt Laila says. "She's waiting for you in her room. You are her daughter. You don't bother with her enough, Amah. Your mother and I both know that."

Amah knows her mother's complaints. She does not look up, keeps eating. Eventually, Aunt Laila sighs loudly and leaves.

Amah takes her unfinished plate to the kitchens. Her aunt's words linger as she watches the cook lay out a soft leaf, paint it with lime and cream, then trickle in betel nut. The cook folds the leaf and hands it to her. She chews the *paan* for relief.

* * *

Her mother is sewing in bed when Amah gets to her room in the palace. Rose incense fills the place. A prayer mat lies over the blue tiles. On the wall, her mother has placed a painting of a procession through Lucknow with their beloved King. Amah's mother and Aunt Laila are part of a group of household staff who surround His Majesty. The two women are dressed in *burqas*, their arms hooked together, their eyes laughing. Because Amah is a part of the Rose Platoon, she doesn't dress in a *burqa,* and she often misses their jokes.

For weeks, His Majesty has protested against the false treaty in Calcutta, hoping to convince the English administration there of the wrongdoing in taking his land. Amah's mother occupies herself with stitching wisps of flowers and fish into handkerchiefs like her husband used to do. She still wears plain yellow, even though Amah's father, and Amah's brother, too, died years ago. She has been waiting for the King to send word for her to take the mail coach with other members of Qaisarbagh's household and join the group supporting His Majesty at his temporary residence in Calcutta. The King will understand if her mother doesn't want to travel, that she might want to stay here in Lucknow with Amah and Aunt Laila, but she's going. Nothing ever stops her mother's cutting of threads, the stitches stubbornly crossed like this mother and her daughter.

Amah's mother finally stops sewing and holds up a jar of pink salve. Amah sits down on the bed and begins to rub the cream into her mother's dry hands, keeping the cream away from her mother's gold bracelets.

"You can't get such salve in Calcutta," Amah says, resting her hands on top of her mother's hands for a moment.

"We'll take enough with us," her mother says, her hands lying still beneath Amah's.

"Mama, you can't go," Amah blurts out.

Her mother is almost as tall as Amah is—a woman with almond-shaped eyes, high cheekbones, thick hair. Amah's grandmother liked to say, "Your mother carries the best of Ethiopia's features." Her grandmother came as an orphan-child from Ethiopia at a time when Queens and Emperors fought there, when the air was thick with war, but the air was worse on the boats that waited to take Ethiopian war-captive slaves to other lands. That was when her anxious grandmother found herself sick on a boat with drinking water brown as tea. Hundreds of Indian men in cotton skirts brought hundreds of boats holding East-Africans sick with fear to shore, where hundreds more Indian men in fancy trousers whirled and leaped around them. The voices of so many people speaking foreign languages made up of liquid syllables swirled around her grandmother overland and upriver, through Cawnpore to Lucknow, where an Indian King purchased her grandmother to make *paan* for the royal family. That was when a pampering world poured forth and anxiousness dissipated in her easy-going grandmother like light rain on hot sand. "And oh!" she used to say. "Such a city of brown faces, vividly green trees wedged between tall houses, sparkling palaces, and armies of jewellers. Statues of gods I had not met conversed with statues of our Allah. There sat Venus and Zeus in roadside gardens." Her grandmother adored Lucknow. "Never leave such a place behind," she said to Amah. "Make your place here. Remember what the European sightseers like to say in English when they arrive: 'You are in Luck. Now.'"

Like Amah's grandmother, Amah's mother made her place here, and she married an Indian, a Lakhnavi. She has a box of opals, pearls, and rubies saved in a cavity beneath her prayer mat. But she's not happy. Cholera took Amah's father and Amah's brother. Her tall father, and her smiling brother, ten years older than Amah, both men bristling with life early one morning only to be reduced by the afternoon to men too difficult to rouse, with sunken eyes and parched lips, both father and brother dead by nightfall. Amah has heard the story many times.

Now her mother pulls her hands away, peers at Amah quizzically, and makes a noise in her throat. Everything in her mother's face says that Amah does not make up for their losses. Even if she sat by her mother day and night, as her mother often requests, even if Amah did that and vanished from life itself, she's not at all sure that her mother would find the solace she craves. Her mother's eyes travel from Amah's cropped hair, over her red jacket to her rifle, as if seeing Amah for the first time. As a little girl, Amah was delicate, with her mother's cheekbones and her father's bright eyes. She wore her hair long, in plaits. Now, her hair— a mass of tiny curls, brown and black—is efficiently kept above the nape of her neck. The jodhpurs she often wears to ride have neat, reinforcing patches. She wishes her mother liked what she likes about herself, the things she's grown proud of. Every day she hopes they'll be better people to each other. But something shrinks inside her. She knows her mother is thinking, What child is this? She says, "Amah, you're coming with me to Calcutta."

"Mama, it's my duty to stay here. To protect the royal storerooms."

"It's your duty to accompany your mother."

Her mother has never seen reason to leave the palace, let alone travel to Calcutta. It's far too far. "It's best for you to stay, Mama," she says, putting the lid back on the jar of salve. "Keep living how we've been living. We must watch out for His Majesty here. I'll help Begam Sahiba record what the English are doing until His Majesty returns."

Her mother's eyes widen. "Begam Sahiba has no authority. His Majesty, the Queen Mother, they wouldn't respect her meddling. You don't know how to choose what's best, Amah."

"Why choose to go and live in a strange place in a strange city?"

"It's here that's become strange. You saw what happened today. I will stay in His Majesty's household there until things are put right. I want to leave tomorrow and not come back until the city is in the King's hands again. You should be ashamed of not doing what I say."

Amah gets up. When she turns around in the doorway, her mother's eyes are hard and far away. "Bring me warm milk in the morning," her mother says.

"Yes, Mama." She's used to that look, and to the tone in her mother's voice. She leaves, closing the door gently behind her.

***

In the night, Amah awakes. She reaches for the drink beside her bed. Beads of lime in water, an earthen cup rimmed with powdered sugar. Through the open window, she hears the shimmering of anklets and the strains of a ghazal, then a round of applause and voices—the sounds of a gathering, faint in the night. A drum beat and cymbals accompany a larger drum, high, low, rhythm ongoing, melody, song. Sweet tobacco and orange kadam blossoms scent the night air. Unfurling hookah smoke trails over bright mustard-oil lights, a smokescreen of sorts against the dark shapes of the auction table, the silent stables, and the ghosts who are beginning to arrive. Still, out her window, the stars are awash, like lit lamps to honour gods. And beyond her, in the darkness of the inner gardens and beneath the frangipani tree that drops its heavy, white flowers, a small pigeon returns home, calling *Yahu* in the night. Amah keeps the cup to her lips even when the sugar is gone, the lime-water finished.

2.

———◆———

AN ENGLISH TAKEOVER hangs in the hot air, and Amah's mother has gone. In the morning, Amah arrives late from the kitchens, spilling the steaming milk as she walks. Still heavy with sleep, she finds her mother's room empty. The prayer mat over the blue tiles is still there but a smaller prayer mat is not. Her mother's white pigeons peck the grass under the kadam tree outside her bedroom. Their breasts still shine from last evening's *ghee*-soaked breadcrumbs. Nothing before ever stopped her mother from feeding those birds.

Amah goes back to her own room, puts on a saffron robe that covers her from head to foot, with a veil she can barely see through. She hides her rifle under the robe, hitching it to a belt at her waist, and walks to the front hall to find Kasim. Her cousin jumps when he sees her, then comes and puts his old face close to hers, cupping his right hand over his heart and patting his chest. His eyes, knotted with cataracts, widen.

"*Adab*. What are you doing?" he asks.

"*Tasleem*. My mother left. I'm going to catch up to her."

"Oh!" he says, his eyes growing wider. "Go!" he says, and pushes her toward Qaisarbagh's front doors.

On her way to Cawnpore Road, Amah stops at Begam Sahiba's home. She finds her friend in her private quarters, bathing in steaming water. Above the bathing pool, Begam Sahiba's portrait hangs on the wall. The King commissioned the painting before the divorce. Now he has given her seven hundred and fifty acres of land from which she gets an annual income—his effort to make up for an awkward separation. In the portrait, the artist has captured Begam Sahiba's elegance—her green eyes and wide brow, her dark-copper skin, and her black hair pulled away from her face.

Amah lifts her veil. "*Tasleem*," she says, and bows her head.

Begam Sahiba looks up at Amah from the steaming water. "*Tasleem*. Listen, I'm requesting a meeting with that English Chief Commissioner. Coming with me?" Her brow wrinkles briefly like a breeze wrinkling water. "I've never seen you dressed so, Amah."

Amah tells her about her mother, that she must find her, bring her home.

"Perhaps the mail coach hasn't left. Go quickly, Amah. Have you received your salary from Calcutta?" Begam Sahiba asks.

"Not yet."

"Take ten *rupees* from the silver box on the table. Find me when you get home."

* * *

On the outskirts of Lucknow, on Cawnpore Road, Amah finds a mail coach sitting empty. The driver is asleep on the bench inside, so content in his dreams he reminds her of Angel Gabriel. When she calls to him, Angel Gabriel gets up in a hurry. "*Salaam*," he says, smoothing his hair, his moustache.

"Any other mail coaches gone today?" Amah asks.

"One early this morning."

Amah tells him she must go after her mother who is very old, who has never travelled outside Lucknow, who does not know what she is doing.

Angel Gabriel gets out of the coach and climbs onto one of the two horses. "Let's go," he says.

It takes eight hours to travel southwest to Cawnpore. Gabriel drives the horses toward the city, over the clay repairs in the road, under the swooping telegraph lines overhead. Lucknow recedes in the red dust. He shows her the new roads leading across the green fields to distant villages. "All of it new," he calls back to her through the coach window. "All of it English. For Awadh."

Amah struggles with his words. She dismisses them and concentrates on the wide landscape outside the coach.

"Have you ever left Lucknow?" Gabriel calls to her.

"Never," she says.

He smiles. "You Lakhnavis are proud people," he calls.

She feels a wave of butterflies rise inside her, then a lunging of protection for her mother who has never gone further than the Thursday evening Sufi prayer meetings in Lucknow, than Qaisarbagh's kitchens for her meals, than her sister Laila's room for afternoon chitchat, than the kadam tree to feed her birds. She pictures her mother on the mail coach, not knowing which direction to pray. She hears her mother trying to understand the foreigners outside the Kingdom of Awadh—English foreigners and foreign Indians in their foreign towns with their foreign languages. Where will she find somewhere to bathe, a place to relieve herself? Amah's heart begins to shake for her mother, and it shakes because her mother will blame her for her hardship because Amah is not there—and then her mother will travel farther away from her, her judgment of Amah sealed, a change of heart not possible. And this is too much for Amah to bear. So she pulls herself up straight and lets the distant trees and the red-clay roads—the very things her mother saw as she travelled the same route—become bits and pieces of kinship between them.

They arrive in Cawnpore in the early evening. Gabriel points her in the direction of the busy main square, telling her that the river Ganges is just beyond it, and where she should find a steamship at the dock. Amah walks toward the square, skirting an English East India Company warehouse stocked with sacks filled with Awadh grain. In the square, she's not noticed by white Company men who strut with their walking sticks past red-and-blue Company flags that hem the area and match those that fly above the warehouse. Vendors sell sketches of London, and pictures of the foreign Queen Victoria. It is a chatty English place with no Lakhnavi musicians or glittering archways.

She stumbles out into the crowds at the water's edge. Her rifle hitched to her waist under the robe is bulky, awkward. The water smells of dead fish. She looks around for her mother in the crowds but there are no old women waiting among the young English families and their accompanying Cawnpore servants. On the steamship that has just arrived, Englishmen with binoculars stand on deck as the vessel's ropes are pulled tight by Cawnpore labourers. Company families begin to stream off the boat with trunks marked in big letters for Lucknow; tiny English children in sailors' suits with flushed cheeks walk behind their mothers' hooped skirts.

They are all people arriving. No one is departing. Amah moves away from the crowd and puts her hands on the wrought-iron gate between herself and the water. Her mother's steamship must have gone.

She closes her eyes. She can feel the morning sun along Cawnpore Road from Lucknow, smell red clay, hear gold bracelets clinking, see an old woman in yellow pyjamas with an embroidered handkerchief in her hands board a steamship, turn her back. She sees her mother turn her back.

She opens her eyes and looks out at the brown water beyond the steamship, smells the dead fish. Amah won't wait for a boat to take her to Calcutta. She won't travel any further. She'll go right home, where they both should be.

She walks back through the square in the growing darkness to find Gabriel. His horses and mail coach are not where she left them. She finds an inn near the square. An Indian man wearing a white coat stands at the door. He smiles widely. "Three *rupees* to stay here."

His big prices match his big mouth. She gives him three

rupees, slipping them into his outstretched hand. He squints at the silver coins, at the little mermaids stamped on them. "They're no good," he says, handing the money back. "Only English *rupees* here."

"I have no English *rupees*. You have to take these," she says, but the man shrugs and turns away, still smiling.

* * *

That night, Amah watches for snakes in the tall grass on the outskirts of Cawnpore. She drifts to sleep, wrapped in her robe, her hand on her rifle, dreams she is travelling on a boat and wakes up, startled. She sleeps again and dreams of *jinn* in brass vessels waiting in the grass. She dreams of a man lying on the ground whose tongue is covered in hot dust and blood, sugar and ashes. *Jinn* in brass vessels wait. Royal pigeons beat their silk wings. She wakes up again in the darkness and lies there stiffly in the grass until dawn.

She longs for a bath, and she's wild with hunger, but no vendor will take Lucknow *rupees*. The morning mail coach to Lucknow is crowded with Company families so she must wait for the late afternoon coach. When it pulls up, Angel Gabriel climbs down from his horse and goes inside to rest on one of the benches, unfolding his newspaper. Amah gets in behind him. She's taken off the long robe to reveal her red jacket and pink silk trousers, her rifle too, none of which make him stare; he knows Lucknow. But he does ponder her for some time. "No mother," he finally says. "But, listen. I heard some good news. The early morning driver told me his mail coach was full of His Majesty's staff yesterday on their way to Calcutta. There is a group travelling together. She will be safe." He cocks his head. "But you," he says. "Cawnpore has worn you out." He shows her a space between the last bench and the back of the coach. It's fitted with cotton blankets. "You can sleep there," he says. "You can sleep all the way home."

Perhaps he was born kind, Amah thinks. Perhaps he spends all his time in Lucknow, not Cawnpore, learning manners, warming his heart on Lucknow's snacks. Perhaps this is the reason for his good nature.

Amah means to go to sleep while she waits for him to read his paper—lie down with her rifle and bundle her robe, curl up into herself. But the air inside the coach is heavy. A mob of mosquitoes, and she finds herself awake, with bumps swelling on her face. She sits up and watches the empty steamship in the distance move against its moorings on the river. She looks the other way, out to the street where skinny dogs and skinny cows roam. "I'd feed them if I could," she tells Gabriel.

He looks up and laughs. "You Lakhnavis would feed them ten-*rupee* sweets." He turns back to his newspaper, tells her the Imambarah College in Lucknow is closing for good. "The English are closing it," he says. "Lots of changes in your city." He taps the paper. "Lots of people are leaving."

"I'm staying," she says.

"Lots of changes in Lucknow," he repeats. His moustache droops, making him look as tired of the topic as Amah is becoming.

An English family arrives and Angel Gabriel gets down to pack up their trunks. A little boy enters first, dressed in a blue sailor's suit, his mouth a thin line as he stares at Amah sitting in the bedding at the back of the coach. Like *Little Boy Blue,* Amah thinks, remembering the English picture book of nursery rhymes in the palace library. The father is a tall man with his gloves in one hand, who waits for his wife to be seated. Amah smells talcum powder and moth balls, sees England rolling off their postures. "There's a really black one," Little Boy Blue says, and folds his face into his mother's wide skirt. He stares at Amah again. "Is it a man? Woman?"

"Hush," the English mother says.

Amah understands only the coldness in their unfamiliar English words.

The mail coach moves forward. Cawnpore is left behind in the dusk. She tries to understand what the boy sees, what he cannot see. One thing she knows with certainty—she cannot see herself in whatever it is he sees.

She shifts her thoughts to home. Amah was once a girl her grandmother loved to watch. She thinks of Begam Sahiba's house, of the little tiger Shahzadi, of potato kebabs. Lamps are lit; incense burns. Begam Sahiba stands beside Amah, letting her embroidered head-covering fall to her shoulders as she reaches out to touch the feathers of her black swans. Little Boy Blue doesn't know these things. In every coach shared by an Indian and an English family, perhaps it is just the same. She leans her head against the side of the coach, closes her eyes, tries to sleep.

"It's so terribly hot," the woman says.

"Frightful," the man replies.

"What a journey," sighs the woman. "I'd never imagined such untidiness. And so many idols. I thought things had got better."

"They say one never gets quite used to it, dear," says the man.

"We'll have to get used to it."

The horses stop. Amah groans softly. She will never sleep.

There is a moment of silence, something odd. And then hell hits Gabriel first; it is as if the two thieves have been spat from the darkness. One of them shows Gabriel a *katar,* a stabbing stiletto, in the light of their lanterns. They pull the English family outside, the woman screaming while she holds her son close, the man shouting.

Amah picks up her rifle and gets out. In the small glow thrown by the lanterns, one of the thieves holds the stiletto against Gabriel while his friend frisks the English family. He throws the Englishman's purse to the first thief, pulls a necklace off the woman. Little Boy Blue starts to cry.

Amah raises the rifle and tells the man with the stiletto to give the weapon to Gabriel. Along with his lantern.

When Gabriel takes the *katar* and holds up the lantern, the thieves become small men who turn their heads to look at Amah, startled as if she's a *jinni* who has just appeared in the darkness. One of the men coughs and coughs. Both of their faces are streaked with dirt. "Don't kill us," the coughing man sputters.

Gabriel picks up the Englishman's purse, his hands shaking, and takes the necklace from the hands of the other thief.

Amah's rifle, still raised, is steady. "Are you mad?" she asks the thieves.

The coughing man continues to cough. "No money," he says. "Please have mercy. We have families. We have taxes to pay."

"You chose to live in Cawnpore," Amah says, lowering her gun. "You'd be better off in Lucknow."

"We are villagers."

"Get out of our sight," she says.

The men back away, then they start to run, the darkness swallowing them.

"Are you coming?" Amah asks Gabriel.

"I'm coming," he says, and he jumps onto one of the two horses.

The English family get back inside the coach. It's more a scramble and a fall, all three too dazed to climb. Amah gets onto the horse beside Gabriel's.

They slap the reins and they ride, the coach wheeling behind them, the horses climbing into the moonlit sky. Gabriel keeps mopping his brow, and wiping the spittle from the corners of his mouth with his sleeve. "That has never happened in two years of driving this road. Those thieves were nervous, edgy—and brave. Attacking English families...."

"Desperate," Amah says.

Gabriel wipes his mouth again. "That poor family would only see it as lawlessness. The act of some sort of savage beasts."

"It was lawlessness," Amah says. "They did behave wildly."

"I can't drive this road with that kind of lawlessness around. I can't stay here."

"You say it's never happened before, and now they are far behind us."

"I will find a new route."

When they get into Lucknow, it is very late and the moon is high. Several Company men are waiting by a carriage on Cawnpore Road to meet the English family. The little group huddles together, the Company men listening intently to the high-pitched voices of the husband and wife that fall over each other while Gabriel pulls the trunks from the back of the coach.

They are all getting into the carriage when the English father stops and turns back. "Thank you," he says to Amah and Gabriel in Urdu. Then, in English, "Thank you very much indeed."

"I'm sorry you were greeted so badly," Amah replies in Urdu. She is not sure if the man understands her, but he nods and turns back to the carriage. In every part of her body she means the words.

In the silence that follows after the carriage leaves, Gabriel untethers the horses and lets them loose in the field next to the mail coach. "It's late," Amah says. "Come with me to the palace and eat."

Gabriel smells of road dust and old newspaper. He limps along the road. They walk, and it feels like they are never getting closer. The pulsing silence roars in Amah's ears. Her eyes sting with weariness. She sees the *katar* across the lanterns, hears the thief's cough-coughing.

In the front hall of Qaisarbagh Palace, her cousin Kasim gets up from where he was resting in front of the royal storerooms, his voice echoing against all the marble. He calls a kitchen boy to take Gabriel to bathe, to bring him white pyjamas and a full meal.

Angel Gabriel barely makes it through the meal where they sit near Amah's mother's kadam tree. He dozes before he finishes. "Like a sister," he says to Amah when she rouses him, tells him to follow the boy to bed.

Amah chews *paan* under the cold stars. She has bathed and eaten, too; she's full and sleepy. Before dawn, she brings her prayer rug into her mother's room and falls asleep across it.

She wakes up when the first rays of pale yellow sunshine lie in the garden outside. The sun's presence nudges her. When she walks out, everything is quiet. Her mother's birds sleep in their cots with their beaks tucked under their wings. No one is up. The air is not yet hot, and the dense neem tree leaves tip in a breeze not brisker than the breath of a baby tiger. The wooden doors of the shops aren't yet open, trainers are not yet being paid five *rupees* to bring home pigeons with white wings splashed with green, drink vendors do not yet play songs with spoons, tapping their bottles of mango, lime, and lychee juices to attract customers, the courtesans are not thinking of new poems, servants are not milking goats, women are not fetching water from wells, colonels are not betting at the racecourse, and Lucknow's storytellers are not conjuring an apparition by three witches in *Macbeth*. The city sleeps. Amah lives in Lucknow, not Cawnpore. Lucknow, Lucknow. The city is settled for now.

3.

⟡

IN THE WEEKS and weeks that follow, hundreds of Englishmen
fall on Lucknow like hard rain bringing down rose petals.
They force themselves into Lucknow's royal buildings, pay
the King's municipal workers to leave, and make new accom-
modations for themselves. Company men move into offices
they carve out of the royal stables.

Amah waits outside the Company's new post office that
replaces His Majesty's service on the main road, Hazratganj.
A palace boy stands inside the building each day, waiting
for letters from Calcutta. Letters for English families, with
stamps of Queen Victoria, arrive in large cotton bags. French
Champagne and Scotch whisky are delivered in crates for the
shops. Amah imagines one of His Majesty's kindly scholars
writing for her mother, to tell Amah her mother misses Amah
now that she is so far away, that nothing will cut their familial
thread. Each day, the boy comes out empty handed. No letters
for Qaisarbagh Palace. No staff payments. No letters arrive
from her mother.

In Lucknow, English telegraph wires hum like flat harps
with news for the English from Calcutta. But the palace has
no news of what is happening with the petitions to reverse
the deposition.

Nor do they receive any news about the Queen Mother who
has gone to London to meet Queen Victoria. His Majesty's
mother is an aristocratic, powerful widow who eats her meals

with a spoon, not her fingers. Amah pictures her on the boat to England, surrounded by bearers, all of them guarded by female African soldiers in uniform with muskets. The Queen Mother is overweight, addicted to hookah, and left Lucknow in bad health. Amah wonders if she was seasick, like her grandmother was on the boat to India. The silence caused by beloved people suddenly gone to other places leans on Amah. The silence leans on Lucknow.

Surely we can stop the Englishmen, Amah thinks. Can't we talk reason, find agreement, laugh together, see eye-to-eye? Under the kadam tree, she feeds her mother's white pigeons, listens to how they utter the sounds, *Yahu, oh God*, as they breathe and coo. Even the pigeons are fed well in Lucknow. She listens to the trickle of the mermaid fountain in the garden tank, to the rustle of paper tassels attached to kites in the blue sky. We've made room for the English for so long, she thinks. Surely, there are ways we can all live together.

* * *

Begam Sahiba looks at Amah over her hookah pipe, her green eyes steady. "I heard that more of the royal household's members left for Calcutta. Did your mother go with them?"

"I think so."

"I waited for you to see the Chief Commissioner," Begam Sahiba says gently. "We need to get back to how we were. Then everyone will return home."

Later that morning, Amah rides the grey mare that belongs to her cousin, Kasim. A crowd of servants follows in oxen carts behind her. Amah perspires in the gold-and-silver-threaded tunic she wears over a pleated skirt and jodhpurs. Behind them, Begam Sahiba travels inside her curtained palanquin carried by four men. She wears an orange cloak, her face veiled in black. The hot sky lacks His Majesty's flock of silk-winged pigeons that used to fly above them to provide shade.

The Residency, the Company's headquarters in Lucknow, is

located on a hill a mile away from Qaisarbagh Palace. Amah's group moves past road-side gardens full of orange blossom and marble statues, by golden spires, gilded spheres, and brass domes, through streets filled with residential palaces built by nobility that sparkle from stucco made from crushed seashells. The group travels around shady archways where Shi'a and Sunni academics publicly debate, and along the river where the royal family's steam-powered boat sits idle. The road has been dug up for new English telegraph poles sunk deep into the sandy earth, the smell of fresh tar hugging the dusty air, the copper wires cutting the sky.

Inside the Residency, English clerks in gold spectacles bow low to Begam Sahiba, then return to their paperwork. The large hall contains men in high collars and black bow ties, white-washed walls, over-stuffed chairs, inkwells, and pencils with rubber tips.

"They've certainly made their place here," Amah says to Begam Sahiba in a low voice, knowing that many of them speak Urdu.

"A business built on our loans," Begam Sahiba says proudly in English, her voice rising as they walk through the hall, heads turning to watch them. "Loans that we gladly allowed to become donations. To help people who needed help. That is our way."

At the far end of the hall, the officer behind the desk blows on a cup of milky tea as he reads the letter granting them an appointment with the Chief Commissioner. He is the Englishman with red hair and a dimpled chin, the man who held Amah back from her horse at the auction. If he recognizes her from the auction, he does not show it. They stand in the middle of the hall, Begam Sahiba deep in their midst, Red Man blowing again on his milky tea. "Hurry up," Amah wants to say. "Hurry up." To gaze around that room is to see arrogance surrounding you—you, Lakhnavi sweeper going up the velvet stairs, and you, Lakhnavi man taking down chamber pots, and you, too, the

Lakhnavi men cleaning the noisy, over-heated telegraph office.

Red Man puts down his cup and ushers them into a sitting room where he stands behind another desk. He knows enough to address Amah and not Begam Sahiba who faces the bookshelves, shrouded by her attendants. He holds up a piece of paper and says mostly in English, a little in Urdu, "The Chief Commissioner has been held up. New land tax regulation. Urgent matter. I have a letter from him. Shall I read it to Her Highness?"

Amah guesses, from the way he holds the letter, that it is up for discussion. Unlike many of his superiors, he does not seem to care to speak Urdu, and his face seems faintly mocking. She glances at Begam Sahiba and forces herself to speak. "Yes, *sahib*," she says in Urdu.

Red Man reads the letter, which is written in Urdu, and it's clear he can read fairly well if he wants to. "The Chief Commissioner wishes to assure Her Royal Highness that pensions and payments are forthcoming to replace those that the King provided. The Chief Commissioner is pleased to offer Her Highness an annual pension in order to reduce the inconveniences while our improvements are being made. We await your response."

"Improvements? How astonishing." Begam Sahiba speaks in English and her voice remains clear even if her face is hidden. "What sort of foolish people do you take us for?"

Red Man looks down at the letter. "Lucknow is a chaotic place, Your Highness," he says in a loud voice. "You will see that there are things we can do to run it efficiently—without lavish spending. The King's ways are ruinous. We are here to rescue Awadh for its own good. Your Highness, the people here are discontented with the King's rule."

"What on earth are you talking about?" Begam Sahiba says. "We are content. And we contentedly gave you millions of *rupees*. Perhaps that was ruinous. You dismiss the town clerks, the newspaper men, the city street cleaners. You close down our post office. You sell the animals, also worth millions of *rupees,* for what—to make one-time payments to all the sacked workers? You build roads to get into Awadh's villages. Why? No one out there would say they need rescuing either. These are not truly improvements but the same sort of sacking story your Company is suspected of in other places. Tell your Commissioner that we are not so foolish as he seems to think. Today he is clearly afraid to deny the facts face to face. He thinks I cannot see that."

She moves toward the sitting room door and out into the hall, the servants following closely behind her. Amah also follows, listening to Begam Sahiba rapidly translate the conversation for them all. Amah's chest burns as she listens. They walk back outside, passing under the Baillie Guard Gate, and into the street.

Abhi, the merchant, stands with several Englishmen. They smoke cheroots. He walks a few steps forward, considering Amah, puffing his tobacco, his face slack under his gold and silver cap.

"Talking with friends?" Amah asks.

"We are all friends," he says. He smiles, flashing his teeth stained red with betel.

Abhi and his forty thieves. Like Red Man and his Chief Commissioner.

"How are your grain stores at Qaisarbagh?" Abhi asks. "Do you need barley?"

"The head housekeeper is in Calcutta. Send a formal letter to our kitchens if you want to know," she says. The light shines in the blue silk hue of his *kurta*. It is a well-pressed shirt, like his cap. His green, velvet shoes are new, like his marriage. "You must feel pinched by the prices kept down by your friends," she says.

He shrugs. "That's fate."

"There's no such thing as fate. We mould our futures." She turns to go.

"Why is it important to say anything at all to me?" he says, following her to Kasim's horse. "You are late now, African palace guard, wife of a rifle. Look how far the others are ahead of you. You don't have time for idle chat."

"I thought you might need to be reminded of who is who," she says.

He approaches her, stands too close. He smells of burlap bags, lavender soap, and stale tobacco. His skin is red under his black beard.

"Company friends are waiting for you," Amah says, mounting the mare and looking out at the glittering city below her. "You have to go."

* * *

The next day, after noon prayers, Amah stops at her friend Mohammed's newspaper stall in the canopied street by the palace on her way to Begam Sahiba's home. English and Urdu newspapers are laid out on wooden ledges, along with sweets in silver paper, and soft, dark-brown halva, *habshi halwa*. Mohammed greets her, moves the sliver of bamboo between his teeth to one side. As always, she offers silver-foiled *paan* from the palace in exchange for reading his papers. She puts down the brown-paper envelope she's been carrying, and picks up an Urdu newspaper. She turns to where selections from English newspapers have been translated into the back pages. "There's a rumour going around the palace that there's news about the Queen Mother," she says, holding out the paper to him. "Can you find it?"

By the time the papers arrive in Lucknow the news is already old. But two months ago, the Queen Mother was a novelty in London, causing crowds of onlookers to climb walls to try to see her while she remained hidden in her hotel, surrounded by Lakhnavi bodyguards, hookah bearers, and cooks who shop in London's Oriental Quarter near the Thames where the river runs into the streets. The Queen Mother's cooks buy lentils, rice, and soap from shopkeepers who sell Indian stores. Mohammed also reads about Lucknow. It is being cleaned up, the writer from London writes, the city is being sanitized. Mohammed reads about teeming millions of Asiatics, his voice not changing. He reads about how Amah the Asiatic and Mohammed the Asiatic need to be cleaned up, how dirty they are, and how child-like too. Sadness finally creeps inside his voice, and he puts the paper down. He smooths it out, returns it to the ledge.

Amah picks up her envelope, feels the weight of it. "There is something we have to do," she says.

* * *

Amah finds Begam Sahiba standing at the door of a small pavilion, her meeting room, at one side of her garden. The sun beats down on several of the city's bankers who are leaving. Begam Sahiba bids them well, her finger tracing the pink scar that has formed from the baby tiger Shahzadi's scratch on the day of her rescue. Little Shahzadi lies stretched out, asleep in the garden, oblivious to the heat and to the black swans who stand under the neem tree.

"*Tasleem*," Amah says, bowing her head.

"*Tasleem*," Begam Sahiba replies, smiling at Amah. "Today is a better day. Those bankers assure me that they have power over the Company's credit. They can take it all away if absolutely necessary." Her eyes suddenly fix on something over Amah's shoulder. "Oh, look. Look who's coming, Amah."

The Queen Mother's advisor, old man Lal, has followed Amah down the canopied road from Qaisarbagh Palace to Begam Sahiba's house. He is the Queen Mother's favourite advisor and prepares her Yunani herbal remedies daily. White-haired Lal follows Amah into the pavilion while he eats a tangerine, his usual addiction. Amah hands Begam Sahiba the envelope.

"It was delivered to the palace from the new English post office."

"Is it from the Queen Mother?" Begam Sahiba asks tentatively, studying the seal.

"Yes," Amah says. "She must have sent it from Calcutta before she set sail for London. It's been opened."

Begam Sahiba puts her hand inside the envelope. "Empty."

"It arrived that way. Everyone at the palace has seen it. Everyone is upset, especially His Majesty's wives, especially Lal. I wanted you to see it. Lal wanted you to see it."

"You think the English opened it?"

"Yes."

"We cannot prove that, Amah. Be careful of the conclusions you jump to."

"No one else would break her seal, Begam Sahiba. We don't have any correspondence from His Majesty. No salaries, either. Even the palace advisors are wondering if they are out of work."

Lal swallows the last of his tangerine and wipes his face with his handkerchief. He fidgets, but Begam Sahiba does not send him away. She hands the envelope back to Amah and takes up her hookah, the cool smoke circling the spiral stem.

"Lal agrees that no one at the palace seems to know what to do," Amah says. "If there isn't a *sahib*, a *sahiba* should carry on with the responsibilities."

"We are documenting what they are doing," Begam Sahiba says. "We'll add this to the record," she indicates the empty envelope. "The King intends to be back soon."

"But we've had no word. Right now, we've no idea. Someone needs to be in contact with the royal advisors in Calcutta, to find out what's going on."

Begam Sahiba continues to smoke, the spiced tobacco scenting the air, while she puts her thoughts together. Finally, she indicates the envelope again. "All right. So, now it seems that the English are spying by reading our letters."

"What we need are our own private messengers. People we can trust to bring our letters, our salaries, safely to us.

You could write to His Majesty's advisors. Tell them what is happening here."

"The English will simply offer bribes to get our letters," Begam Sahiba says. "They are not above that."

"We will find loyal people," Amah says. "Messengers the English won't discover."

"The palace advisors would not want me to have anything to do with royal correspondence. Think of the Queen Mother. They'd be afraid they'd lose their jobs."

"Right now, it looks like they have lost their jobs, Begam Sahiba. They need to get through to the King. Lal needs to stay in touch with the Queen Mother for her medicines. We are only doing a good deed."

Begam Sahiba contemplates Lal, the wisps of white hair fallen over his sunken eyes. She puts down her hookah. "I'll send a boy with payment to Gulbadan at the *kotha*. Work with her to find some secret messengers, Amah." She leads the way to the door. "So, now the English have us doing something we've never dreamed of doing, not in a thousand and one nights."

4.

———⊙⋅◈⋅⊙———

L UCKNOW WAITS IN the clobbering temperatures for the monsoons to arrive. In the front hall of the palace, Amah's cousin, old Kasim, and another cousin, Fatima, who also guards the royal storerooms, take out pressed hand-kerchiefs and mop their brows. His Majesty's wives hide away in their bougainvillea-covered rooms. In a pavilion deep in the gardens, palace advisors talk in low voices, their bare feet ca-ressing the cool marble floors. In the city, some of the English have left for better weather up in the hills; their procession of elephants, oxen carts, and hundreds of servants weighed down with luggage, creeps along under the hot sun. The rumour in Lucknow is that this year most Company men will not join their wives but will stay in the city, despite the heat, to continue with the so-called improvements. Vendors watch the Company men in their blue tailcoats come and go from the new offices established in the King's buildings. The vendors' eyes are not unkind; they are trusting souls, souls that trust change. But, Amah thinks, there are things they don't understand.

She leaves the palace in the evening light to meet Gulbadan who's already been notified about the need to find messengers. Gulbadan is an older, plump woman with black-and-grey hair pulled tightly away from the delicate pearl clusters that cover her ears. She manages the wealthy *kotha,* a set of apartments belonging to the King's courtesans—some of his favoured poets, singers, and classical dancers who live above the main market street, Chowk, situated west of Qaisarbagh Palace, on the other side of Residency Hill. Begam Sahiba completed some of her training privately with Gulbadan before her marriage to His Majesty. After marriage, she replaced her courtesan friends with tigers, black swans, her son Birjis, and Amah.

Amah climbs the stairs to the *kotha* and finds Gulbadan in her little pavilion at the top. Her back to Amah, she sifts through papers in a wall of drawers. She wears a green, silk *kurta* with a short-sleeved, tight blouse underneath, and wide pyjamas tied at the waist. A light *duppata* is draped over her head. As Amah waits for Gulbadan to turn around, she daydreams about being invited to recline in the open-air courtyard against one of the pillows, as if she were a royal patron waiting for an evening of poetry and music, while Sai, Gulbadan's nephew, serves her puffed *puris*, chicken in creamy gravies, and almond milk when she asks.

"*Tasleem*," Amah finally says, bowing slightly, and touching her forehead in respect.

"*Tasleem*. I'll talk to you about the messengers in a moment," Gulbadan says, not turning around. "Go and do something else for a little while."

Amah leaves to find Gulbadan's nephew, Sai. In the court-yard, a group of Indian nobles are seated for dinner and a performance of *ragas*. They've brought ruby bracelets for the courtesans and laid them out on a low wall for marvelling. Serving boys offer the guests fried kebabs with mint and pepper chutneys. Sai, a small, young man, places mosquito coils around the courtyard and supplies salve for bites. He supplies the guests with cool water to relieve their hot mouths. The men thirst for the possibility to touch a courtesan's black hair, want to have their dry tongues quenched by smooth skin, men who return for these soirees like homing pigeons. Sai offers cool water to the courtesans, young women with green eyes, gold-flecked brown eyes, and bright, black eyes, women who own homes and shops and goats, who tutor young boys in manners, and who write poems that come from their fresh mouths—poems that hang in the warm air above the marigolds and blue pillows embroidered with silver fish that match the silver stars, poems that wink in the air like the diamonds on the courtesans' delicate noses, that shimmer like the silver spangles on the women's chiffon pyjamas. Delicate syllables rest in the air, then disappear—courtesan song written on the breeze.

At the well by the kitchen, Sai refills the water pitchers and greets Amah. "*Adab*," he says, his head bowed slightly. He cups his hand over his heart and pats his chest twice.

"*Tasleem*," Amah replies.

Over the years, she's seen her friend Sai decorate the *kotha* for Ramadan, Diwali, Jain saint days, the Jewish New Year. They played together as children, like siblings, throwing mangoes at each other while being chastised by Gulbadan. "Milk sweet?" he asks, holding out a dish. "Sister, look. The colour of dark honey. Like you."

"Too kind, my friend, but no." Sai loves milk sweets so much that, watching him, Amah can taste the ones he eats.

The strains of a band practicing a waltz can be heard from Residency Hill. Sai twirls barefoot around the well, humming and sucking the sweet, mimicking the stiff-legged English couples performing their drills. Finally, he sits down beside her, still sucking on the sweet.

"That music makes my head sore," Amah says.

"Those new telegraph wires make my eyes sore," Sai says.

"Shall we cut them?" she asks.

He glances at her in surprise.

She hesitates, realizing she means the words. "Shall we cut them?"

"Is that some sort of foreign joke, Amah?"

"I'm serious. Their telegraph wires bring them news, and we receive empty envelopes. I think we should cut them."

"We would land in jail. The royal family has some leeway—

you might have some leeway even—but I would land in jail. Most likely a new English jail."

"There must be a way to slow the Company down."

"It's better to proceed through the right channels. You know that."

Amah keeps thinking.

"I would never do it, you know that, too," he says. "However," he adds, nodding in the direction of Amah's rifle, "perhaps you would." Sai gets up and stretches. "Sister, I'm not going to agree with you about something that will get you hurt. Leave the idea alone." He picks up the water pitchers and stands there, waiting for her.

She lets the thought go for now and gets up to follow him.

In the courtyard, notes from a sitar curl through the air like questions. The gathering of captivated men listen, eat *habshi halwa*, and reflect. Gulbadan walks across the courtyard toward Amah, pausing to speak to two men in capes, seated behind the others. They are not Lakhnavis, and Amah cannot read their long faces. "Who are they?" she asks when Gulbadan reaches her.

"Rasheed and Akbar. From Calcutta. They work together, know villagers who they can stay with for a *rupee*. They know how to travel carefully, resting with villagers, making sure they stay alert. They can bring your correspondence from Calcutta through Cawnpore to here."

"How do we know we can trust them?"

"I think they are trustworthy."

"But Gulbadan, how do we know for certain? Have they done this work before? We need to be sure."

"Begam Sahiba will know that if I think they are trustworthy, then they are trustworthy," Gulbadan says, her voice rising, her face setting. "They are good men. Where is the letter for His Majesty's advisors? Stop wasting time."

Amah hands it to her and bows her head. "Thank you," she says.

* * *

Lucknow stands still the next afternoon, the first afternoon of monsoon rain. Amah waits with her cousins, old Kasim and Fatima, at the doors of the front hall, looking out into the street where the water flows clearly from the drains, drenching the thirsty flower beds. The rain dampens their skin. A scrubbed warmth fills the air. "I wonder what the cold feels like in London," Amah says. "Our Queen Mother must be watching the cold rain. And in Calcutta, what do those people see? I wonder if the rain in Calcutta chokes the streets as it never does here."

Her mother's angry absence washes over her. She suddenly wants to lie down and leaves the front hall, hurrying through Qaisarbagh's gardens, rain trickling behind her ears, the wet azaleas brushing her arms. She means to go to her room, but she finds herself at her mother's door and goes in.

In the corner of the room, Amah picks up her mother's prayer mat to check her mother's box of precious stones. Amah has already taken some to sell, to pay the royal cooks who wait, like she does, for their salaries to arrive.

Amah hears footsteps and, when she turns around, Aunt Laila stands in the doorway holding glass prayer beads. "You couldn't even bring her warm milk," she says to Amah, lifting her voice above the rain hammering on the roof.

"Auntie, my mother took the early coach to Calcutta. If she'd stayed I would have brought her warm milk in time."

"Since when do you do things for your mother? It's shameful that she had to travel alone. And now your mother's room is as empty and silent as your heart is of prayers."

Amah studies her aunt's face. Like Amah's mother, she has high cheekbones, almond-shaped eyes. Aunt Laila's son, Amah's cousin Hasan, a royal jockey now out of work, shares these delicate features. Except for Amah's cropped hair and her father's height, they all look related. Their differences lie in a deeper place.

She doesn't tell Aunt Laila that the silence in the room seems tranquil after her mother's clucking sounds of disapproval that her aunt, it appears, has taken up. Instead, Amah excuses herself, and leaves.

She walks in the canopied street by Qaisarbagh Palace, under the dripping trees and some unseen birds who, to use her grandmother's old phrase, make a clatter like pastry pans. In the distance, newspaper buyers huddle around Mohammed's stall. She stays away, thinking about her mother, how she would wait for Amah's brother to come away from his court meetings to eat, how she would give the palace cooks orders for her son's daily dishes. Her mother often told her about her brother, and also about her Lakhnavi father. She spoke in an insistent, chastising voice, as if that would help Amah not to forget them. Amah does not remember them well.

She stops to contemplate the mosquitoes gathered above a puddle on the road. Lucknow is an ancient city, she thinks. Struggles have come and gone. Surely, this one with her mother can come and go, too. They will all come home, and there will be no more choosing. When Amah looks down, there are mosquitoes clinging to her ankles.

5.

———•—×—•———

ULBADAN'S MESSENGERS, Rasheed and Akbar, leave for Calcutta with Begam Sahiba's letter, alerting the palace advisors there of the immediate need for a new means of correspondence, and asking them what is happening with the King's petitions to restore Lucknow to the royal family. Begam Sahiba includes a list of changes the English have made—the sale of all the royal animals, the takeover of buildings, the closing of the college, the surveillance of land taking place in and around Lucknow. The messengers take a small parcel for Amah's mother, a black *burqa* for the Prophet's birthday that Amah has purchased from the courtesans' shop in Chowk. With no letters from her mother, Amah tries not to wonder if her mother is so disappointed that she wants to forget her. With her small gift, she insists her mother remember.

While they wait for the weeks it will take the messengers to return with news, Begam Sahiba arranges a thirteenth birthday celebration for her son at the *kotha*. The preparations relieve Amah of the silences at the palace. They also take her mind off the people wandering the streets out of work, and the whispered conversations in the alleys about leaving Lucknow for good. The preparations for a *tamasha* help her to forget about the smell of new whitewash when she passes the English post office.

The night of the *tamasha* is even better. *Mashallah!* The sharp scent of marigolds fills the lamplit courtyard. Like a royal king, Amah finds her place among the guests, lying in silk pillows. Boys offer copper hookah bowls. The guests admire His Majesty's courtesans, women versed in Persian and Urdu, women with word skills whispered to them by third-century Persians and Afghanis, women who pass on their poetic turns, whose turning hennaed feet and jangling anklets play with a *tabla's* drum beats, women whose silk pyjamas set fashions, and whose silver and gold coins fill Lucknow's banks. These women are powerful patrons of the city, who teach Lakhnavis the art of placing visitors first, who are ready to offer guests savory *pulaus*, golden, braised meats, and a popular confectionary trick: sweets fashioned to look like pomegranate seeds filled with almonds, pear juice, and sugar.

Begam Sahiba's son, Birjis, runs to Amah, and she reaches out her hands to him, kisses the boy on both cheeks. Birjis is dressed as a yogi in saffron robes, the way his father, His Majesty, dresses on his own birthday, ashes of pearls smeared on his body and cheeks, pearls around his neck, and a rosary between his fingers to counteract any evil stars shining down on his precious day. Amah can't help thinking that the evil is not in the sky above Lucknow's brass domes. It has come to roost in the city's streets.

Several cooks produce a large pie that they open to release some small, white pigeons who fly away above the hushed crowd.

Sai finds Amah and Birjis. He gives Birjis a turkey wing that turns out to be spun sugar when Birjis, their ash-covered kite-fighter, bites into it. The boy laughs.

"I want to make you laugh, too, Amah," Sai says in a low voice. "Sister, try not to worry. Let your lovely eyes twinkle like the jewels on your tunic." He smiles at her, and she eventually smiles back.

Sai. So kind. She can't recall her mother ever praising anything about the way she looks. His words warm her. Together, they watch Birjis break off another piece of spun sugar and eat it.

"You will get bumps on your tongue," Amah says to Birjis.

"Those types of bumps are lie bumps." Birjis holds out the sweet to her. "I don't lie, so I am immune. You?"

She waves it away.

"Birjis, Amah," Sai says. "Let me tell you a good story. An English story."

In the gardens of the English bungalows on the other side of the Gomti river, Sai milks goats for Englishwomen who have purchased the animals from the courtesans and pay for a milking service. The Englishwomen tell him to leave the milk buckets on kitchen sills, on verandah steps where English town planners peer through binoculars, and beside dining room doors where couples speak too loudly at lunch. Everything they say carries over the warm air, under the goats' udders, and into Sai's ears.

Tonight, Sai is quickly surrounded by birthday guests who lean in closely. "So," he says. "I was asked to come inside since there was a serving man absent. I stood against the wall across the table from the other men who work in Mrs. Gunning's dining room. First, the English ate a small hog that had been placed upon the table, and several other sorts of flesh, along with a great quantity of wine which doubtless was the cause of all the loud noise that went on for some time. They stood up four or five times and called, '*Hip Hip*,' before they drank some more. I didn't look into the eyes of my fellow servers, nor even glance in their direction, so distorted I felt by a fit of laughter daring to overcome me. Finally, when I could not stop my eyes from watering, and my cheeks had small cramps, I fell into a heap of coughing to try to stop the convulsions. But after dinner, when they performed their usual dance drills—pulling about each other's wives—I had to escape to the kitchen where, my serving friends informed me, my helpless whoop was mistaken for a lost hyena's yelp. But then I got the hiccups, and I was told by Mrs. Gunning, who came in for more Champagne, to get out."

The guests laugh. "And they call our teetotaler King immoral," someone says.

More guests wander up the stuccoed stairs from Chowk, the main market street. Amah offers Muslim teachers *paan* with cardamoms wrapped in edible gold foil. She helps Sai prepare betel nut boiled in milk for Hindu landlords. Around them, the courtyard is filled with the low, warm voices of Lakhnavi friends. She leads the way to the courtyard for an old Shi'a scholar who tells her as he walks, his face creased with knowledge and joy, that his sole purpose here is to find the places in the conversations where he is needed to instruct. Two elderly Somalian *paan*-makers wave to Amah from where they sit; the women knew her grandmother well. A young Hindu man and his friend, a young Muslim, both dressed in fine silks, recite their newest Persian verses while the crowd encourages them with responses in Persian of their own. The old Shi'a scholar raises his voice, waving his hands to get attention, to lecture them all on grammar and logic.

Amah's aunt's scoldings are far away, across the city. The English waltzes are also far away, across the river. In the *kotha's* courtyard, fireflies wink and dance. The guests put away the day's worries to gather in old female ceremonies, picking tea-stained teeth, hunger satiated by *pulau*s, and smart women's attentive, kohl-lined eyes. And later, guests accept beds in breezy rooms with warm baths, silk covers, and lullabies.

* * *

At dawn, the first birds sing tentatively and the musicians give into them, their final notes dying away. A few guests, including Amah, are still up, lost in old songs.

Somewhere on the road below, a gun cracks. It is a rifle and not a watchman's musket. They hear the high trumpeting of an elephant. Confused, Amah leaves the courtyard to fetch her rifle from where she left it in Gulbadan's pavilion and waits, listening, at the top of the *kotha's* stairs. The gun cracks again and this time the elephant screams like wild pigs.

She hurries down the staircase and through the empty Chowk, running all the way to the farthest end of the road, guided by the elephant's cries and kicked-up red dust. Amah finds the animal next to a broken wall. Black blood pours out of one eye and out of the elephant's mouth, staining her trunk. Prakash, her attendant, holds a silver harness. His lips tremble and his teeth chatter as he prays for her life to the elephant god, "*Ga-ga-nesh, Ganesh, O-o-m Vakratundaya H-Hum.*" Amah puts her hand on the elephant's sunken temple, her dry skin. Prakash is sobbing, telling her an English auctioneer ordered the elephant to be shot since they could not sell such an old beast. Even though Prakash had pleaded, the English officer with the red hair and dimpled chin, a man who had no idea how to kill an elephant, came to do it. The elephant broke her ropes and charged down the road. There is no sign of the dimpled Red Man who fumbled the job.

Amah takes off her scarf and holds it to the elephant's bleeding mouth. Prakash scrambles off the animal's side, tears off a piece of his *lungi,* and holds it over the elephant's eye. It is barely light in Chowk. The elephant's drool, mixed with blood, slides onto Amah's hand and down her arm. She is kneeling in pools of saliva. The elephant's drool is thicker and warmer than blood. Mixed with blood, it is shiny red. Amah's legs are warm, wet. Her tunic slides on her skin. She whispers to the elephant that she loves her as she searches her mouth. There are bullets in her tongue, and the blood leaks from the back of her throat. Amah could fill buckets with the stringy, bloody drool, and pour it onto narrow paths to quell the dust. Her fingers dig the bullets out from the elephant's mouth. The elephant trembles with pain, her grey body more crumpled than the moment before. She nudges her head toward Prakash's chest. Amah stands up and prepares her rifle. She's never shot an animal. She's never shot a living thing, and she likes it that

47

way. The rifle becomes the bark of a tree, a necessary herbal remedy. The elephant watches her with one beautiful eye, and Amah wills her fingers, which do not seem to be her fingers, and she shoots into the elephant's heart. The elephant will stay in Lucknow, she thinks, pushing her head against the animal's warm brow. She is going to stay in Lucknow, sweet old beast. Prakash wails goodbye, his voice bouncing off the wooden doors of the shops.

* * *

The next day, Amah goes to a Muslim neighbour's women's quarters with her cousin Fatima and other members of the Rose Platoon for the tenth day of the sacred month in the Islamic calendar. She prays for their elephant. The women's songs soothe Amah. Afterwards, there are meat dishes and sherbets. She eats a little, listening to the hushed talk about lost jobs, about how Abdulla the landlord can no longer afford his usual generosity. He is leaving the city with his family, which means that Sai's job milking the landlord's goats is finished. And there is one less wealthy patron coming back to the *kotha* like a homing pigeon.

The women's quarters are full. No dish of sherbet is permitted to melt, no passion-fruit ice turns to water; elegant old women leave, overloaded with pots filled with pea curries and half-moon *parathas* and dishes of rice pudding. On her way out, Amah sees Hasan, Aunt Laila's son, coming out of the *imambarah* with some other men down the road. Abhi, the English lover with teeth stained red from betel, is also on the road, mingling with all the men. He needs to be watched. But she passes him now, and catches up to Hasan. "*Salaam*," Hasan says. "Good evening, older cousin; praise be to Allah."

And Amah looks down at him and says, "*Tasleem*. Good evening, little cousin. Praise be to Allah. Where are you riding dressed in silk jodhpurs?"

"I am walking home," he says.

"With those fine clothes, you don't need a horse; you can fly like a kite."

Hasan laughs and asks her to walk with him. "The filth in the streets is piling up. With a guard in well-laundered clothes like you, I will be sure to take the cleanest route."

"Walking with you, Hasan, keeps my mind off the streets getting so dirty. I only feel warmth."

"But it is getting cold," Hasan says, gazing up at her. "I don't think it feels like this in Calcutta."

"We are warm enough."

"The Company is not paying any wages to dismissed royal jockeys as they said they would. Their promises are empty. You have not received your salary from the King. Shall we go and see what it is like in Calcutta?" He stops in the road, his dark eyes pleading with her.

"No, Hasan," she says, quietly. "We have plenty here. We should stay where we're needed. At home." She turns from him, ducks into an alley, and walks ahead.

* * *

The next day, Amah watches the old elephant being cremated. The English have refused to transport her to the elephant cemetery to be buried three miles away. Amah stands in the thick crowd of onlookers in the rain, all of them wrapped in shawls and headscarves. Ten English soldiers stand between them and the animal, giving orders. The workers the English have hired cover the ground with straw and dig an enormous hole beside the dead animal. Amah holds an urn for Prakash, the elephant's attendant. Ganesh, the elephant god, has been carved onto the urn by Judea the jeweller—a gift from Begam Sahiba. "Prakash is us; we are Prakash," Begam Sahiba said.

Prakash stands on the elephant's flabby side with an axe, where he carves out white chunks of elephant meat to lighten the carcass. He cuts up and down the body, crisscrossing the droopy grey skin with white slicings, his face heavy and creased. The rain stops. The elephant is roped and pulled into the muddy hole, her tattered old ears turning inside out, the workers sweeping the straw after her in the lengthy task of covering her. A burning stick is lodged in her mouth. As the flames are kindled and begin to leap, the hole shimmers, and everyone around the hole shimmers, including Amah.

The shopkeepers move away, their eyes clouded with confusion. Prakash's lips tremble and his teeth chatter as he whispers his tales of auctioneers and a red-haired officer's mistakes to town gardeners, bookkeepers, and street cleaners—people who stand around these days with nothing to do. The hired workers continue to feed the roiling fire. They chant songs to Ganesh, throwing prayers into the churning air, breathing the heat, singing farewell and new-life songs, waving their words out to the meadows, under the fish-shaped archways, and above the city's brick minarets. Lucknow's people move away but Amah has seen their eyes. Each of them takes a little fire with them, smouldering pain that will not be relieved by a monsoon rain of broken English promises.

6.

——◦•✦•◦——

A SERVANT BOY at the palace finds Amah with Fatima and several other guards standing outside His Majesty's storerooms off the front hall. He gives her the news to go to the *kotha* at once. The messengers are back. Amah runs through the gardens to the kitchens where Kasim is eating pieces of bread mixed with *ghee* and sugar. She asks him to take her place guarding the storerooms. On her way out, Aunt Laila stops her near the kadam tree where her mother's white pigeons peck the dirt.

"What is going on with Hasan?" Aunt Laila asks Amah, fidgeting with her prayer beads. "This morning he told me he would not come with me to Calcutta."

"What did he say?"

"That there are ways he can make money here."

"Perhaps there are," Amah says.

"Don't be coy, Amah. Hasan is my son. He should come with me to Calcutta until this business is finished with. Tell him to come. He is a *Habshi* jockey, a respectable man, and people expect good of him."

"Auntie, I must go," Amah says.

Her aunt raises her voice behind Amah. "Just like you. You can never do what's expected, or be respectful and kind. Don't poison him like a cobra-woman, barren of prayer. You are nothing like your mother. Not one bit."

Amah passes quickly through the gardens while she hears

her aunt continue to curse far behind her. She fixes her gaze on all the bees that hover in the yellow-tinted jasmine, then stares at the reflection in a water tank of a pigeon in the air. She leaves behind her aunt's words.

Outside, she hurries past homes designed by French and Italian architects, past artisans' workshops, past terraced roofs and tall columns, past water fountains filled with lotus flowers, and past the public spots reserved especially for poets' gatherings since there are more poets in Lucknow than in the rest of India. She passes the *kotwali,* the police headquarters, with an attached jail in Chowk. She sees the Company officer with the dimpled chin and red hair come out, the Red Man who cannot shoot an elephant. She watches Red Man smoke a cheroot with his tall, Indian friend—the *Kotwal*, the Lakhnavi Chief of Police. She scans the area for Abhi in his silver-and-gold-threaded cap, but this time he isn't there.

At the stairs leading up to the *kotha*, the gate-keeper, Gulbadan's brother, nods to Amah. He is fat and nervous, a peasant who owns a strip of land in the province of Awadh. He is staying here while his petition against the Company's Summary Land Settlement is pending. The Company moves as swiftly as pirates to take new land in rural Awadh, but they do not move swiftly to their sea of petitions.

Upstairs in the courtyard, plump Gulbadan sits with a young woman who holds her long plait in her hand. Gulbadan glances at Amah and pats the air impatiently. Amah sits down.

The young woman is full of dark shadows, a stranger who has probably crossed fire to get to this place of rescue. Her posture makes Gulbadan's brow furrow. She says, "Nothing happens here that you don't want to happen. But first, let's undo what has been done."

Amah fidgets, half-listening to the girl—that her husband died during the first month of marriage and that she ran away from her husband's family who marked her as ill-starred. The courtesans are called from their rooms to make jokes about fathers-in-law who slap girls for immodesty, and mimic old husbands with obscene gestures. The girl listens. They sing about Persian love, Urdu love, English love, and passionate love. They sing about moulding fate like clay, about the game of love, the art of pretence, and the importance of saving a little fortune of silver coins and red rubies to purchase income-producing property in Lucknow in order to retire with rooms of their own. "Make your place here at the *kotha*," they say to the girl. "Stay here and become rich, and then marry again if you wish."

Amah has often watched newcomers become sisters at the *kotha*, a place for young women to change their fate. Here, ears listen. Hearts love. How easy that is. Hindus become Muslims, Muslims become Parsis, Parsis become Christians, and Christians become Hindus. Women are women.

But she wishes that this time Gulbadan would not make her wait. Impatient, she gets up and goes to find Sai, who she finds sitting outside his room with an almost-empty bottle of whisky in his hands.

"What are you doing?" Amah asks.

He laughs. An enormous hiccup interrupts his laugh, and that only makes him laugh louder. He gets up and stumbles between his room and the kitchen, tripping on his slippers, so Amah urges him to stand still while she pours warm water down his throat. He throws up.

He takes the water pitcher from her hand and tries swinging it at her, but she stops him, urging him to sleep. She pushes him into his room and makes him lie down on his bed where he weeps apologies, still hiccuping, and eventually begins to snore.

"What's going on?" Gulbadan asks, appearing as Amah cleans up the mess outside.

"Sai was drinking whisky, but he's asleep now."

Gulbadan goes into Sai's room, and Amah can hear her scolding his sleeping body as she takes up his twisted sheet and unfurls it. Then she comes out and asks Amah to follow her.

At her pavilion, Gulbadan puts on her spectacles and goes to her wall of drawers. "He's got a weak constitution, my nephew," she says. "His mother, may she rest in peace, would be horrified. I do not like that." She retrieves a set of keys. "Whisky! Since when does he drink whisky?"

"I don't know. But it is not a good time to behave in an undignified fashion. Gulbadan, tell me, did the messengers run into any trouble on the roads? Night-time marauders? A thief with a bad cough?"

"Of course not. They know how to avoid trouble." She picks out a key and goes to another drawer and opens it. "But it is true that there are all sorts of superstitions in the sky these past nights. If I believed, I would be worried."

She takes out a small brown-paper parcel and turns around. "Listen, Amah, watch Sai. Don't be led astray by your friend. When you were a child, you made good plans. You planted a kadam tree to shade your parents' room. Now you've become an important member of the royal household. You know how to make good judgments."

Amah feels a glimmer of guilt as she takes the parcel. Gulbadan would not agree with her persistent desire to cut the telegraph wires. Amah thinks about it. If Lakhnavis have to find messengers to run overland in disguise from Lucknow to Calcutta and back, if they have to go to all that trouble, expense, and time, then surely, surely the English telegraph wires can go.

**

At Begam Sahiba's house, the black swans croon under the neem tree. Shahzadi is growing so quickly her bamboo enclosure appears small. In Begam Sahiba's meeting room, Amah holds up the parcel. "*Tasleem*," she says, and bows her head.

"*Tasleem*," Begam Sahiba says as she takes the parcel, pulls it open, and studies the letters inside. She picks out one of the letters. "Look at me trembling. It's really from Calcutta. And addressed to me." She turns the letter over. "From the King's advisors. The seal has not been touched. It's unopened."

Amah watches her friend's face as she opens the letter and reads. She waits for light to come into Begam Sahiba's eyes but sees nothing. "What is it?" Amah finally asks. "What is the news?"

"They tell us to wait for the King's return, that they don't expect it to be much longer," Begam Sahiba says, still reading.

"No salaries?"

"We are ordered to pass on this letter to the palace advisors here. Staff will receive their salaries upon the King's return. The advisors are optimistic about the latest petition before Governor General Lord Canning to restore the province of Awadh to the royal family. And a new Chief Commissioner will be taking over the English East India Company in Lucknow. He is apparently a good man, fond of Lucknow. They urge Lakhnavis to welcome him when he visits to survey the city, ahead of taking his new position." She gives Amah the letter. "The King sends a strict reminder to all his military men in the city not to take up their arms. As a sign of good faith. You must relay that message far and wide, Amah."

Amah adjusts her rifle. "No response to what we document-ed? The auction? All the demolition?"

"Only that we must wait for things to go through the proper channels."

Begam Sahiba takes out the other two letters from the brown-paper wrapping. "From the Queen Mother. For Lal. And there's one from your mother." She offers Amah one of the letters and holds the other up. "We must call Lal."

Amah does not open her letter. She doesn't do anything.

"I'll call a boy to get him," Begam Sahiba says. She goes out and comes back.

While they wait, they do not say a word. Amah cannot say what they do but they don't look at those letters. They wait until the Queen Mother's old advisor arrives. White-haired

Lal breathes hard and offers tangerines. Begam Sahiba gives him the letter and he tries to give it back to her. "Read it to me," he says.

"You know that she would be angry," Begam Sahiba says. "It is not my place."

Lal presses the letter into her hands. "Please," he says, his voice catching. "Read it to me."

"Let's not waste time," Amah says.

Finally, Begam Sahiba breaks the seal and opens the envelope. She takes out the letter and scans the pages, beads of sweat lining her upper lip. "She has not yet met with the English Queen," she says. "Queen Victoria is pregnant with a ninth child and remains in confinement. The Queen Mother has received visits from Company and Government representatives who tell her that she can't expect Queen Victoria to change what has happened. They tell her it doesn't work that way in England, that their Queen doesn't have that kind of power over a business such as the English East India Company. But the Queen Mother is determined to ask her to return the Kingdom of Awadh to her, to plead her son's case." Begam Sahiba looks up. "I hope she is not making another mistake," she says.

Amah glances at her. They both know His Majesty divorced Begam Sahiba to make his mother happy. His mother believed that Begam Sahiba had a suspicious birthmark on her neck in the shape of a coiled snake. That was before his advisors told His Majesty that the mark on the nape of her neck was a birthmark—that the idea of a coiled snake was nothing but superstition. But the deed had been done; the divorce issued. "Let bygones be bygones," His Majesty had pleaded with Begam Sahiba who had finally, bitterly, consented.

Begam Sahiba continues to read about the Queen Mother's needs for *Rasayana* tonic mixed by Lal. "She says England would fit into the province of Awadh like a Pomeranian puppy fits inside a teacup. Masses of grey birds and grey dogs. Her handkerchiefs are black with soot. Indian Bath Soap at luxury prices. Her veil is an entertainment theme in their papers. On her arrival, they mocked her, sketching her in their papers as a nude damsel." Begam Sahiba's eyes flash. "My goodness. Now, that is discourteous."

Lal looks away. Begam Sahiba folds the letter, creasing the pages hard with her fingers, as if to erase what they've just heard. If she still harbours resentment about the Queen Mother, the resentment against the English is growing stronger. "She's not giving up. Queen Victoria's baby is due in four months' time. She'll stay until their Queen is out of confinement and she can meet with her. She'll stay until the government in London has read her petition. She wants to make sure they read it in London. She feels that no one really seems to be paying attention to the fact that the only reason the King is in Calcutta is to dispute and rectify the treaty, and that it remains unsigned."

Begam Sahiba contemplates Shahzadi in the garden. "Cities are overtaken by Englishmen. Cultures fail. Towns are renamed. In the Punjab, the Sikh Maharaja has been pensioned off and brought to England, a man who is nothing but a royal lap dog for Queen Victoria. It happens everywhere, all over the world. Dozens of times a year, hundreds of times a century, to people much more vulnerable than us. Each has its aspects of a slur."

She walks the length of the room. "But we will not be the ones to injure. No injury, no requital. We must be courteous, Amah, and rise above such misbehaviour." She stops and looks at Amah pointedly. "I've risen above things, many things. So, we can rise above this matter. Now, your letter. Shall I read the letter from your mother?"

The letter does not take long to read. It is a simple note written by a staff writer on behalf of her mother, telling Amah the King's residence at Matiya Burj has all the necessities. She is well despite the circumstances. Her mother doesn't mention the fact they did not say goodbye. She does not ask after Amah. She does not say when she plans to return.

When Amah looks up, her friend is studying her. Begam Sahiba says, "I will arrange to meet with this new Commissioner who is coming. We will get your mother home soon."

* * *

At first, Amah stays in the crowd at a distance from the carriage, watching Red Man brief the visiting Chief Commissioner-to-be. Sir Henry Lawrence is a man with sharp, blue eyes and a long, white beard. When the carriage pulls up to the shops being pulled down around the new English post office on the main road, Hazratganj, she ventures closer, right beneath the carriage, to listen to Red Man. She considers his tone, tries to catch any English words she might know. The man says, "That stucco, such flimsy stuff. Just as weak as the natives."

"But parts of Lucknow have fallen into disrepair," Sir Henry Lawrence says with dismay. "The alleys are full of filth. The sanitation ditches are choked."

Red Man says, "We must keep ourselves apart; we need to keep ourselves clean."

Amah strains to see the new Chief Commissioner-to-be. He frowns as he gazes out of his carriage, not happy, she guesses, with what he sees. The man says, "I find all of this alarming. I find this very wrong."

Red Man's chin dimples. He says, "Sir. Sometimes you've got to do things for them. Show them what's worth keeping."

A crew of beggars pulls down the shops. One of the beggars used to be the King's best newspaper writer. Now he is a seventy-five-year-old demolition worker pulling down the shop where he used to buy his ink.

Amah thinks, perhaps the new Chief Commissioner-to-be with the noble, white beard will read the petitions and call a halt. Perhaps he will write a letter to his superiors in Calcutta.

Sir Henry Lawrence never seems to mind Amah as she walks near the carriage. Red Man does not recognize her. Again. He prods her with his boot, spits at her as she tries to raise up the old newspaper writer from where he dozes near the old shops. Later, in the afternoon, he tells her to move along while she stoops to gather pieces of statue in the rose garden between the Residency and the stone church, yellow butterflies dancing on the fresh-turned earth. Red Man is the same demolition officer she's seen smash Begam Sahiba's favourite Venus and Napoleon statues in the city, the same man who hits her with a stone now in the English rose garden. "Leave it be, filthy boy. Get along," he says in Urdu. On Sundays, she knows he becomes still as a statue, kneeling in the stone church.

Her red jacket is dirty from the man's boot, and his spittle has dried in her hair. She picks up a clod of dirt from the flower bed and imagines the Chief Commissioner-to-be isn't there. He is safely inside the Residency, reading their petitions. She sees only Red Man with his dirty mouth and dimpled chin, smirking at her. She almost misses him, but the clod catches his chin, dirt flying like fireworks. She hears him curse, enraged, as he spits mud from his mouth.

What Amah has failed to see is Begam Sahiba's palanquin carried by four men, and the group of servants standing by Begam Sahiba as she waits under the Baillie Guard Gate at the Residency to meet Sir Henry Lawrence for the first time—a veiled Begam Sahiba with angry blotches around her eyes, her hands clenched at her sides while she watches Red Man, who jumps out of the carriage and runs forward to grab Amah. Amah has failed to see that her action would confirm Red Man's words that they are dirty weaklings.

* * *

In the *kotwali*, the police station, Red Man smacks Amah across the cheek. Dust settles. Amah imagines Begam Sahiba saying coldly, "See? Discourtesy gets nowhere." The officer— Red Man—has become a drunk jailor, a man who receives Company rewards for bringing in Indians like her.

A single smack bruises; the second and third break the skin. Things happened so quickly—it has been an hour since he caught her throwing the clod of dirt on Residency Hill. His body fills her cell. She smells sweet wine and cheroot smoke in his coat, sees the butt of a rifle swoop in close to her chest.

One throw. Why such fury? Red Man walks out and locks the cell, pocketing the coin that has fallen from her jacket. Amah says in Urdu, "The royal family is not subject to your laws."

And he whispers, a mix of English and Urdu, "By Jasus, you will be, boy." He tosses her coin in his hand. "Finders, keepers," he says.

He is disgusting. Like the holding cell. Filth clogs every crevice; flies cling to old feces carpeting the floor. His scorn seeps into the wounds on her face like salt. In the cell across from Amah, a man dressed in a glittering shawl is also being made to suffer shame. "Have they read my petition?" he asks Red Man who sits at the desk in the middle of the room. He gets no reply.

The prisoner's name is 'Ali Shah. He retches at the back of his cell. All the stinking filth is too much for him. The *Kotwal,* the Indian Chief of Police, comes out of his side office. Paid handsomely by the King for years, the tall man with a grey moustache has been bribed by the English over the past months to work for them. He wants to make 'Ali Shah eat. "To stay well," he says to Red Man. "For the inspection."

In the late afternoon, 'Ali Shah rests against the iron bars of his cell, staring out, a pot of rice hanging from a nail, untouched. Amah hears men shuffle and cough from the small jail through the back door of the police station. Outside the front doors of the station, Red Man and the *Kotwal* have gone to smoke.

The shouts of vendors in Chowk and the jangle of anklets shroud conversation. With the cells' bars between them, formality breaks down and 'Ali Shah and Amah talk in low voices. 'Ali Shah is a *taluqdar*, a village land-owner, who has not paid the new land tax. He wears a handsome shawl, what his father wore before him. What they've worn for generations. Centuries.

"It's better than the Straits," Amah says. "We are not going to Singapore, Penang, or Malacca."

"Who is?" he asks.

She shrugs. "Whoever they want to punish most. Manual labour. You never come back."

'Ali Shah won't accept Amah's offer to help him get the money he needs for his release. They've taken his family's land and he's fighting that with a petition. The clerks are mired in paperwork. "They behave as if we've been squarely beaten, as if Awadh is a conquered country," he says. "Except there's been no war."

Amah tells him about the clod of dirt, about her duty to His Majesty, to her friend, Begam Sahiba, about how what she's done only fulfils the Englishmen's worst slurs against them. "I was discourteous," Amah says.

"Perhaps we have to be," he says. "To get their attention."

"You should eat," Amah says. "Don't hurt yourself."

'Ali Shah considers the pot. Then he eats every grain of rice. The *Kotwal* comes inside, pours wine into a pewter cup, and drinks. He goes to 'Ali Shah's cell and looks into the pot. "See, you needed that," he says.

Amah dozes on and off all evening, ignoring hunger. The *Kotwal* and Red Man talk loudly in the side office, the squeaks of cane chairs on the floor, of iron keys thrown down, of bottles clinking. Their wine, that smell! Like sweet vinegar all around Amah, clinging to her damp cheeks.

She wakes in the morning wanting salmon and rice. Mango in ice chips. A chicken kebab with sweet onions. She can't stop thinking about puffed *puris* and gravy. It's Begam Sahiba, she thinks. She is sending me these thoughts to punish me.

* * *

Amah waits until the *Kotwal* is alone. Crazed bluebottles keep hitting the station's walls, a sound that makes him frown. His breath is sour wine. Tall and muscular, this Chief of Police's grey moustache matches his bleary eyes. So attentive to her request to be freed, to her explanation that she is the female bodyguard to the King, and good friend to Begam Sahiba, that he seems like the old days. He stands at the desk in the middle of the room and pulls at his moustache. He checks Red Man's records, calling the Englishman a Mr. John Graham, a name Amah has never heard. The *Kotwal* rubs his chin. "Mr. Graham thought you were a servant boy. I thought you were a pest." He stares out the window. "All the inspections. We can't keep a woman here."

He loves Begam Sahiba, too. He knows who she is.

He goes to the side office and brings out three cages of silk-winged pigeons, the cages full of golden-green flutterings. He isn't afraid to have purchased the birds at the English auction of the royal animals. Through the wire, he strokes them with his finger, and feeds them bits of old *chapati*. "On loan with me," he says. "My good deed for His Majesty." He is going to bring them back, he says, once things settle down.

Amah hates herself for letting him rid his conscience of guilt by telling her this. She hates telling him he's treated the birds so well that Begam Sahiba will reward him. "I have to get home, too," she whispers to the pigeons in their cages on the floor, as the *Kotwal* goes to get his keys.

* * *

In Begam Sahiba's garden, Amah keeps her eyes fixed on Shahzadi who whimpers in her sleep.

"What are you going to do next?" Begam Sahiba asks her icily. She has sent a servant boy with payment for 'Ali Shah's release. Begam Sahiba stands very still. Perspiration dampens her headscarf and seeps into the neckline of her rose-coloured shirt edged with *chikan* embroidered flowers.

"Stay close to you."

"No more rudeness?"

"Not again."

"It's not what we do," she says, her voice tight with anger. "That man Sir Henry Lawrence will be the new Chief Commissioner sometime in the new year. He has sense. He knows the city well, and he does not agree with all this change." She stares at Amah. "And Sai told me you were conspiring with him to cut the telegraph wires. Don't you dare do that either."

Amah's eyes drop. "No," she says.

What could she do instead? She could try to repair Begam Sahiba's favourite Venus and Napoleon statues, re-stucco the mermen near the pulled-down shops. Blue as indigo, pink as bougainvillea, white as seashells.

"Promise?"

"Promise."

"All right," Begam Sahiba says, her eyes softening, her voice changing. She loosens a strand of pearls from one of her earrings that has caught in her headscarf. "Now listen. We all could do with a jolly occasion. Let's hold a *tamasha*, invite Lakhnavis to join us. We'll tell them about Sir Henry Lawrence. Send out notices to every single sacked worker in the city and invite them to come. Everyone—all the King's old army men wandering around pensionless, our courtesans, noble families, vendors, bankers, kite-fliers, Shakespearean actors, merchants. Everyone must come to the *tamasha*."

7.

⊷•⊷

LUCKNOW IS THE most optimistic city ever in a takeover. The sky is full of colourful rockets and the *pop-pop* of crackers as Hindus and Jains celebrate Diwali. Muslims are at morning prayers. Company families are at the stone church for advent. Old mango trees are being decorated for Christmas in the spirit of Queen Victoria who has made public her intentions to decorate a fir tree for the coming holiday. Bagpipes play ceaselessly on Residency Hill.

Amah walks past high garden walls laced with pale yellow flowers and gives one of Begam Sahiba's newsletters to a nobleman's wife who is picking off dead heads. She and her husband have not left for Faizabad, a city eighty miles to the east, where other Lakhnavis have packed up and gone. The older woman scans the newsletter inviting Lakhnavis to Begam Sahiba's *tamasha*, her face registering surprise and then approval. "*Mashallah*," she says, tucking the newsletter under her arm. "Amah, you are looking well. You have done well. Your family must be proud."

Amah bows her head. "Come to the *tamasha*," she says.

* * *

At Begam Sahiba's *tamasha*, held inside her garden, the *Kotwal* arrives first. "The pigeons are back," he says to Amah. The three cages of green, silk-winged pigeons sit in the shade of the sprawling tent. Begam Sahiba stands near them, but ignores

64

the birds. She glances at the *Kotwal*, but her eyes are far away and her eyelids flutter. Amah studies her. Perhaps she is asking Allah, "Was it right to invite someone who drinks with them, who has profited from all the change?"

Amah goes to stand at the garden's iron-rod gate to watch who arrives. Neighbours spill inside—the King's soldiers who've lost their pensions, grain contractors, book-binders, royal boat crews, animal and menagerie attendants, portrait painters, actors, newspaper writers, municipal workers, architects, some noblemen and their families, *paan*-makers, dancers, and peacock-fan bearers—all of them out of work. Shi'a poets and Sunni administrators come. Female members of the Rose Platoon, like Amah, come. Lakhnavis come from apartments in the alleys, from smart homes in Hazratganj, from shops in Chowk, from every quarter of Qaisarbagh Palace. Even some of the King's wives who bicker about who is who, and look at Begam Sahiba with wounded eyes, come to listen. Courtesans disguised in black *burqas* come. Courtiers and lawyers arrive; they are the descendants of East-African sailors, soldiers, merchants, and slaves who came from across the Indian Ocean, blown here by monsoon winds and perfumed breezes to marry Lakhnavis—East-African-Indians whose memories of ancient African homes dance with memories of ancient Lucknow, East-African-Indians who these days share some of the loyalty they feel for His Majesty with Begam Sahiba. "*Salaam,*" these men say to Amah as they file past her into the garden. They settle themselves on Begam Sahiba's carpets and on her grass.

The merchant, Abhi, approaches the gate, and Amah steps forward. The man is alone, without his English friends. "Nothing better to do?" Amah asks him.

"Everyone has been invited," he says, holding up Begam Sahiba's newsletter.

She closes the iron-rod gate. "Too late, the garden is full," she says. He smiles, his teeth stained red, looking at her through the bars. She stands there watching him until he turns away.

Under the tent, she sees Gulbadan but not Sai. Old Kasim and Fatima have stayed at their posts in Qaisarbagh Palace's front hall with some of the other palace guards. Aunt Laila stands against one of the tent's poles without Hasan. At the palace, the rumour is that out of desperation her baby cousin has taken a job grooming horses at the new Company Tax Office—the horses belonging to tax collectors who ride out to demand hefty sums from landowners like her old prison-mate, 'Ali Shah.

Amah walks up to Aunt Laila. "*Tasleem*, Auntie," she says.

Aunt Laila keeps her eyes on the crowd. "*Tasleem*," she finally says. "While you were in jail fooling around, the messengers returned with news about the royal staff in Calcutta. Gulbadan had a boy bring the note to the palace."

Amah waits.

"Your mother is ill," Aunt Laila says, her eyes still on the crowd.

"What?"

"She has taken to her bed. She wants Yunani medicine, prepared here."

"I'll send it today," Amah says.

"Too late. I gave it to the messengers already." Still, her aunt does not look at her.

"When do they leave?"

"Tonight."

From the front of the crowd, Begam Sahiba beckons Amah. Without another word, Amah walks up to the front and stands near Birjis. Birjis smiles at her like a sweet, fat tiger, but Aunt Laila's news has removed Amah from the garden. She struggles to concentrate on Begam Sahiba, on her long shirt and pyjamas, her headscarf embroidered with little lace fish, her gold bangles. Several wisps of dark, wavy hair escape from her friend's headscarf and fall about her face. The news Aunt Laila has delivered will not move aside. Amah forces herself to think about duty. She wonders if Abhi stands on the other side of the wall, straining to listen. The stone walls are high, and it would be difficult for him to hear. The news about her mother shifts a little. The messengers are still in Lucknow, and it is only late morning. She has a bit of time to send something.

"Greetings and peace, my dear friends," Begam Sahiba begins. "The English have stated that Indians forming a crowd is against their new laws. I reminded them that those who are registered at Qaisarbagh Palace have legal immunity. It doesn't matter that we do not all live there. You need not be afraid. They will never tell us apart."

A titter moves through the crowd.

"His Majesty has not yet come. We wait for news of his latest petition in Calcutta. Her Royal Highness is still in England. The Queen Mother waits to meet Queen Victoria."

"Begam Sahiba." An old architect who worked for the King gets to his feet and bows. "All our petitions in Lucknow are being ignored. The English are making every attempt to drain our wealth."

"Yes. The royal family is trying their best to bypass the Company in Lucknow and insist in London and Calcutta instead that they return the city to normalcy. What has happened is astonishing. The English owed us millions of *rupees*, which we let go, and now the bankers tell me that the English have stopped the production of His Majesty's *rupees* in order to bring Lucknow their own English *rupees*. And on the pretence that you are discontent—you, our people—they took our animals and some of the King's property. On the pretence that they are rescuing us."

A nobleman calls out, "No ruler ever experienced such devotion and loyalty as His Majesty. We do not need to be rescued. Begam Sahiba, we cannot put up with this nonsense."

Begam Sahiba raises her hand. "No, we can't. But let's do keep our wits about ourselves," she says. "Disarray won't do us any good. Their greed must remain beneath us. There is plenty of financial assistance to be had. I've made contact with many of you already about how I can help you. Others should meet with me. I've spoken to those among us who have retained their wealth, and we are proof that there are still plenty of resources. There is a new English Chief Commissioner coming. A man named Sir Henry Lawrence. He arrives here sometime soon. Lawrence is known to be a decent man, with a deep love for Lucknow. I have met with him. In the meantime, don't leave our city. Build the virtue of patience. I can help, like a parent, so come to me if you need help. Now, please. Let's rise and eat together."

Everyone is getting up when the *Kotwal* comes forward, bowing low to Begam Sahiba. He invites her to tour the jail, to see his good work. She takes in the top of his head, the curve of his ears. Her green eyes are soft, but, by the time he stands up, they've become globes of hardness. "You are a foolish man to agree to work with them after His Majesty left; you're a fool to be bribed," she says. "I trust that you will not forget that members of the royal family, including divorced queens, remain above you by law."

* * *

In the afternoon, Amah leaves behind the conversations in Begam Sahiba's garden and walks quickly up the road to Qaisarbagh Palace. She goes to her mother's room. In the corner, she digs out from under the blue tiles their box of savings—pearls from her father, rubies the size of quails' eggs that the King gave to Amah for her riding skills, a jar of opals from Amah's brother. Her heart grows heavy with the sadness that her mother's empty room passes on to her and a sadness, too, over the savings she's spent. She takes a large pearl and finds one of the servant boys in the garden, the boy she trusts the most, and tells him to sell it to Judea the jeweller for *rupee* coins.

"Money is running thin, dear Amah," the little boy says. "Can I have a pearl of my own when I get back?"

"My mother is ill. Make sure Judea gives you His Majesty's *rupees* and not English ones. He might be trading in both but ask for our own. Take the money and go to Chowk's perfumery to purchase some honey-scented oil, the oil extracted from kadam trees."

"And then, dear Amah?"

"Go to the Yunani Medical Clinic and have them prepare the best Yunani remedies. Buy her some *habshi halwa* too. Take it all to two men named Rasheed and Akbar at the *kotha*. Bring my mother a little bit of Lucknow."

"She will be very pleased, dear Amah. And then, dear Amah?"

"You will have a pearl of your own."

"*Mashallah*!" The boy smiles and touches her feet.

She puts her hand gently on his head. "Go now," she says and watches him run between the azaleas to the back of the palace where he leaves by the back door.

When Amah gets to the front hall, her cousin Kasim greets her, his face solemn, his right hand cupping his heart. "*Adab,* Amah. Why were you gone so long?"

In the hall behind him, a crowd of Company men in blue uniforms stands under the oil paintings of Lucknow's *nawabs*. "Give me that rifle," one of them says to Amah as soon as he sees her. She smells the saltiness of unwashed skin, sees the look of hatred in his parrot eyes. Unlike pigeons, she thinks, parrots do not easily go home. Reluctantly, she gives the rifle to him.

"Who does this rifle belong to?" the man asks in Urdu, examining it.

"His Majesty," Amah says.

"Stay over there with your other black friends," he tells her.

Amah flinches. His scorn revolts her. As always. But she must be careful. She goes to stand with old Kasim and Fatima, and the other East-African palace guards, in front of the storerooms.

The man with parrot eyes paces in front of them. "Where are the King's possessions, Amazon slaves?"

None of them answer. The Englishman steps forward and

raises Amah's rifle at Kasim. "Where are his possessions kept?"

Kasim gestures at the brass doors covered in fish mosaics behind the palace guards.

"We are here to conduct an inventory," the Englishman says.

"His Majesty has not ordered an inventory," Kasim responds.

"Open those doors. All of the King's possessions must be accounted for."

"His Majesty's permission must be received in order for anyone to see his possessions," Kasim says, his voice getting harder.

The Englishman with parrot eyes pushes the rifle into Kasim's shoulder. Kasim grabs the rifle out of his hands, turns it on him, and tells him to leave. The Englishman puts up his hands. "Steady on," he says in English. "Steady on."

The Englishman's friends step up, their pistols pointing at Kasim's face, their mouths like thin lines, and Kasim drops the rifle. The Englishman with parrot eyes turns to Fatima. "Now, open the doors, Amazon," he says in Urdu. "We have an inventory to complete."

Fatima finds her keys, but she doesn't move. One of the men with pistols takes the keys. He unlocks the doors. Amah moves forward to bar the way to the rooms, but another man with a pistol pushes her back, holds his pistol to her shoulder. She dares him by struggling to go forward again, but he keeps the pistol pinned to her.

The man with parrot eyes and several others move into the rooms. None of them take off their shoes. They survey the sea of white sheets that protect delicate possessions from dust and prying eyes. One of the men moves forward. "Don't touch!" Amah yells.

The man freezes, but the one with parrot eyes jeers him onwards in English. The pistol at Amah's shoulder moves to the side of her neck, warm and pushing hard.

Company men's hands pull back the sheets, force the valuables to reveal themselves. Men's fingers caress bags of opals and rubies, and follow the curves of the King's gold throne.

The Englishmen touch tents and silk carpets, embroidered coverings for elephants, gold-threaded shawls, trunks of pearls—the possessions are carefully noted by the Company men whose eyes grow heavy with envy. They consider the oil paintings of Cleopatra, Zeus, and Hercules; the volumes of French and English books; the Queen Mother's favourite plays. They write down gold-plated book titles—*The Merchant of Venice, Othello, Hamlet*. They handle a silver tea set from Prince Edward, Queen Victoria's father. They take their time. Even the dozens of English suits that are a part of His Majesty's wardrobe are fondled.

When they are finished, the man with parrot eyes comes up to the guards, his friends behind him. He smiles, as if something has changed between them while they stroked the King's belongings.

"There's no need for you to stay here," he says in Urdu. "Perhaps you do not realize that we've abolished slavery."

The guards say nothing.

"Ignorant," one of the Englishmen says in English.

The man with parrot eyes replies in English. "Curious faces. Something between stupidity and physical beauty. Look," he says, switching to Urdu. "India remains in the dark ages of slavery. Like America. But we've abolished that medieval institution. Leave the King and we will let you go free. We will release you from slavery."

"Those poor black sods in America would do anything to hear those words," one of his friends says in English, and they laugh. "We'd hear their caterwauling from here."

The insults are obvious in tone even if they are not completely comprehensible. How curious it is, Amah thinks, that men who cast slurs can appear so proud. "We have no reason to leave Qaisarbagh Palace," she finally says.

"What on earth keeps you here?" the man asks.

"Lakhnavis usually lead very good lives," Amah says. "Usually."

The man laughs. "You're under a stupid spell. Perhaps you like the lazy life." He turns to his friends but continues in Urdu. "Good company for a debauched patron. I imagine they make each other very happy."

"Happiness keeps everyone in Lucknow," Fatima says. "Even you."

The man shrugs his shoulders in an exaggerated way and turns to go. The palace guards move quickly, escorting the men to the front doors, freeing themselves of them. Amah turns back to the storerooms, picks up the sheets from the floor. However long the English have been here, they don't understand the glory that breathes in the old Lucknow gardens, that bobs with the honeysuckle, that stirs the water of a courtyard basin that reflects a blue pigeon tumbling in the sky. She lets the white cotton sheets fall gently over golden clocks, blue-green opals, and English slurs. She leaves the rooms, locking the doors with Fatima's keys, and picks up her rifle from the floor. She goes to find Begam Sahiba.

II. THE RED YEAR

8.

———◦•◦•◦———

HOT WINDS BLOW in the new year, 1857, the year that will become known as the Red Year. Old English newspapers lift and unfurl from where they lie on their ledges at Mohammed's stall. Displaying sketches of a pregnant Queen Victoria in her flowing gown, the papers drift through Lucknow's streets, wrap themselves around shopkeepers' ankles, wedge themselves in the doorways of noblemen's homes, cling to the rosebushes in the English garden by the Residency, and lie in the muck of clogged drains. Begam Sahiba gathers together Jai Lal Singh, a powerful courtier at the palace with strong ties to the royal army, as well as several of the King's best army men. In Begam Sahiba's meeting room, Amah finds the men sitting against cushions, all of them dressed in *achkans*, long coats fastened with buttons and edged with lace. Begam Sahiba paces. She pulls a loose strand of hair away from her damp face, and tucks it back under her veil. "I'm thinking of a new Force that will be loyal to me," Begam Sahiba is saying to Jai Lal and his friends. "Can you assemble them?"

Jai Lal Singh glances at his friends who remain expressionless. Jai Lal has a sharp, intelligent face that matches his sharp figure. He bows and says, "*Huzoor.* His Majesty disbanded us to show good faith."

"Come now, Jai Lal. The inventory. It appears that we cannot all sit and watch while they plan to take everything they can get their hands on. Our good faith seems to be only whetting their appetites." Begam Sahiba walks up and down, her em- broidered shoes tossed aside. "You know, I've been thinking that the King won't come back unless and until every single thing is restored to him. He is trying his best with his own petitions, but they haven't agreed to petitions one or two. Does he really think they'll listen to petition three or four? It's apparent from the inventory that we can no longer afford the luxury of waiting for His Majesty. Lucknow is a pool of water with idle English snakes on its shore. Can you assemble a different Force, a new Force?"

Jai Lal shrugs. "There are no salaries, *Huzoor*."

"I'll pay the salaries myself."

The men with Jai Lal shift in their seats. Envious, Amah thinks. Because Begam Sahiba holds the admiration of their citizens. Because she has *lakhs* of *rupees*. *Lakhs*. Amah wants to tell them: No matter what you think of her veil, she is as strong as you.

Jai Lal gets up and looks through the doorway at Shahzadi, the lanky tiger lying in the grass. "But what about Lawrence? What will your new friend think of such a Force?"

"We must stay on good terms with him when he arrives. It would be better to settle this matter properly with him instead of reducing ourselves to threats. But that should not stop us from having a Force ready in case we need to remind them that our numbers are much greater than theirs, that they should listen to us, that they cannot touch any more property. Any- one's. We must organize underground," Begam Sahiba says.

"They have spies," Jai Lal says. "They will find out."

"I will watch for spies," Amah says.

Jai Lal continues to study Shahzadi in the garden while ev- eryone else is forced to study the lace on the back of the man's coat. Finally, he turns around and looks at his friends. They all glance away. "This idea will cause trouble," one of them says.

"Yes, it would cause trouble at the palace," another says.

Jai Lal contemplates his friends, his eyes steady. He bows

his head respectfully as he turns to Begam Sahiba. "*Huzoor*, we will prepare quietly."

* * *

Underground, Jai Lal spreads the word about a new Force. Above ground, vendors boil milk sweets, the heat of their fires fanning Lucknow's hot air. Boys' kites wilt in the bright skies. The courtesans send bags of coins concealed in wardrobe boxes to support Begam Sahiba's efforts. Underground, Lakhnavis are quiet but not tranquil. Above ground, at least at first, the English sleepwalk.

Company men cut off newly-paved streets from Lakhnavis. Sai brings back tales of his employer, Mrs. Gunning, who cuts a swathe of lilies out of her cantonment garden with a volley of pistol fire—a woman who sometimes whips servants, cutting into their backs, a woman who offers lashings of whitening cream to the darkest of her attendants.

* * *

Honey-scented oil from kadam trees drifts all the way to Calcutta. Rasheed and Akbar, rested and disguised as dandy poets, have gone with more of Lal's tonics for the Queen Mother and medicines from the Yunani Medical Clinic for Amah's mother. At the palace, Amah sees her aunt sitting outside her mother's old bedroom, her fingers working her glass beads while her lips work in prayer.

"Go and rest," Amah says.

"No!" her aunt shouts. She grips Amah's arm. "You have to persuade Hasan, and we will all go."

"Being between here and Calcutta for weeks of travel will not help anyone," Amah says, speaking as if the prayer beads have suddenly got stuck in her throat.

"She could be dead!"

"We have sent our medicines. She will get the best of everything with His Majesty at his residence at Matiya Burj," Amah says. Aunt Laila grips Amah's arm harder. She starts to cry. Amah holds her by the shoulders but Aunt Laila makes a face and pulls away. Amah walks past her and out into Lucknow.

***

She walks the streets and prays for her mother. Bagpipes play in the distance on Residency Hill. She listens to the learned Lakhnavi men who list under the weight of the bagpipes they are forced to put their mouths to. The bagpipes hum and drone, sending tortured sounds into the pale sky. In the late afternoon, she arrives in front of one of Abhi's apartments deep in Lucknow's alleys where several women talk together in low voices. She looks beyond them to the boarded-up windows of the apartment and at the litter mounting before the doorway. The alley smells of sour rice, rotting mango, and a traitor's greedy breath.

"Have you seen them?" Amah asks the women, nodding at the apartment.

"She left for Faizabad," one of them says.

Amah thanks them and turns to go home. On her way back, the sound of the bagpipes drives her into the Chattar Manzil, a royal building near Qaisarbagh Palace where Jai Lal holds his meetings with Lakhnavis, a few at a time to avoid detection.

She practices with her rifle in the cavernous room where the Rose Platoon and His Majesty's army used to practice military drills for parades. She shoots rounds of cartridges. She hits rows of little clay pots faster, she thinks, than six hungry hunters. She is Zeus bringing thunder. She is in charge of a weapon that can threaten the sound of bagpipes belonging to men who threaten her commitment to courtesy.

***

Lakhnavis silently step into Jai Lal's underground, and, above ground in Chowk, the old Somalian *paan*-makers who knew

Amah's grandmother trickle fragrant spices onto lime-green leaves, and do what Amah asks and watch for spies. Over the next weeks, Amah collects several of the best rifles from the Chattar Manzil and keeps them in her room. The rains are still months away, and, when she is not on duty in the front hall, she lies under the kadam tree, sweating and longing for a cotton compress soaked in chamomile. The small, white pigeons sit in their cots, waiting for the plain seed Amah feeds them instead of her mother's breadcrumbs coated in *ghee*.

Amah waits for Jai Lal's list to expand. She waits for Sir Henry Lawrence to come to Lucknow. One afternoon, chewing *paan*, she listens in her mind and waits for her grandmother's voice to come into her ears. She strains to remember the pitch of her grandmother's words, the tenor and lilt of her joy. Her grandmother's words escape into the grass and up into the orange kadam blossom.

* * *

"*Tasleem.* Where is Sai?" she asks Gulbadan at the top of the stairs to the *kotha*.

"*Tasleem.* Across the river. Milking in the cantonment," Gulbadan says.

"He should be listening carefully to conversations there these days."

"They don't think we can accomplish anything," Gulbadan replies. "You really shouldn't worry about Jai Lal being found out. But be quiet, Amah. We have English guests."

"Who probably made you take English money?"

Gulbadan does not respond. She turns toward her pavilion.

Amah walks to the edge of the courtyard. A group of Englishmen, including Red Man, lie against the gilded fish pillows and eat *shami* kebabs with green chillies and coriander served on platters of saffron rice. They are not anything like noblemen in black velvet hats but men with faces flushed with wine who dismiss green gourd, cut to resemble flowers, on silver-hammered plates. They are naive men in hungry postures, gleeful for the opportunity that evenings abandoned by exiled royalty and departed noblemen now afford them, all of them aching for the attentions of a courtesan who will bring forth new Persian poems that these unversed men, Amah thinks, surely cannot understand.

She studies the four courtesans who are getting ready to perform. They wear loose trousers and long shirts. Their faces are painted like their conversations, women trained in the art of disguise. Cosmetics are not something Englishwomen wear, not something an English citizen would approve of, so why are these men even here?

She turns her back and goes to Gulbadan's pavilion. "I am eager to get on with things," Gulbadan says as soon as Amah comes in. She gives Amah a silver-plated betel box and taps its domed lid. "Another donation. In support of Jai Lal's new Force," she says. "Keep us informed."

Amah bows her head, thanks Gulbadan, and leaves.

On the way out, Red Man passes her as he, too, walks to the stairs going down to Chowk. "You are everywhere, black man," he says, entirely in Urdu.

"You might want to remember that."

He stops and looks back at her in surprise, his red eyebrows digging roads into his forehead, perspiration beading in his dimpled chin. "You might want to remember that the English are everywhere, all over the world, for a reason," he continues in Urdu. "Civilization is not otherwise to be found here," he says, gesturing toward the courtyard. "English ways will only do you all a lot of good." He turns to go down the stairs while Amah watches him strut his Red Man strut.

* * *

Christians wait for Easter, Jews get ready for Passover, and Hindus prepare coloured powder for Holi. Cows walk the alleys and poke their noses into pilgrims' shrines. Sai finds

Amah in the front hall at Qaisarbagh Palace. He bows his head and cups his heart, pats his chest twice. "*Adab*. Mrs. Gunning bought a new floral gown this morning," he whispers loudly. "For an occasion. Sir Henry Lawrence has arrived. Gulbadan wants to know what he is going to do. She is impatient, like you."

Amah rides Kasim's grey mare on the lookout for an English procession to welcome Sir Henry Lawrence. She doesn't find one. Englishmen smoke cheroots in the streets. She waits by the rose garden near the Residency but she does not see Sir Henry Lawrence enter, or leave.

But the next morning at dawn, when she is out riding, she meets him. He sits on a shiny, black Waler at the intersection of two narrow lanes in an old part of Lucknow.

She pulls on the reins of Kasim's mare to let him pass. Sir Henry Lawrence is tall, perhaps a little gaunt. He contemplates Amah's horse, then Amah in her red jacket and rose-coloured silk trousers, and cocks his chin. He doesn't think that many of his officers can hold the riding posture she does, he says in Urdu. "You must be from the Rose Platoon of Female Africans, are you not?"

"Yes," she says. "Sir."

He nods, smiling at his own correctness, and passes her.

* * *

During his first week, Sir Henry Lawrence is found to be everywhere in Lucknow early in the mornings. Sometimes Amah dares to follow him at some distance. He surrounds himself with brick minarets with brass finials, frills of green pottery, and mango groves. Lucknow's buildings, covered in the fine stucco made from crushed shells, polished to a glittering finish, trot gaily past his horse. His horse cuts through the large grounds belonging to a Frenchman who once upon a time set his home right in the Gomti river to keep the home cool. Now it is the grand old Frenchman's mausoleum.

Near the end of the week, Amah spots Sir Henry Lawrence riding the stretch of the Gomti where she is washing Kasim's grey mare. The horse nuzzles Amah's neck from time to time with her wet nose and her whiskery mouth as Sir Henry rides up to her. "Do you know where the statues of Jupiter and Zeus are?" he calls.

Amah stands up at once. She smiles.

They ride through Lucknow's streets, ducking under rose-bound arches, past Sikanderbagh, the mosque and summer house with its pink walls, past European-styled palaces owned by deceased *nawabs*, beside ancient royal tombstones where English parties like to picnic, and through gates with wrought-iron railings to get to the statues. The reins are light in their hands, and the pale yellow sun bounces off their shoulders. Red-breasted birds chatter around the Commissioner's slim build and white beard. After some time, a blue-eyed officer spots Sir Henry and rides up alongside him, in between Sir Henry and Amah, and says something in English to Sir Henry about a shipment of cartridges. Cartridges. Amah considers the word. The officer nudges his horse fully into Amah's place, ignoring her presence.

"What is wrong with the old cartridges?" Sir Henry Lawrence asks the man in English, and Amah hears his irritation.

"They are depleted."

How awkward for her, for her mare, to try to ride beside this rude officer. So Amah shifts her mare and rides ahead, leading the way down Hazratganj for Sir Henry.

The sun gets a little higher in the sky. The smell of warm, red dust surrounds the horses. Worry about the lack of a salary prods her. She forces her thoughts elsewhere and tries to think of one of her grandmother's tales from old Ethiopia, but her grandmother drifts quickly to Qaisarbagh Palace, as if caught in shackles of clear, gushing water, as if her Muslim grandmother came out of a palace fountain and put her clean, bare feet firmly into the oceans of gardens at Qaisarbagh, and the royal family and Amah's mother and Aunt Laila dive with her grandmother in lilied bathing pools. Her grandmother stands in her garden of gurgling fountains, marble wells, passels of blue pigeons, and ponds of fat, merry goldfish while she offers *paan* and listens devotedly to Sufi bandsmen, for the ecstasy tucked into their music. Amah listens carefully, and as she leads the way for Sir Henry Lawrence she hears her grandmother's voice clearly this time—the old dialect mixed with Persian and Urdu words that pour together into sentences like liquid honey, her words containing a sweetness not present in Amah's mother's voice. "Find your place," her grandmother says.

Amah leans forward and watches the red dust coat the grey mare's hooves. One of the King's golden-green, silk-winged pigeons, an escapee from last year's auction, sits on the side of the road and coos. She coos at Amah, and she coos at Sir Henry Lawrence. She is a cooing, approving pigeon.

They arrive at a broken-down garden near La Martinière College. Inside the school, English boys, soon to set sail for England, are dressed in blue jackets, trousers, and ties. They sit at desks and read their books. Inside the garden, blue statues lie in pieces on top of the churned-up earth. Sir Henry Lawrence gets off his horse to stand with Amah, who had not thought that these statues had been touched. The blue-eyed officer waits, his face mottled with impatience despite his efforts to conceal it.

They contemplate the broken statues. "I cannot be here after all," Sir Henry Lawrence says to Amah in Urdu. He turns, at a loss. "These were my deceased wife's favourite statues. I cannot be here."

Amah is both sad and relieved at the man's reaction.

Sir Henry mounts his horse and looks over to her. "Is there a good *chai-wallah* nearby?"

* * *

Under a shady covering in a bougainvillea-laden lane, the *chai-wallah* pours milky tea back and forth between two clay cups to cool it. He gives the milky tea—how the English like to drink it—to Sir Henry. From an urn, the vendor pours well-water that sparkles like diamonds. He boils the clear water in a silver pot over a ruby fire and cuts emerald-green limes with sugar and lets the mixture steep. Then he offers these diamonds, rubies, and emeralds to Amah, and she brings them to her lips, slips them into her mouth, and holds them in her cheeks to protect them before letting them slide down her throat. The steam that rises from the cup dampens her nose and cheeks, and the steam from the *chai-wallah's* silver pot twirls like flutes in the air, like the twirling flutes that once carried Persian and Arabic melodies all the way here, steam rising high as the heads of Ethiopian women who would travel high seas.

"Her riding skills are remarkable," Sir Henry says to his officer in English while he brushes drops of milky tea from his beard.

His officer barely nods. "Her?" he asks.

"Yes. Her intelligent eyes hold a singular amount of energy, much like a man's, and her gestures and manners will not be familiar to an Englishman new to this land, like yourself, as those that belong to the fairer sex. The dress at court for these famously-skilled guards is the same for women as it is for men."

The unfamiliar English words pour over Amah. Impossible to understand.

"You know," he says to the officer. "I will never go back there, to those statues." He looks over at Amah and says to her, to his officer, too, in Urdu. "It should never have happened, all this change."

It should never have happened, Sir, Amah thinks, and bows to this English saint.

The officer on his horse studies the construction of a road in the distance, but his eyes register shock at his superior's words, that he's said what he said in Urdu.

"I have been to Lucknow so many times," Sir Henry Lawrence continues, addressing Amah. "This is the Paris of the East. And when Lady Honoraria and I first came to this city, it reminded her of *One Thousand and One Nights, The Arabian Nights*. It reminded her of Moscow and Constantinople."

We used to have many European visitors, Sir, Amah wants to say.

"I think it was a Russian bishop who said Lucknow is even more impressive than Moscow," Sir Henry Lawrence says. He turns to his officer and switches to English. "Qaisarbagh Palace is bigger than Versailles. But you would call Lucknow a picture of Oriental confusion. A town that has grown haphazardly, without any order to it. A town that is as effeminate, as weak and characterless as its King who does not love the military life but instead fancies building things." Sir Henry Lawrence sips his tea. "My dear fellow, I keep very early hours, eat sparingly, and scarcely touch wine, beer, or spirits. I believe I can stand fatigue of mind or body with any man in India. I have repeatedly ridden eighty and a hundred miles at a stretch in the hottest season of the year, and I have worked for weeks twelve and fourteen hours a day at my desk. I have built a boarding school far from here, near Simla, for orphans and children of British soldiers who have come to India to serve. It is very successful. I have another one at a hill station in Rajasthan. I have plans for yet another. I know this country like the back of my hand. And yet my warnings this week about what your new generation is doing in Lucknow go unheeded. Past generations of Englishmen in India would not agree with you. The last Chief Commissioner was, let's say, rather tactless. You would be wise to ponder the delayed salutes some of our best native military men are offering these days."

The sullen officer's face softens just a little. Sir Henry Lawrence's black Waler and Kasim's grey mare stand together. They pull up the new grass with their whiskery mouths. The vendors whistle as they walk to work, and little boys in muslin pants swim around Amah like wriggling, merry fish, ordering lime and sugar cordials for patrons. Sir Henry gives his empty cup back to the vendor. "Good bye," Sir Henry Lawrence calls to Amah. She bows to him as he leaves with his sullen, blue-eyed officer.

She lingers, thinking about Sir Henry Lawrence, and watching the Lakhnavis. Some of them do not read Begam Sahiba's newsletters, nor answer little boys' requests to meet Jai Lal. They travel down the lanes, skirt the newest roads as instructed by Englishmen, and leave Lucknow to find work.

A crowd of thirsty buyers swarm the *chai-wallah* and conceal for some moments Abhi, that 'Ali Baba, and his conceited smile that shows his red teeth. Fresh flowers in the hair of a group of little girls briefly cloak the man's perfume as he approaches her.

"I see that you have a new English friend at last," he says to Amah. "Perhaps you understand the need to have new friends, lonely African maid."

She lets him pass by. Then she walks to him, turns him around suddenly. He jerks in surprise at her touch. He frowns, staring at her red jacket, her silk trousers, and up at her cropped hair.

She takes her hands off him. "The man has benevolence," she says. "The man is a friend to Lucknow, unlike your friends."

"Is the man's benevolence of use? Is that helping you?" he asks, his smile returning. "Is it making the city better like the new road there is making the city better? What is he doing that is helping your Queen?"

When Amah rides home alone, the freshness of her drink fades away, and the silk-winged pigeon she saw earlier does not coo. She has disappeared.

9.

———•••———

AT QAISARBAGH PALACE, the old advisors, men whose long faces match their long robes, wait in rooms with velvet sofas, silver-topped tables, and gilded walls. They wait for a reply to a letter they've written to Sir Henry Lawrence asking him about his intentions in Lucknow. Amah waits, too, for the reply. A letter comes and after the palace advisors read it they give it to Jai Lal who gives it to Amah to take to Begam Sahiba. Amah repeats Jai Lal's words as she hands her friend the letter, "Sir Henry requests time as the new Chief Commissioner to assess Lucknow and what has happened."

Begam Sahiba reads quickly. "We must give him his time," she says. "We must relent for his sake."

Amah worries that time is moving more swiftly than Sir Henry is able to move, more swiftly than they are moving. At the Chattar Manzil, she views Jai Lal's list, now close to a thousand, for the new Awadh Force that they are officially calling the Organization of Awadh Soldiers. Loyal men mill around the Chattar Manzil, just a dozen at a time. "The men are restless, too," Jai Lal says as he watches Amah come and go.

"It would be easy to show the English the huge numbers of Lakhnavis who are ready to defend what is theirs," Amah says. "The longer we wait, the more money we need for salaries."

"Patience," Jai Lal says, his sharp face lowered respectfully. "I am thinking we should do things more formally. We should be thinking about a temporary ruler to put into place. Birjis may be the right choice. One of the King's sons. Restore the royal family for Lakhnavis' sake. I need to find the right time to discuss this with Begam Sahiba."

Amah considers what he's said. Jai Lal is strong-minded. Intelligent. Resolute.

"Patience, Amah," he says. "We need to organize carefully."

Amah paces the streets. She paces at the palace. The messengers, who left so long ago with Lucknow's medicines for her mother, have not returned from Calcutta with news about her health, or about the King's plans to return. Everyone is waiting. Waiting. She is passing through the front hall at Qaisarbagh Palace when Fatima comes to complain to her about a man waiting outside. "He's been there since yesterday."

Amah frowns, impatience continuing to stir. She goes to the front doors and opens them. The man stands under a tamarind tree that has grown up by the palace wall. He wears blue pantaloons, curled slippers, and a thin muslin shirt. His skinny pony is tethered to the tree with a piece of coir rope, her head bobbing to disperse the flies. The man is small, with wavy hair that is not cropped or oiled, and he carries a dirty, white bag. He contemplates the busy street with dull eyes, and keeps clearing his throat. "A villager," Amah says. "Go and see."

Fatima approaches the man. He responds quickly to her questions, his eyes fixed on the ground. She walks back to Amah who waits at the front doors. "His name is Pavan. He needs to pay the new English land tax for his village. He has protested but he has to pay it. He does not have enough. He hopes the royal family might help him, give him some work."

"Many of us are out of work. Did you tell him that?"

"Yes. I told him."

"If the King were here it would be different but right now he will have to leave."

"I told him that, too."

Late that afternoon, the man is still there. He has dried spittle in the corners of his mouth, and his pony looks thirsty, too.

Amah tells a boy to bring them inside the palace, to feed, water and wash the skinny pony. "Keep her away from Kasim's grey mare. That pony is sick with something," she says.

The man Pavan might be sick, too, she thinks. He coughs when he stands in front of Amah uncertainly, his head bowed. Perhaps he's never seen a woman dressed in riding jodhpurs before. He's probably never seen a rifle before. She studies him more carefully, listens to his cough. Yes. The man on the road from Cawnpore. The coughing thief. "You'd be better off in bed," she says. "How long did it take you to get here?"

"Two days."

"There is no work here. Not now."

"The Settlement Officer came to our village." The man clears his throat. "He said we must pay the new tax or go to jail. I thought there must be something in Lucknow. You have more than we do." He clears his throat again, his gaze fixed to the ground. "It was you who told me about Lucknow."

"This is not the time to look for work here; many people who were never poor are now poor. And I have other things to do. I cannot be distracted. Come and eat something. Then it would be best to leave."

The next morning Pavan's hair is wet, combed, and no longer full of dust. Because he is a Hindu, he has rested in a *puja* room reserved for Hindu guests at the palace. His clothes and slippers are washed and dried, and Amah thinks he wears his desperation a little better too. His face is soft, like a fig.

She relents. After breakfast, Pavan secures his dirty white bag to the pony and waits while Amah gets Kasim's grey mare. They ride to the *kotha*. The man does not help her to keep her mind off her own money worries. She has sold more of her mother's opals, rubies, and pearls to purchase semolina, dried fruits, and milk for Qaisarbagh's kitchens. Everyone is using their savings to keep going. Things have to change, she thinks, things have to change. She pulls her rifle closer. She contemplates pointing it at a thousand Company men while

an English knighted saint nods his head at her. She pictures
a thousand white handkerchiefs waving from English hands
toward ten thousand Lakhnavis dancing a King's dance, and
ten thousand Lakhnavis waving back, bidding the foreigners
adieu as the English bow and retreat out of the city of Lucknow.

***

At the gate leading up to the *kotha*, Gulbadan's brother says,
"This is not a good time. Gulbadan has many meetings."

"Gulbadan is expecting me," Amah says, feeling a little leap
inside her caused by the fib. Amah and Pavan follow the man
as he heaves himself up the steps, his bare feet like plump
cushions for his fat calves.

The courtyard is filled with bankers, poets, musicians, busi-
nessmen—Muslims, Hindus, Jains, and Jews. None of them
smile. Amah can hear Gulbadan speak loudly to her brother
in her pavilion—that she isn't expecting Amah and that her
meetings are not to be disturbed, so why is he disturbing her?
Her brother's mouth hangs open and his breath comes shorter
as he walks out, with Gulbadan behind him, to stare at Amah
and Pavan. Silver combs hold Gulbadan's black-and-grey tresses
in place. Over her spectacles, she glances at Pavan, taking him
in, and then she studies Amah. "Amah," she says. "Don't play
silly jokes. You want to speak to me? You'll have to wait. All
these people were here first."

In the courtyard, one voice climbs over another. Two hours
pass before Gulbadan's brother sourly beckons Amah and
Pavan into Gulbadan's pavilion.

Inside, the older woman is putting away a large silver box
in her wall of drawers. "The worst thing of all," Gulbadan
says, "is the restrictions being placed on printing newspapers.
There's a rumour that someone in Calcutta wants to stop them
altogether. To keep us in the dark."

"That is a place we must not be," Amah says.

"At any rate, everyone is feeling slightly better," Gulbadan continues. "They need money for this new land revenue tax collection. We can help Begam Sahiba with the task of keeping Lakhnavis out of jail, but the new Commissioner must actually do something soon." She locks a drawer and calls for water. "Now," she says. "What is it that I can do for you?"

"Dear Gulbadan, is there something you can do for this villager? Do you have some sort of job he might do?"

Gulbadan takes off her spectacles and rubs her eyes. "You've come to do some heroic duty for this man?" Her face shines with perspiration. "No, Amah," she says. "We don't need another mouth to feed. These are cautious times. Why are you here with him?"

Amah doesn't tell Gulbadan about her first meeting with Pavan. She tells her that he hoped for help from the royal family, that he, too, needs to pay the land tax, that he is looking for work. Amah shrugs, glancing at Pavan.

"Perhaps Sai knows someone," Gulbadan says. "Sai! Where's my nephew? Where's the water? That nephew of mine slips in and out. Sai!"

Gulbadan gets up and mops her face with a large handkerchief. She takes up a cold compress and puts it around her neck. Amah presses her toes on the cool marble while she watches a hot breeze play with the curtains. Sai finally comes in, his head bowed while he mumbles apologies, his face flushed with sleep while he pours water for his aunt.

When he hears why Amah has come with the villager, he says, "Mrs. Gunning has lost her sweeper. Her neighbour's cook is gone. The English are finding it difficult to get new help."

"What?" Gulbadan adjusts her compress. "Lakhnavis need money."

He shrugs. "Astrologists say there are signs of danger."

Pavan clears his throat.

"Do they see it in the skies only?" Amah asks.

"So far," Sai says, glancing at Amah. He puts down the pitcher. "Come with me this evening when I go to milk the goats."

"I do not like to cross the Iron Bridge," Amah says.

"Do it for the man's sake," Gulbadan says crossly.

* * *

In the early evening, the kingfishers over the Gomti whoop like musical accompaniments. As they cross the Iron Bridge, Amah feels a terrible urge to hold on to Lucknow and keep it safe. Not so very long ago everyone in the city knew the art of fine tricks with confectionary. They knew how to make chocolate look like eggs, and glazed blueberries appear like chicken. Even the English liked a good joke at the table—they were the first to laugh out loud at the disguised sweets. All travellers were welcome here—people collected from the world, different plates on the same table. Lucknow is still full of the jangle of anklets, muslin shawls glittering with spangles, the songs of sitars and stray silk-winged pigeons, an oasis under the starry skies with its billowy rooms, its poetry, its hushed murmurs, its statues of Roman gods, its secrets. She feels a small moment of uncertainty about the gathering of the new Force but that dissipates quickly. Tranquillity is all they want, she tells herself. Lucknow's past is all they want. Their lives before the English takeover is all they want.

* * *

They ride to the cantonment gate and dismount under the late afternoon sky where stars will emerge at dusk and whisper about danger. The call for prayers from within Sikanderbagh's high pink walls floats thinly across the purple sky. Amah and Pavan follow Sai through the gate, into the cantonment, and past several white-washed bungalows with rose gardens. Eyes from the verandas watch them. Mouths murmur words, quick as telegraph lines. Sai's little group walks around to the back of Mrs. Gunning's bungalow. They stand with her goats and an aviary housing golden-green pigeons in the garden. A pair of eyes from the next garden watches them.

"There you are," Mrs. Gunning calls to Sai through a back window. Sai goes up to the house, and, although his voice is low, almost a whisper, not like Sai at all, Amah can hear him ask in Urdu if *memsahib* needs to hire anyone. Mrs. Gunning comes outside, an older woman in a floral dress and straw bonnet, her hair dyed black with acids. "This is Pavan, *memsahib*," Sai tells her. "He is looking for work, *memsahib*."

Pavan clears his throat and fidgets with his dirty white bag.

"Is he sick?" the lady asks, her Urdu all English-y. She studies Pavan. Pavan keeps his head bowed.

"Well, perhaps we can fix whatever it is in return for good work," she says. "Lucy," she calls in English to the eyes watching in the next yard. "Here's a new sweeper. It simply must have been a streak of bad luck."

"Perhaps," says the mouth that belongs to the eyes that belong to a younger woman with blonde hair in a bun, a woman who wears a hooped skirt. "Where has he come from?"

"Sai has brought him. Sai wants to find him some work." Mrs. Gunning continues to study Pavan. Inspecting all of him, Amah thinks. An English inspection.

"Once you start to get into the servants' business, Mrs. Gunning," the woman from next door calls, "it is difficult to disentangle yourself. It's best to leave their affairs alone."

"Not this time," says Mrs. Gunning. She disappears with Pavan into her kitchen.

Sai fetches a bucket and kneels to milk a black-and-white goat. The pretty birds in the aviary murmur together. A lone cricket bleats in the oncoming dusk, and a child cries from somewhere in the cantonment. A strange smell of meat, cooking, comes from Mrs. Gunning's kitchen, and Sai turns to smile at Amah. He says, "First time in an English garden?"

"Yes."

He smiles again. "Go for a stroll up the road before you go. Say you are with me if anyone asks. The ladies know me well. I milk so many of their goats." He turns to Mrs. Gunning's black-and-white goat, puts his cheek against her taut belly, and hums.

"I saw that traitor Abhi in Lucknow several days ago," Amah says.

"He lives in Lucknow, Amah. He is allowed to walk our streets."

"He was walking streets forbidden to other Lakhnavis. He's living too close to us. Like Red Man and his friends are living too close to the *kotha*."

"You worry too much, my friend," Sai says, turning to Amah. "Now go up the road and have a look around. It will do you good to stop thinking about those men. Go, Amah."

Amah walks slowly up the road and looks at the row of bungalows fading into the dusk. She contemplates the houses and walks in the middle of the road with her hands at her sides. She does not carry her rifle here, as Sai requested. A show of good faith for her friend, and also, of course, what His Majesty would prefer.

The air is close. She glances back at the brass-coloured twinkling across the river where *nawabs* once gave away brass gift boxes filled with coins, where brass-framed oil paintings of European buildings and brass mermaids are kept in vast palace storerooms behind brass doors, and where Yunani remedies for ill mothers are stored in brass vessels. In the cantonment, the gardens at night appear dark green and inviting. But there are mosquitoes everywhere, and things rustle in the hedges. On the verandahs, candles stuck in tin lanterns drip wax into the camphor that repels the insects, and the light keeps the hedge things away.

She walks for a long time. The night comes on. A thousand pink hibiscus pass her as she steps over a thousand drops of sweat that have dripped off women with bent backs who pitched this English road that leads her away from Begam Sahiba, from a grandmother's love, and closer to London where a diabetic Queen Mother frets while she waits.

A thousand cooks have not added enough salt to the soup, a thousand canes rule Asiatics by fear, and a thousand tamarinds that drop heavily from trees are picked up by a thousand sweepers while a thousand English citizens sit on verandahs drinking a thousand cups of milky English tea while a thousand *ayahs* feed laudanum to a thousand English children to stop them from crying.

No one bothers her. She walks as far as the English ballroom with its blazing light. The brass of the orchestra belts the air. Chandeliers gleam, and women in silver-embroidered gowns sashay across the floor. It is a tremendous raucous with shrieks of hilarity. Amah imagines Sir Henry Lawrence sitting outside, the dancing making the widower melancholy. Company fiddlers try to welcome him with that lively tune, "All the dames of France are fond and free...," but Sir Henry Lawrence, Amah imagines, will not join the glittering *tamasha*. Instead, he observes the soldiers in their mess tent just a little further on who are playing cards by the light of candle stumps while their wives knit their husbands' socks.

She retreats back down the road toward the cantonment gate and tries to make sense of the conversations inside the sitting rooms where, she's heard from Sai, sacred tiger skins lie. Men's and women's voices compete with the chorus of frogs outside, frogs who watch her from their hidden posts. She conjures the posts of sweepers inside the homes who beg not to sweep the verandahs of dead birds since it breaks their caste; the posts of cooks who roast pork flesh and beef flesh to present to men in bungalow dining rooms who read letters from Calcutta about tranquil Lucknow and the timeliness of a quiet introduction of English East India Company rule; the posts of Muslim bearers who readily accept the miracle birth of Jesus and who dust off bibles and imported jars of marmalade; and Hindu *ayahs* who hail Mary, the mother of miracle births, among their Hindu icons—all of them servants who hold the fans that overlook the dining tables, who cut back the invading bushes that overlook the front gardens, who clean the windows that overlook the road, and who polish the boots of Englishmen who overlook their feelings.

Amah rides back over the Iron Bridge in the darkness, above the Gomti's winking waters.

10.

————✦————

"FINALLY. He has written to Calcutta to express his alarm about any more changes taking place." Begam Sahiba looks up from the second letter from Sir Henry Lawrence that Amah has brought to her from Jai Lal, who got it from the palace advisors. "He wishes to stop the so-called reforms, and return Lucknow to us."

"One man against the rest of them," Amah says.

"He is the Chief Commissioner, Amah. You can be sure of his power."

But later that afternoon, Amah is not so sure.

A young Indian soldier from the Company's army comes to Begam Sahiba's house. His wispy beard belongs more to a boy than a man—a light shadow of facial hair covering his cheeks. Until now, this boy with gold earrings and soft eyes has been loyal to the Englishmen he works for. The boy's father and grandfather also worked for the Company army—a family tradition resulting in English pensions. But this afternoon, he speaks nervously, quickly. "An English officer gave us orders to use new cartridges, each of them wrapped in paper greased with pig and cow fat. With the old cartridges we could tear the grease paper off with our hands. Now we are ordered to bite off the paper greased with pig and cow fat and spit it out. These are the same new cartridges that have been offered elsewhere in India, that have already shamed other men. 'We will not use those,' men in other parts of India said to their officers. 'You know that we cannot bite off the tips of cartridges greased in forbidden meats and defile our gods.' Well, we heard about those men's complaints before the new cartridges were offered to us this morning. The English know as well as we do how loyal we are to our duties. There was no violence. Simply, one by one, as they presented the cartridges to us, we said, 'No, Sir.'"

"And what now?" Begam Sahiba says.

"They are not happy," the handsome boy says. "But we hope we will not be made to use them. We are writing our superiors a letter formally requesting the continued use of the old cartridges instead."

"What about their Chief Commissioner? Was he there this morning?" Begam Sahiba asks.

"No, *Huzoor*," he says.

Begam Sahiba turns to Amah with wide eyes. "Is the man asleep?" She turns back to the boy. "Make sure you send your letter directly to Sir Henry Lawrence."

Outside, the telegraph wires flash in the low sun. Palace walls made of crushed shells glitter. Englishmen on horseback call to each other, alert, sipping water from their canteens, as they watch the soldier boy depart from Begam Sahiba's house.

Later, Amah will think that perhaps they were doomed from the start. It is like trying to water red dust in the noon heat. It is like trying to step on shadows. They are not dogs in Jain funerals who walk ahead, can see death.

* * *

Not all of the officers are in church this Sunday. Amah watches them carefully. They patrol, asking men who wait for snacks in Chowk to disperse, calling them *pandies*, a word Amah does not know. The officers separate five women buying silk cloth for a wedding. They break up a group watching a man train pigeons to do somersaults in the air. Since the officers are paying attention to Lakhnavis, Amah knows they must be worried.

Begam Sahiba and Amah walk the road by the Gomti. Begam Sahiba, too, wants to keep in touch with the English climate. Entirely veiled in black *burqas*, the women remain unseen, like petitions from landowners, like the worries of a Queen Mother who resides behind curtains in an English hotel. Begam Sahiba holds up her pyjamas underneath her *burqa* so the mud doesn't dirty the hems. When they reach a part of the road that has been swept, Amah takes Begam Sahiba's hand and pulls her along. Her friend is light as a butterfly, fiery as chillies.

They walk past the Gomti's Iron Bridge and over to Chowk lined with shops and apartments, the street fairly quiet in the mid-afternoon heat. Outside the police station, English Company officers on horseback watch. In Chowk's apartments, women with babies point to red-breasted barbets in green neem trees, and a herd of goats in the road. Inside dim interiors, shopkeepers sit cross-legged on white sheets, their sandals beside them. Elsewhere in Lucknow, shops have vanished to make way for the English desire for grass. Elsewhere in Lucknow: a city of broken water pipes.

One of the vendors who stands in the shade, preparing his cart of fruit ahead of the evening crowds, sings out to the officers on horseback, "Man-go, Man-go."

"Better to wield mockery than swords," Begam Sahiba says to Amah.

Amah shrugs. Near the police station, she stops to purchase bird seed from a vendor with some money Kasim has given her.

The young man pours the seed into an old Urdu newspaper. She watches as the little hill covers the words. "How is your mother?" the man asks.

"We've waited for news for a long time now," Amah says.

"I will pray for her today," the man says. He folds and ties the parcel, passes it to her.

Amah sees her old prison friend, the landowner 'Ali Shah, walking on the road. He bows his head and greets Amah who in turn tells him that it is Begam Sahiba who stands beside her. "Such kindness, *Huzoor*," he says, bowing his head to Begam Sahiba. "I was spared the scars your guard still shows around her eyes. I will stay here in Lucknow, *Huzoor*. I will help however I can."

The sash around 'Ali Shah's tunic hangs down; his gold turban is creased with black. Amah wonders if he fears going home. No land. No fort. His family scattered. Perhaps this is the reason he has stayed. She has seen others like 'Ali Shah in Chowk. Who knows how suddenly groups of like-minded strangers might form?

Outside the police station, Red Man leans against the wall, under an awning. The man with red hair and a dimpled chin has a cheroot in his mouth. He searches his pockets, doesn't find a match. Amah watches him as he contemplates 'Ali Shah, stares at the old welts around Amah's eyes, probably wonders whether the woman standing next to her is Begam Sahiba. So close he is, and yet there is nothing he can do.

They walk on. Sai calls to Amah from the courtesans' textile shop. Amah means to go to him to ask him to lead them on to the *kotha* for water and lime, perhaps a courtesan's poem, before they return home. But the hot rains come down, and send them all running for cover.

In the courtesans' shop, embroidered shawls and scarves sway in the breeze that starts up in the rain. Several crafts-men stop work near the shop's doorway where their needles make silver knots of stars on muslin. The courtesans' young shopkeeper, Geeta, touches Begam Sahiba's feet and stands with them among the many silk and crêpe samples hanging down from the low ceiling, wilting in the damp air.

Sai appears and disappears among the samples. "Any news about your mother?"

"Not yet," Amah says.

"Hopefully the illness has passed," he says to her. "Milk sweet?" He offers a small box, his voice muffled by all the cloth.

"Thank you, no. But I'm glad you've returned to sweets. No more whisky. Quite silly."

"Not as silly as sleeping late and missing the mail coach that took your mother away. If my mother was in this world, I would be certain to have accompanied her."

Amah does not answer.

"Let's tell jokes instead," Sai says. "Yesterday, I saw two of His Majesty's procession bearers who used to carry the ceremonial sticks in your parades. Remember those fine silver sticks? Well, the men's titles and their sticks were taken away from them months ago, and they put in a petition to get the titles and the sticks back. Yesterday, the petition was heard, and their titles as procession bearers were reinstated. To lead His Majesty's non-existent parades. And somehow, they forgot to give back the silver sticks!" He flings out his hands, the silks clinging to them.

"Not so funny, my friend," Amah says.

"Oh," he says, peeling the silks from his hands. "How about a story then?"

"What is this word, *pandies*?" she asks him.

"The name of some poor soul who resisted using cartridges in paper greased with animal fats. Pande was his name. In Barrackpore or somewhere. Pande wounded some of his superiors. So now they are calling us all *pandies*."

The women are silent. Outside, the road toward the police station streams with water. Red Man has found a match in all this wetness. He stares in their direction through curls of smoke. Several Englishmen under enormous parasols continue to sit on their restless horses in the noisy downpour.

"The English are nervous," Begam Sahiba tells the little group inside the shop.

Geeta says, "They finally see they've gone too far, and now they're worried."

"Not for what they've done," Begam Sahiba replies. "Still only for themselves. But perhaps Sir Henry Lawrence will get through to them."

"That Red Man is everywhere," Amah says.

"He was with the Company clerks who showed up to survey Gulbadan's land. The new taxes," Sai says. "He showed more interest in the courtyard, hoping to see a courtesan, than in his clerks' task. Gulbadan wants to remind you she is ready to assist further, to help with the Force."

"It is time to remind them that they are outnumbered," Amah says.

"Soon, Amah," says Begam Sahiba. "Soon."

Amah closes her eyes and opens them. Soon is not soon enough. She concentrates on the noise outside. Red Man is calling to one of the officers under the parasols. The officer kicks his horse and rides up the road, dismounting in front of the shop. He shuts his parasol and comes in, stopping in front of Sai, the water from the parasol running onto Sai's feet. "Go home," the officer says to him. His Urdu is rough, like his voice. The officer's hair sticks to the sides of his face. His coat is wet. Amah smells oil, a gun just cleaned, greased cartridges.

Through clenched teeth, she whispers, "No discourtesy." The officer doesn't hear. He is batting away the swathes of silk that stick to his face.

Sai slips away. Gone. Begam Sahiba and Amah are eyes with beads of moisture on their brows. They are hidden away inside the wavy silks, inside their cloaks.

"What's your purpose here?" the Englishman asks in Urdu.

"We are getting out of the rain," Begam Sahiba replies in English. "Like people do."

The officer holds up the parasol, swings it around, gets it caught in silver patterns.

"What do you usually do?" Begam Sahiba asks. "Stand in the middle of a road with its overburdened irrigation system—due to the misuse of the city's drains as dumping sites for beloved buildings being pulled down? Is that what the English do in England? Stand around in puddles and avoid shelter? Here, we bring up our children to stay dry in the monsoons, not wet."

The slick-haired officer shrinks a little where he stands, a stillness in his bland features where confidence usually rests. He is trying to place her, knows suddenly that he is dealing with royalty. He becomes quiet, worried about his senior officers, Amah guesses. The man becomes an English slave.

Begam Sahiba grabs Amah's hand. "Home," she says in Urdu, turning her back on the Englishman and moving into the rain.

At the police station, Red Man is gone. Water spouts from the corners of rooftops. Their veils are wet; Begam Sahiba's pyjama hems, along with their embroidered shoes beneath their cloaks, are speckled with mud. "Let's just get home," she says, her voice sick and tired.

Outside the station, an officer on horseback blows his horn. He kicks his horse, takes the others with him in a sudden gallop.

Amah and Begam Sahiba watch them ride into the distance, in the direction of the Iron Bridge.

A letter has been intercepted from the soldier boy with golden earrings and soft eyes who came to see Begam Sahiba. The letter suggests the use of violence in response to the forced use of the cartridges. But the horses galloping away don't tell Amah or Begam Sahiba this. They don't understand what will happen next. Not yet. In the meantime, Amah and Begam Sahiba enjoy Chowk with no foreigners in its streets, the rain stop, stop, stopping.

They turn around and walk in the opposite direction of their homes. Outside the shops, statues of Venus and Mother Mary call to the stars, a muslin shawl glitters with spangles.

They climb the steps to the *kotha*. Gulbadan's fat brother is nowhere in sight. Nor is Sai. They slip past the courtesans' rooms, past the jangling sound of anklets, past trails of bougainvillea, past several small, white pigeons cooing, *Yahu, oh God*. With every step up the stony hillside behind the rooms, the two women slip back a little, but they continue upwards. Finally, they overlook the city.

Amah's mother's absence hangs heavily in the air. They sit there at the top of the hill contemplating Lucknow—the brown ribbon of the Gomti where kingfishers whoop, the stables that are now English offices, the empty Imambarah College, the new post office, and the silent meadows where no animals roam. Begam Sahiba and Amah both see ghosts, feel their thin residues of comfort, hear skeletons of melodies they once knew. Their hands pick at the stones beneath them. Stones that border the English rose garden near the Residency, that were used to build the old English church.

Amah and Begam Sahiba could sit on these stones, Amah sees, and not make their way among them. Or they could move back down the hillside, stand fast, the stars above them. They have this choice. "We must change our fate," Amah says to her friend. "We must change our kismet."

11.

————————

AMAH STOPS AT Mohammed's newspaper stall, which has more sweets than newspapers on its ledges, and picks up an English paper from Calcutta. "Where are the other papers?" she asks.

"There are few dailies coming anymore," Mohammed says, shifting the sliver of bamboo in his mouth.

The English paper is, as usual, over two months old. Mohammed provides a summary as she glances over the page—a star is photographed for the first time; there's a new coat made with some sort of durable fabric. Nothing about the Queen Mother waiting patiently for Queen Victoria to give birth and be released from confinement. Nothing about His Majesty and his loyal staff living temporarily at Matiya Burj near Calcutta. Nothing about Lucknow. While she examines a sketch of a ceramic milk bottle, she asks Mohammed about the strange news she's heard in Chowk—that an intercepted letter from the young soldier boy's regiment to another regiment had suggested a plan for the murder of English officers. A murderous *tamasha*.

"I don't understand that," Amah says. "The boy came to see Begam Sahiba. Their plan was to write a formal letter of request to their superiors, asking if they could go back to using the old cartridges."

"No, I don't think that was their plan. The letter the English intercepted clearly suggested murder. Sir Henry Lawrence himself confronted the men who were involved. A panic broke out. Twenty mutinous soldiers are now sentenced to hang. A shocking business," he says.

"No one's talking about the shocking cartridges," Amah replies.

Cartridges greased in pig and beef fat that insult everyone's gods. You might grease the cartridges in mustard oil, and Muslim and Hindu men might gladly bite off the tips with their teeth, Amah thinks. Or you might grease cartridges in golden *ghee* and serve them to His Majesty. Or you might just put the English paper down and walk away.

***

In Begam Sahiba's meeting room, Begam Sahiba stands with Jai Lal and several of the King's Indian and African soldiers. As Amah enters, Begam Sahiba says, "*Tasleem*. I saw your aunt just now. She should go to your mother before she dies of worry."

"*Tasleem*. She won't go without Hasan, and Hasan isn't around much these days," Amah says. She's seen her baby cousin in the yard of the Company Tax Office grooming their horses, but she hasn't seen him at the palace. She turns to Jai Lal, asks what she came to ask. "Have you been recruiting the men from the regiments who were insulted by the new cartridges?"

"That would be dangerous," he says, his voice firm. "The English are watching their units. And I don't know those men. We need to be careful not to get caught up in that business."

"They are going to hang Lakhnavis."

"Men who planned murder."

"I can't believe that young soldier boy was caught up in any such affair," Amah says.

"Amah's right. Those men were completely loyal to the Company," Begam Sahiba says.

Jai Lal takes out his handkerchief and mops his brow. "I

don't know. But regardless, our Forces will be orderly," he says. "We must proceed in an orderly fashion."

Amah sighs. Her worry seeps into the letter she holds, bent and damp with perspiration. She gives it to Begam Sahiba.

"Rasheed and Akbar have finally come?" Begam Sahiba asks, her face lighting up.

"No. An errand boy gave it to me as I was coming in your gate."

Begam Sahiba opens the letter, takes out the single page, and reads quickly. "Well," she says. "An invitation. Sir Henry Lawrence invites me to attend his *durbar* to honour the men who intercepted the letter of betrayal of their officers." She gives the letter to Jai Lal to read. "Of course I cannot go," she says. "I have felt nothing but goodness about the Chief Commissioner the whole month he's been here, and I think he really does want to rectify what's been happening. So I don't want to appear rude, or unsupportive, but I cannot go to his *durbar* and be seen by our people to be taking sides over this intercepted letter business. I cannot go and sit on a sofa beside those Englishmen in such a setting."

"Write to him," Amah urges. "Tell him about our meeting with the young soldier boy, that we believe in the innocence of those soldiers, that there is some sort of mistake, that they could not possibly have written such a terrible letter. Did he see the letter himself? Write to him, Begam Sahiba, and I will bring your letter to the *durbar*. We should do everything we can to stop him from hanging Lakhnavi men."

* * *

Amah takes Fatima with her. In front of the Residency, carpets have been laid out over the fine, green grass, and the two women stand with other Lakhnavis behind the chairs arranged in rows facing the building. Company men smoking clove Zanzibar cigarettes stand near their wives who carry rainproof blankets from Nepal, and who wear scarves coloured with Indian dyes. Some distance away, sofas have been pulled onto the Residency verandahs for the officers. Amah recognizes Sir Henry Lawrence chatting with the men.

From a top window of a large home beside the Residency, a plump nobleman with a towel around his bare shoulders watches. Down below, what could be a whole village of Indian servants in crisp white *dhotis* offer palaces of cucumber sandwiches stacked like stuccoed bricks on trays. Fingers pluck sandwiches to place in welcoming mouths. The lawn buzzes with proud Company men and tall, bearded Lakhnavi men from Company units, all of them in long, silk coats. Company wives fill the seats, women with straight backs and elegant hands, women who ride side-saddle, who toil on menus, who learn to buy eggplants that look like balls of gold, who learn never to buy mangoes that, rumour has it, taste like turpentine, women who helplessly watch moths flutter and flop into their food, who strive to grow into good wives, but are lonely women who sit alone for hours sketching Lucknow's yellow birds, women who dearly love their Lakhnavi *ayahs*, women who greet each other now with polite nods and pretty smiles. They offer each other silk fans that send small breezes over soft, delicate skin, their fragile blue eyes fluttering from time to time over to the empty platform set up for a speech. One of the women stares at the crowd behind the chairs. Two blue eyes rest on Amah, on Fatima, and the woman who owns the eyes smiles at them.

Her warmth penetrates Amah, and she knows it's done the same thing to Fatima because they both smile back. Glad to be smiling. The feeling in her lips, in her face, in her whole chest fills Amah. There are delicious things to eat, hot tea to drink, light talk, and comfortable chairs. Perhaps we are not really on opposite sides of the river, she thinks. A fleeting, welcome thought.

An old servant with a tray of sandwiches passes close to them, and Amah holds out the letter, indicates Begam Sahiba's seal. "Please," she says. "Please can you get this to Sir Henry Lawrence?"

The old servant in his crisp white clothes studies the seal and bows quickly, formally. "I will place it on his desk. He will have it at the end of the *durbar*. Will you take a sandwich? His Majesty's mother was fond of these," he says.

"Thank you," Amah says, and takes one.

When he is gone, Fatima juts her chin out to the crowd. "There's Abhi. Friend of thieves."

"Do you know those men he's standing with?" Amah says, feeling for bits of cucumber behind her teeth.

"No," Fatima says. "And isn't that our tamarind tree fellow over there?" She looks toward a group of horses being cared for—by Pavan—away from the crowd.

"I thought Sai's English friends needed a sweeper," Amah says. "Not a stable hand."

"Perhaps they've lost their stable boy, too."

"He does not hold the effects of a festive occasion in his posture," Amah says.

"No, he does not look so happy, even in a fresh *dhoti*."

"Scared, I think," Amah says. "Not convinced of English security."

"Maybe just his worried self," Fatima says.

* * *

At half-past one, the marching band trumpets; a tremendous royal salute goes up, and pigeons circle and cry overhead. Sir Henry Lawrence smiles at everyone when he comes out to the platform on the lawn, followed by several servants carrying gifts. "The cucumber sandwiches in Lucknow are marvellous," he says. A titter goes through the crowd and everyone smiles. Amah and Fatima smile.

He calls forward the two English and the two Lakhnavi soldiers who intercepted the letter. One of the men who steps forward is Red Man; his red hair and blue eyes seem to stand out even more against his white coat. Sir Henry Lawrence awards them three hundred *rupees* each, a shawl, a sword of honour, a jacket, and an embroidered cloth. Amah doesn't see the other men. She is studying Red Man's face, the wink of satisfaction resting in his eyes. There is something wrong, Amah thinks, something very wrong.

"Sir Henry Lawrence is giving the gifts with his own hands," Fatima says quietly to Amah. "A good man. Look at all of them beam."

Sir Henry Lawrence addresses the crowd again. "I want to emphasize to you the handsome pensions that the native men in our army units can hope to get for themselves and for their families. Only last week, in this very city, three hundred men were sought for new units equipped with these tremendous pensions, and thirty-two thousand men, clamorous for service, eagerly rushed forward to partake of the bounty."

Fatima whistles between her teeth. "Thirty-two thousand," she says in a low voice.

"Our saintly Englishman does not recognize his irony," Amah answers, finally taking her eyes off Red Man and turning to Fatima. "Thirty-one thousand, seven hundred did not get the jobs. Thirty-one thousand, seven hundred army men remain desperate for work to feed something more than scraps of cucumber sandwiches to their families."

"There are too many hungry people," Fatima says.

"Hungry for work," Amah says. "Let's go."

* * *

In the dimness of the early dawn the next day, Amah is riding Kasim's grey mare along the same roads Sir Henry Lawrence likes to ride, hoping to see him. Surely by now he has read Begam Sahiba's letter about the soldier boy's loyalty, about Begam Sahiba's own request that Company regiments simply go back to using the old cartridges not greased in cow and pig fat, about not making the grave mistake of hanging loyal men. If they cross paths, perhaps he will give her a message for Begam Sahiba.

She doesn't find him along his old routes deep in the city, so she takes the main road, Hazratganj, and then a road along the river toward Residency Hill. In the low light, she sees a dark line stretching from the road below the Residency all the way up the hill. The dark line flickers. As she gets closer, the line becomes a convoy of Lakhnavis silently pushing cart after cart. She rides beside them, peering into the carts at the grain, firewood, charcoal, cattle fodder, and ammunition. Up the hill in front of the Residency, men are digging up the fine, green grass where cucumber sandwiches were served, turning the lawn into muddy lumps. Some of the men dig trenches. Others are shaping earth embankments as barricades. In the homes around the Residency, Lakhnavis hammer slats of mango wood across the empty windows. Others circle trees that front the homes with axes in their hands.

Amah stops in the street below the hill, and the Lakhnavi men pass her on their way up. The men carry sacks of flour and push carts filled with tins of peaches, asparagus, and ham. Other carts hold barrels of water drawn from the wells situated in front of deserted Indian palaces that long for the old days when Englishmen came for supper, dabbed their moustaches with silk napkins, napped in palace gardens under shady neem trees, lay on chaises in airy pavilions watching a King's plays while dreaming of loans granted on thick paper stamped with red seals, sealing endless agreements for borrowed stately homes, grants of saltpeter, and an ongoing supply of powdered dyes that poured forth from a glittering architectural maze that first beckoned Company merchants from long ago who came two by two into Lucknow's stables that held Australian Walers, a city that welcomed, too, their child who lay in the manger by offering him warm milk.

"What is happening? Which Englishman ordered all of this?" Amah asks a man in a turban. The man shrugs as he moves past her. She spies a friend of Hasan's, a young man who also used to be a royal jockey. "You aren't a labourer," she calls. "What are you doing?"

"I'm not a labourer," he calls back to her as he continues to push his cart. "They pay us three times a labourer's daily wages."

There are bare-footed boys, too, pushing a cart of grain, and Amah gets down from her horse and walks alongside them.

"Is it true they are paying you three times a labourer's daily wages?" she asks one of them.

The child looks up at her questioningly with his bright, dark eyes.

"There's a month's worth of food in this cart," she says.

"Ali, don't do any talking if you want to keep working," a Lakhnavi man calls to the boy.

"I want to keep working," the boy says, still looking up at her.

Amah stares down at him, filled with sadness, confusion. What's obvious is that whatever is happening has nothing to do with getting rid of cartridges greased in pork and beef fat. It has nothing to do with helping the Lakhnavi men condemned to be hanged. "Drink lots of water when you get to the top of the hill," she says gently to the boy. "Your lips are cracked from thirst."

* * *

When Amah tells her what she's seen, Begam Sahiba says, "Perhaps they are leaving! Perhaps Sir Henry Lawrence is preparing for a full departure."

The palace advisors send another letter right away, asking why the English are buying up Lucknow's supplies. Amah walks the road back and forth below the Residency. Earthen parapets have been thrown up around the enormous building. No one is unpacking it of its tremendous stores and taking them in another convoy down Cawnpore Road.

"No," Amah says to Begam Sahiba later. "They are not

leaving. And we are drifting along like old newspapers."

In Chowk, Amah walks through the crowds of shoppers who exclaim about the lack of goods for sale. No one knows what the English shopping spree was all about. The heat of the day is fierce, like a growing heat of quite another kind.

She stands clear of a bullock cart filled with Lakhnavi men and a driver who shouts at his bullock, trying to stop the heavy animal from bolting one way and then the other across the road, parting shoppers like the sea.

The cart comes to a stop, and Sai scrambles out of it. He looks hot and dirty, and comes right up to Amah, his breath halting, his hand over his heart. "*Adab*. They are leaving."

"*Tasleem*. The Company is leaving?"

"The women. The women and their children are moving into the Residency. I helped them load their goats into their carts. The officer with the red hair was there. Do you remember him?"

"Yes, I remember him. Was Abhi with him?"

"No. That Englishman was giving orders to the women and he did not want me there. But every bungalow was a scramble of women packing bags and children, and I wanted to help them with their goats. The animals are frightened. One of Mrs. Gunning's goats kicked me as I was getting her into Mrs. Gunning's cart. Why are they leaving their homes? Do you see anything dangerous, Amah? The vendors are playing their glass bottles, and the boys are flying their kites."

Amah follows Sai out of Chowk. On the Iron Bridge and along the road to the Residency, another convoy has formed. In carriages, children travel with women who wear worry like heavy shawls, suitcases and animals piled high in carts behind them.

"I've got to let everyone know," Amah says and starts to run toward Qaisarbagh Palace.

Sai keeps up with her. "No more milking," he says. "No more work there. A big job lost." Sai's shirt is creased with red and brown soil, and scratches cover his smooth arms. He gets caught in a group of half-naked boys who scamper up to him on the road. He slips out of their teasing tangle, moves to catch up with Amah again, running beside his silent friend, breathless. Sai is like a young god, resisting scampering children who pull and push him and try to drag him down.

12.

———

LAKHNAVIS TIE DAMP, red cloth around pitchers to cool the water. Clouds trail the sky like an English crusader's white, flowing hair. Englishwomen and children move into the Residency's dark shadows.

Amah interrupts Begam Sahiba's meeting with Jai Lal and several bankers. Sir Henry Lawrence's letter, which Amah has brought with her from the palace, is brief. Begam Sahiba reads it out loud. "I have housed the ladies under my attention as a simple precaution against possible native unrest. I also wish to send on a reply to Begam Hazrat Mahal, addressing her concern about the innocence of the men condemned to be hanged. No misunderstanding has taken place. The men admitted they wrote the letter that Mr. John Graham brought to me upon its discovery." Begam Sahiba looks up. "John Graham? Who is Mr. John Graham?"

"The officer with red hair," Amah says.

Red Man. Amah is the first to understand. "Those soldiers did write a letter ... but perhaps not that one. Perhaps our soldier boy and his friends did not write the letter Sir Henry Lawrence received. Perhaps they really did write to ask him formally about using the old cartridges. But that man with red hair, that red man, if he gave the letter to Sir Henry Lawrence ... it was another letter. Or our soldier boy's letter after it had been tampered with. Perhaps his intention was to make the Chief Commissioner harden his heart toward us."

Begam Sahiba, Jai Lal, the bankers are silent. Finally, Begam Sahiba says, "And if we were to suggest this to him, Sir Henry Lawrence would never believe that one of his trusted officers would betray him."

Jai Lal says, "No, *Huzoor.* He would find that preposterous and that would be the end of any communication at all that we have with him."

"For the sake of the men condemned to be hanged," Begam Sahiba says, "to get rid of these new cartridges that are still in use, as far as we know, we should pursue—"

"We cannot pursue this, *Huzoor,*" Jai Lal insists. "Moving the English ladies into the Residency means he is convinced of unrest in Lucknow. The use of the ill-greased cartridges has caused sparks to fly in other places in India. Many soldiers thought that the introduction of those cartridges greased in beef and pork fat was yet another deliberate attempt to turn men into Christians by having them betray their own religions. A few of those men's reactions were violent. And now that Lawrence has received such a letter suggesting murder here, he must be worried. So he is acting with the utmost caution. Putting up barriers, digging those trenches, barricading themselves."

"Yes. And perhaps they know what you are doing, too, Jai Lal. Gathering the Force," Amah says. "There are even more English joining them inside the Residency. Company men from offices around Lucknow. And I saw some of the Company's pensioners back at work—artillerymen. They are being paid well to guard the Residency."

"Perhaps they do know about our Force," Jai Lal says. "Either way, we should move forward and take advantage of this situation, of the fact that they are all moving into the Residency." He is standing across from Amah, and she watches his eyes meet the eyes of the bankers. "We have begun the re-production of our own *rupees, Huzoor,*" Jai Lal says.

Begam Sahiba's eyes open a little wider. She pauses before she says, "All right."

"Our Force is building nicely. We have well over a thousand Lakhnavis signed up," Jai Lal says.

"Be careful with the *Kotwal*," Begam Sahiba says. "He is on watch for the Company."

"We will continue to recruit, *Huzoor*," Jai Lal presses. "Surely you agree that it is time to make them leave. The banks are going to cut off all credit to the Company."

Amah watches for Begam Sahiba's reaction. Her friend hesitates again. Then she says, "When you are quite sure the Force is ready we can send a letter about the lack of credit now available to them, and surround the Residency in great numbers. What we must do, Jai Lal, is communicate clearly that they are free to leave peacefully by Cawnpore Road. Yes, we will help them any way they need us to help them to leave. But we must remain tranquil while we show them the way out of our lives. With all their bags and whatnot packed with them. Be sure to communicate that very clearly."

"*Huzoor*, we could also plan for the crowning of your son, in his father's name. That would make everything we are doing more official."

"I'm not sure we need to go that far, Jai Lal," Begam Sahiba says, and begins to pace.

"It would be an important move for the sake of formality. Lucknow's citizens would very much approve of a son standing in for His Majesty," Jai Lal says. "And with a figurehead in place, with you both at the palace, we can make an even stronger request for their departure. Move back with your son to Qaisarbagh, *Huzoor*."

"I am very happy where I am," Begam Sahiba says. She stops in front of him. "And you know that His Majesty would not like that. Nor would his mother. I have no right to move there."

"You yourself said that we cannot continue to wait for their return. We cannot wait anymore for whatever it is that is going on in Calcutta or London. We have been patient for a long,

long time. We should officially restore Lucknow for them. Let us go forward with a coronation at the palace."

"The other wives would not like it. Not one bit. You know that, too."

"We will make you comfortable at Qaisarbagh," Jai Lal says resolutely. He glances around at everyone, his eyes brightening. He indicates Shahzadi, stretched out asleep in the sun outside. "We will make preparations for the tiger's comfort as well," he says. "And the swans. We will move them all to the palace with you. For all of this to work as well as it can possibly work, *Huzoor,* we must have you all at the palace."

"For all of this to work, " Begam Sahiba says, "Birjis won't be giving any orders. And neither will you."

Jai Lal bows his head, his face reddening.

"I will make the arrangements for your quarters at the palace," Amah says.

"All right. Make the arrangements," Begam Sahiba replies.

* * *

The *Kotwal's* men seek skirmishes. They slam the weak in jail, prepare the most unlucky for the Straits, pour gin for English officers, and collect rewards. Jai Lal continues to guard his new recruits by training them in low numbers inside the Chattar Manzil until the Force is big enough to easily surround the Residency. Rooms at the palace are dusted and scrubbed for Begam Sahiba's arrival. One of the palace gardens is selected for Birjis' coronation.

Amah rides along the road by the Gomti. Servants ride donkeys who pull carts piled high with bags—carts that lean as they go up Residency Hill, a picture smudged by dust and heat.

She wipes the spittle from her lips with a handkerchief and goes to a well beside the road to draw a cup of water. She gets down and leans into the well, pulls up a full bucket of water, takes up the cup tied inside it, and drinks. She drinks while Company soldiers at the Residency's Baillie Guard Gate wait for the bullock carts filled with La Martinière College teachers, and school boys in blue uniforms, the carts that carry along bespectacled clerks and their files of papers, the labourers who grasp the luggage of Christian missionaries who look down from their carriages at loyal Lakhnavi bearers, cooks, and the men who carry blue and white basins who walk alongside, and the carts that bring bandsmen and sweepers, all of them clambering up the hill toward the looming, newly-barricaded, heavily-guarded Residency where a man with red hair ushers them inside. Amah draws the bucket up again, splashes her face with cool, clear water. When they have all disappeared inside, there is silence from the abandoned cantonment, in the Company offices that still smell like hay, on the roads shimmering with hot sand. Amah hears nothing but the bucket's clink, clinking inside the well.

But then she hears something in the distance—the rising sounds of voices. Riding along the Gomti, past Residency Hill, toward the noise, she finds herself at the Macchi Bhawan Fort where a crowd has gathered. Wooden gallows, with two long cross beams, are set up outside the fort. A row of Lakhnavi policemen guard the six young men in khaki uniforms who stand with their hands tied behind their backs. At once, she recognizes the young soldier boy with gold earrings and soft eyes who came to see Begam Sahiba. She dismounts quickly and leaves her horse tied under a neem tree on the road.

Company soldiers, both Lakhnavis and Englishmen, surround the crowd of Lakhnavis who've heard the appalling news about the hangings. Lakhnavi policemen walk into the crowd, watching and listening. Amah thinks she spots her baby cousin, Hasan, at last, but when she makes her way through the people to stand with him, the man turns and it is not him. But she sees Nawab Mirza and Sharif-un-nissa, brother and sister, nephew and niece of His Majesty, nearby. Sharif-un-nissa is smaller and slimmer than her brother who is plump and flirtatious. He combs his hair back, and rubies stud his ears. He wears satin pyjamas and a tight, embroidered waistcoat. In the old days, Amah brought gifts from Qaisarbagh Palace to their house. Nawab Mirza would greet her in their hallway, wearing only his pyjamas. She sometimes dreamed of him inviting her into his pillow-strewn rooms, offering her roasted cashews, sitting down right beside her, panting sweetly as he thanked her for the gifts from Qaisarbagh Palace. Instead, he would stand in the hallway and call to her, "May the grace of God grant you safety on your way home."

Now the royal cousins greet Amah warmly when she goes to them. "They are hanging twenty of them," Nawab Mirza shouts over the crowd. "This is only the first group. We will help the palace in any way we can."

"Hush," Amah says. "Be careful. The police are everywhere."

The *Kotwal* paces in front of the condemned men. Lakhnavi policemen hem the crowd and listen. An unmanned eighteen-pounder long gun points down at them from its place above the Macchi Bhawan Fort's entrance. English East India Company officers, wearing white trousers and short red coats with gold buttons and gold braiding, stand near the hangman at the gallows. Red Man emerges from the group and approaches each of the young Indian soldiers dressed in khaki uniforms. He strips them of their badges, tossing the badges into the bag that he carries. The big gun above them rules the world like the English rule the world, like Red Man rules, like the *Kotwal* rules—like the hangman rules. The big gun watches. It tells the crowd to be afraid.

Amah thinks, But one must be careful of Englishmen who are becoming afraid, who surely can see that they are a small group in a big city, men who are clearly frightened of whispering Lakhnavis who form crowds.

The hangman readies six nooses made of thick coir rope across the two long cross beams. Made from the tough fibre extracted from the husks of coconuts, the rope will not break. A sturdy, wooden chair, the kind made for English offices, is placed beneath the first noose. When the boy soldier with gold earrings whimpers and will not come forward when Red Man calls him, the hangman becomes furious and pushes him, the boy's hands still tied behind his back, across the distance to the gallows. Amah moves up to the front of the crowd, past the cousins, right in front of the gallows. A wall of English officers step forward to stop her, to stop anyone, from moving any closer. The boy looks at the ground, lost in himself, this boy whose new beard grows like down on his cheeks. She watches while the boy is helped up onto the chair by two officers. The hangman brings a stool and climbs it in order to place the noose around the boy's neck. He says something to the boy, and the boy stands on his tiptoes in his sandals so that the noose falls under his chin and frames his head.

Damn you, Amah thinks. Damn the evil *jinns* and human devils that inspire each other. Damn you. I will lift the boy with his shadowy hair that lies on his soft cheeks, and I will take him away down a Lucknow lane with demolition debris in its open drains. I will walk past those drains and go down the lane and out the other end far up the Gomti where His Majesty's boat lifts and drops in the water by the shore, waiting for us to sail it into the river to catch the soft breezes. I will wear a gold tunic on the boat to match his gold earrings, and, the soldier boy and I, we will point these Englishmen in the direction of the performance we are here to watch, a scene from one of His Majesty's own plays where a chorus of women dressed in coloured silks sewn with gold thread will sing while vendors with broken, betel-stained teeth sell iced water and while white rubber balloons sail with the pink kites that dot the blue sky and remind us of His Majesty's stage painted with white, pink, and blue. Damn you. I will feed the soldier boy soft *habshi halwa*. I just have to slip the coir noose out from under the boy's chin, and I will take his hand, and wait for the gleaming royal boat so that we can watch His Majesty's play. This is what I will do.

But the hangman gets off his stool near the wooden chair where the soldier boy is on tiptoe with a noose that lies against his neck. The hangman stands on the ground, aloofness in his eyes, as Amah turns green, the colour of the Gomti, the colour of the bile rising in the soldier boy's stomach, the colour of silk-winged pigeons in the King's shaded gardens, the colour of the khaki English coats on the condemned men.

The hangman asks, "Boy, why did you do this to yourself? Here, I have removed a loose thread from your uniform. I am even doing away with the blindfold. Listen, at least this way, you will save your fellow man. You will be offering other soldiers a good warning against mutiny, and there will be no more worrying about greased cartridges."

"We are still using the cartridges," Amah imagines Sir Henry Lawrence's clear voice, his polished Urdu. "We continue to use them, the ones that have shamed men."

"What are you saying?" the hangman looks up at the soldier boy who is mumbling, his face flushing pink. "Not a good time to mumble," the man says. He walks behind the boy, puts his hands on the back of the chair. "Your time to talk is nearing its end."

"I did not do anything," the boy says.

"Talk like that," the hangman says, "it's what they all say when things have got this far."

The soldier boy, his eyes turned toward the ground, starts to cry. After another moment, the hangman slowly pulls on the chair. It moves a little and scrapes the ground.

"I didn't do anything," the soldier boy cries out.

"It's time. I have given you more attention and kindness than the others will get." He puts his hands firmly around both sides of the back of the English wooden chair. The hangman drags it out from underneath the boy, and he drops, his feet just shy of the ground.

The weight of the boy's body tightens the noose around his throat, and the boy's body becomes immediately limp. He gasps for air against the tight noose and the weight of his body that is supported only by his neck and jaw.

One of the English officers calls, "Hangman, how long?"

"Twenty minutes."

"Better start with the others," Red Man says. "We'll miss the lunch hour."

Several of the officers smile. "That's a good hang," someone says.

They bring two more men up to the gallows, and make them stand on chairs on either side of the soldier boy who is slowly dying of strangulation. Amah forces herself to stay in the crowd with the gun looking down at them, the boy's distorted, purpling face looking out at them, the police searching for protestors to arrest in the crowd. But the crowd is weak with shock, and there is only a breathless silence. A breathless crowd, breathless as an old *nawab* tomb, as a soldier boy.

Light glances off one of the soldier boy's gold earrings, and it hurts Amah's eyes. The soldier boy's eyes have gone red with bulging blood vessels. The vessels begin to pop and blood pours forth from his eyes. She hears the boy's brain swell, hears his lungs shrivel like burst rubber balloons. When his face is completely purple, when blood streaks his face and his lips stop moving, Amah can no longer hear his heart beat.

The hangman orders the last three men to stand on the three chairs now waiting under the last three nooses attached to the second cross beam. "Up!" the hangman calls. Three officers come forward to help the men climb onto the chairs. On the cross beam in front of the men who stand on the chairs, the first three men's bodies slowly rotate. Amah's eyes hurt as she stares at the mottled face of the soldier boy.

The hangman wastes no time with the last three men, roughly collecting the chairs he's moved out from beneath them.

Ten thousand threads gathered from the husks of coconuts are woven together like the golden braiding on officers' uniforms. Coir rope is braided and knotted for golden nooses while His Majesty listens to Sufi court singers. Musical assemblies of devout Sufis sing out to cause excruciating ecstasy while orders from Sir Henry Lawrence sing out to cause excruciating agony. One of His Majesty's eyes is Sunni, the other is Shi'a, and he listens to Sufi songs, traces with his fingers Hindu paintings, tastes fish the way Jains like to cook it, talks quietly with Jewish jewellers, and wears English-tailored suits made of golden silk. Sir Henry Lawrence, a man who Amah thought reasoned with his heart has insisted on a sour change of heart, so Amah has stayed in the crowd to watch a young boy's heart stop and thereby harden into cold stone her own. Sir Henry Lawrence was a man who once had one English eye and one Indian eye. He has shut one eye. He has shut one eye. His Majesty has both eyes wide open—that Shi'a eye, that Sunni eye—but Sir Henry Lawrence has shut one eye and the veins in the soldier boy's eyes burst and bleed from the pressure. Shi'a priests lead Friday prayers and Sir Henry Lawrence leads his Englishmen away from Indians who are no longer good, good, good but bad, and there is bad, bad, bad in Lucknow. Hanging men is bad, bad, bad. Damn you, Amah thinks, the boy's ashes will glitter like gold unlike yours that will burn like an evil *jinni's* ashes burn in a dirty fire.

Sir Henry Lawrence approves of these Englishmen who look with their hooded eyes at the crowd of Lakhnavis—these men in white pants and red coats who swagger in front of six hanged men and in front of the Lakhnavi people who wear gold-threaded slippers and gold-threaded shawls, who are now bad people who will learn lessons by watching Indians in loose-threaded khaki uniforms die while the Englishmen in gold-threaded coats share the common thread of arrogance with their arrogant leader Sir Henry Lawrence. His Majesty drinks iced water and sails far away while Sir Henry Lawrence does not remove ill-greased cartridges but instead he chooses to break the necks of men with coir rope, rope that usually tethers goats. The winking light of hope Amah once felt for the Englishman, that winking firefly light, is dead.

Amah steps away from the crowd, but Nawab Mirza and Sharif-un-nissa are speaking too loudly to friends around them. The *Kotwal* and his men rake the crowd with their eyes. She makes her way back to the cousins, takes Sharif-un-nissa by the hand. "Let me take you both home," she says, beckoning Nawab Mirza to follow them. "Let us not witness one more moment of this shaming."

* * *

Outside the Macchi Bhawan Fort, six men are left hanging, and later that day Amah is down the road in the English East India Company Tax Office looking for her cousin, Hasan, the royal jockey who has taken the job of grooming tax officers' horses. She waits at one of the two Tax Office counters covered in blotting paper to protect them from dirty fingers. Behind the two officers who sit at the counters, a Lakhnavi clerk collects ledgers and packs them into wooden boxes. The Company's tax officers seem determined to complete their first land revenue collection before they move themselves into the Residency with everyone else.

The English officer behind Amah's counter studies his log book to see if Hasan is in. His tea waits, a saucer on top of his cup to keep the flies from drowning. If he asks, Amah is not trying to find her cousin to urge him to come with her to join Jai Lal's Awadh Force, which today has grown quickly in numbers because of the hangings; she simply wants to invite Hasan to tea.

A man clearing his throat comes up to the next counter, and Amah sees that it's Pavan, his wavy hair filled with dust. He speaks nervously to the tall officer who peers at the villager's land tax certificate. Pavan does not see Amah. Instead, his eyes and ears hang on the officer's response in Urdu. There seems to be a problem with the certificate's seal, a question of forgery. Pavan clears his throat. "The certificate was sent like that," he says.

"It might have been Johnson, when he first arrived," the tall officer says in English to Amah's officer who listens idly while he scans the log book. The tall officer in front of Pavan circles something and taps the paper. "At any rate," he says to Pavan, returning to Urdu. "You are past the deadline. That's a twenty-five *rupee* fine."

The certificate lies between them. Its existence seems to startle Pavan, such a worn-looking man, whose face, a crumpled face, seems more creased in the sunshine falling across the counter—a face that questions every ray of daylight slanted with English decisions.

Pavan clears his throat again as he counts with his eyes the *rupee* coins he pulls from his dirty white bag. Outside, his pony whinnies.

"No, the black boy Hasan has not been in for days." The Company officer with the cup of tea snaps his log book shut.

Amah doesn't move. She listens to Pavan's chattering while no one else in the room listens. He got lost in the city; he needed food for his pony. His odour, the lonely smell of the unbathed, reaches Amah, and the noise of the whinnying pony, a sick sort of sound, enters the office. "Three hundred won't do it," the tall man behind the desk is saying. "Three hundred and twenty-five, *pandy*. Three hundred and twenty-five."

Twenty-five *rupees*. Amah will borrow it from Begam Sahiba. She moves swiftly across the room to leave for Begam Sahiba's home, cursing the men behind the counters who make poor men's lives an anxious hell.

Pavan runs out the door past Amah and two Lakhnavi guards stationed outside, his feet slapping the ground, his hands reaching for the coir rope that hangs across his sick pony's ribs. Amah shouts at him, tells him she is going to get him the money he needs. He doesn't seem to hear her as he tries to pull himself onto his pony and fails. He is shaking badly.

"Bag that *pandy*," Red Man yells in English from where he rides in the road, his duties at Macchi Bhawan Fort evidently complete. He gestures wildly at Pavan and the two Lakhnavi guards drag the man from the pony and hold them both fast. The pony pulls up and down, whinnying loudly, her ears back. The two English officers from inside stand at the door. "Take him in on possible forgery and the inability to make the payment," the tall officer says in Urdu. "Any breach right now is a security breach. And do something about that pathetic animal."

* * *

In Begam Sahiba's meeting room, the ex-Queen's papers and newsletters are being packed into boxes by servant girls. Begam Sahiba sits against some cushions, her dark hair held back by an orange headscarf. She is eating a piece of jackfruit when Amah, breathless and drenched in perspiration, comes in the door. "*Tasleem*. Hasan has been found," Begam Sahiba says at once. "He's taken up residence with some foreign men in the royal observatory."

Amah looks at her friend, confused and still trying to catch her breath. She kneels beside her. "He is staying at Star House? With foreigners?"

Begam Sahiba smooths her teeth with her tongue, removing strands of fruit. "There are Indians roaming the country, restless, with any number of complaints against the Company. None of them are people we want in Lucknow, but some of them have come here. They are unpredictable strangers. Possibly violent. We must keep an eye on those men. Hasan is crazy to go and stay with them."

"They must be recruiting Lakhnavis to join them," Amah says.

"They are recruiting Lakhnavis. We need to keep Lakhnavis focused on our new Force."

"The coronation should happen now."

"I am moving to the palace just as soon as everything is packed up. Don't worry, I am going to support my son's coronation."

"All those young men have been hanged."

"Yes. Sickening. Jai Lal and I agree that we will not succumb to such vile actions. We must take the high road and request a peaceful surrender. Amah, as soon as the wardrobe is packed, we will move to the palace. As fast as we possibly can."

"We didn't do a single thing to help that poor soldier boy. I am desperate to do something. What I came for ... I want to borrow twenty-five *rupees*. A sick Hindu I know who has a sick pony did not have enough to pay his bill in the Tax Office. I do not have the extra he owes. I will sell another of my mother's pearls, but I need the twenty-five *rupees* now. They have taken him to the jail. They are nervous. If I go quickly with the money the man owes, or better, if you come too, we might change the situation. The man is sick. The pony is sick."

Begam Sahiba holds her wrist up, her fingers wet with fruit. "Perhaps it's time to talk to the *Kotwal*, to make sure he is guarding against new Indian foreigners. Regardless of the fool's allegiances, we need to give the *Kotwal* a warning about men like the ones in Star House. Nobody wants those people here stirring up trouble. Amah, send a boy to take him up on his offer that I tour his jail." She gets up to rinse her hands. "We can get two jobs done at once."

* * *

In the evening, the air is not much cooler. Amah rides Kasim's grey mare ahead of Begam Sahiba's palanquin, carried by four young men. She leads them past the Chattar Manzil where Jai Lal bids his latest group of recruits goodnight. She rides along a lane where several noblemen sit smoking hookah on their balconies, cracking fresh pistachios, rinsing their fingers in blue-china bowls of water. Women stand at ground-floor windows, women with red lines of paste smeared down their parted, oiled hair, women who light incense in ancient Persian reading rooms, prepare tumblers of scalding tea, and watch the day sink into dusk, observing the growing darkness extinguish the cries of sentenced men and the routines of life in Lucknow; women whose sweat beads on their eyelids and makes dark arches under their arms.

The police station sits in the shadows, a small, flaming torch at its entrance. Amah rides past the station and around the corner to dismount. Behind her, Begam Sahiba gets out of the palanquin shrouded in a black *burqa*. She gives Amah twenty-five *rupees*. "Did you see that? Did you see what I saw? That pony over there."

Further away, near another flaming torch in front of a shop, Pavan's skinny pony lies on a flat cart, her head matted with clotted blood. Her eyes show the wild terror she felt at the end. Begam Sahiba pulls her cloak around herself and walks a few steps toward the animal.

Heaviness moves within Amah. Pavan.

"May Allah grant you deserved peace on your journey," Began Sahiba says to the pony, walking right up to her.

"Whatever happens inside, Begam Sahiba, I must help this man," Amah says. "I must."

"Yes," Begam Sahiba says. "I understand you, Amah." She pulls out a silk handkerchief, lays it gently over the pony's face.

When the two women enter the front room of the station, Amah looks at once for Pavan, but only sees the six Lakhnavi policemen who stand at attention. The *Kotwal* appears to have barely collected himself. He wears a new shawl. Amah wonders if he forgot they were coming as he bows low to Begam Sahiba, jerking like a bird, his eyes busy putting thoughts into place. "You've been recently honoured. Congratulations," Begam Sahiba says, her green eyes steady on the man. The *Kotwal* bows again. They can smell his breath. Celebrating the rewards of the job. "Such a shiny shawl, and a gift of *rupees*, too, no doubt," Begam Sahiba says. "Who did you round up this time?" she asks, glancing at Amah.

"We need to keep the city safe, your Highness," the *Kotwal* says. "Skirmishes must be put down." He clears his throat.

He seems quite alone without his friend, Red Man. Amah walks further into the room, past the desk covered in papers, and glances into her old holding cell, looking for the dusty Hindu man, Pavan. No one. 'Ali Shah's old cell is empty, too. She sees something odd. A bottle of French wine and a half-empty glass on the desk. That's when Amah notices the dirty white bag, loose, among the papers. The tax certificate lies there, too.

The *Kotwal* is still talking. "I was honoured today by the Chief Commissioner Sir Henry Lawrence himself. You can imagine my surprise at the arrival of the honourable man from the Residency. Your Highness, please follow me to inspect the criminals brought in. Let me also show you the gifts of ammunition the Company has given me for the protection of Lucknow."

Begam Sahiba and Amah lock eyes as the *Kotwal* and his policemen walk ahead of them toward the back of the room. Amah points at the things on the desk and motions to her friend that she is looking for Pavan. Begam Sahiba tilts her head, approving. The *Kotwal* leads them all through the back door into a small jail—a row of cells lit by glass lanterns. Except for the braggard's voice, it is quiet. The men in the shadows inside the stalls bow silently to Begam Sahiba as she passes. Amah listens for someone clearing his throat. She searches the stalls. No sign of the Hindu. She hangs back from the *Kotwal* who has fully recovered his poise. He stops at the last cell with Begam Sahiba to explain that the prisoners are fed, the place is clean, and that there is much more room now than the King ever provided.

Four of the six policemen have followed him to the end of the row of cells. The other two stand halfway between the *Kotwal* and Amah. "There are a lot of wandering fellows who have come to Lucknow," Amah hears Begam Sahiba say to the *Kotwal*.

The two policemen follow Amah at a distance, talking, as

she moves back into the front room, pondering again the two empty holding cells where a new criminal should be. The cells have been washed down; no doubt the *Kotwal* cleaned things up for an important visit from the Residency. The door to the *Kotwal*'s own office, off the front room, is closed. Amah wonders. The two policemen near the back door to the small jail are still talking. She moves quickly, aiming for the office door, and shoots the brass handle with her rifle. It doesn't unlock, so she aims at the wooden door itself, blowing holes in it, and kicks it open.

Inside, an ivory bookcase is down on its side, the books strewn over the floor. She stays by the door, despite the policemen's boots pounding toward her. She surveys the scene—blood on the floor, the ivory edges of the bookcase broken, sharp. The *Kotwal*'s office door is penetrated with jagged, unfixable holes. Breaking in was a rash decision done properly, a quick assessment of what had gone on that day, and Amah is proud of it.

Beside her, the two Lakhnavi policemen stare into the office, too nervous about how to handle her, a woman with a gun who has discovered something they evidently were not aware of. She moves away from them, from Begam Sahiba who has promised to understand, and she goes outside. She must find Pavan.

She rides through neighbourhoods with walled gardens, and feels her rifle lean into her thigh. She reaches the open riverfront and its long stretch of *ghats*. The muddy river air creeps onto her hands and loiters under her eyes. She gallops closer to the water, and the air clings to her face and enters her throat. She rides past the *ghats* where *dhobis* throw wet clothes against rocks in the night, the river filled with evening bathers, and she rides to the funeral pyres where the embers are cold, the marigolds piled on top of wealthy bodies by eldest sons are gone, and today's ashes have been taken away. She reaches a plain site at the edge of it all, a pyre hidden by neglected trees with dusty leaves and bins of barbed wire. She dismounts and ties the grey mare to one of the trees. She feels a drumming in her veins, Gomti air in her lungs. The attendant for the fires, a low-caste man in a *lungi* and an old shirt, is stacking wood by a wall for the next day. He puts his hands together in greeting. "*Namaste*," he says.

"*Tasleem*," she answers, and shows him Begam Sahiba's *rupees*, motioning that he should follow her into the pyre area. She gives him one *rupee*, looks at the poor man's shirt, and gives him another two. Across the river, a gun cracks from somewhere within the empty cantonment. The sound fills the black-and-silver sky for some moments. She asks the man for a list of deceased, those with no money or relatives, those found dead from hunger in the streets, the long list of those who have been given a decent end, whose ashes have been put into urns, taken out by the man, and shaken into the Gomti. He counts off the day's corpses: an old artist, a snack vendor, even a distant cousin of the King—a lady who had become more destitute than the destitute. And then the villager who met with a bad end, an accident of some sort. The man keeps talking. Perhaps Amah has some of the details wrong, but she has some of them right, she knows that—Pavan's last struggles, the man fighting back at a time when the *Kotwal* did not care to have a sick man fussing in the jail, the procession from the Residency to honour the *Kotwal* on its way. Perhaps a decision to put Pavan in the *Kotwal's* office was too hasty; the toppled bookcase might have been an accident caused by a struggle, an accident that had to be hastily taken care of. The attendant talks. He is grateful to the royal family who paid his wages to keep the pyre going, a salary from His Majesty that the English East India Company feels obliged to continue, what with the need for this service, for this perpetual fire for warm spirits without means.

Across the Gomti, an orange ball of light grows brighter, wider. Across the Gomti, the cracking of guns, waves of shouting. Amah watches the orange ball of fire roll through the empty cantonment—the bungalows in flames—the sky above them lit up by burning trees, the pop-pop of branches exploding. She watches the orange rolling fire glow on the Gomti, shimmering upon the dark, silent waters where ashes vanish.

13.

◆◆◆◆

A MAH'S NEWS OF Pavan's death shrinks against the news in the streets that three thousand angry Indian men from four English regiments stationed in Lucknow set fire to the cantonment bungalows. These men were devoted to the Company for years but were nonetheless forced to come to Macchi Bhawan Fort to watch the hangings of their fellow men. Flames and volumes of smoke cause destruction before the men are put to flight and dispersed by advancing English sergeants. Some of the men are arrested, their resistance halted, their regiments disbanded. This time, Jai Lal goes ahead and recruits from the disbanded English regiments. He no longer keeps his Force hidden by training them in low numbers. The several thousand who've joined the Organization of Awadh Soldiers mill in and around the Chattar Manzil where the King once served pancakes to his actors. Many of the soldiers take up rooms there. Jai Lal orders them to show themselves in large numbers in the empty streets until Begam Sahiba has moved to the palace and Birjis has been crowned.

That night, old Kasim calls Amah from her restless sleep. "The messengers have come," he says.

The messengers. At last. In the thick midnight air, Amah shakes *jinns* from her mind as she makes her way to Begam Sahiba's candle-lit meeting room. Inside, Rasheed and Akbar, dressed like Delhi poets in English trousers and Indian *kurtas*, eat kebabs with yogurt. Begam Sahiba leans against the wall, wrapped in a shawl.

After all these months of waiting, Amah wishes to exclaim out loud, to ask what's happened, to welcome them back, but the silence tells her not to. The messengers' long faces greet Amah as they eat; their serious eyes tell her they have serious news. A mosquito whines at Amah's ear, and she slaps at it. Jai Lal lurches into the room, his face covered in perspiration. He bows his head. "*Huzoor,*" he says.

Begam Sahiba begins to speak as soon as he enters. "Rasheed and Akbar have just come through Cawnpore. All of the English there have moved into a makeshift entrenchment. For safety. They fear violence because they've heard about resistance to the English in the whole of Awadh."

"The English in Cawnpore are behaving with great caution," Akbar says. "They are not taking chances."

"The point is," Begam Sahiba says, "a peaceful escape for the English here in Lucknow via Cawnpore might not be possible."

It dawns on Amah. "And surely Sir Henry Lawrence knows about the English situation in Cawnpore. He must be communicating with them. Surely, this is the reason the English have moved into the Residency." Her head swims.

"Of course he must be communicating with them. We've not seen that spy, Abhi, around for a long time," Begam Sahiba says.

"*Huzoor,* Sir Henry Lawrence won't go through there," Jai Lal says.

"The countryside is hostile," Rasheed agrees. "Travel is tricky. We had to lie low, take rest where we could find it, move very slowly. It is essential to be extremely careful at a time like this. They say Awadh is on fire in many places and full of volatile men. Those men are marching everywhere to fight the English. It's become clearer that the Company has been trying to get rid of Indian rulers everywhere. There are men roaming around, dispossessed, and angry with the Company. Indian soldiers working for the English are fed up with being paid less, they have realized, than any Englishman. They are fed up with being scorned by new English officers who only speak English. In Delhi, they found out that the cartridges in use there had impure grease. Some Indian soldiers began a resistance. The English ordered other Indian soldiers loyal to the English to shoot them. Those loyal soldiers would not shoot Indians but joined them instead. They have taken over Delhi. Then there are some plain looters roaming around, stealing in Delhi, and in other places. Criminal opportunists. All sorts of men roaming. Marauders. There is talk of men coming here, too."

"We have a few of them already. We don't want any of those kind of men here," Begam Sahiba says. "It would be impossible to tell who is who. Chaos."

"Newspaper sales have been banned in Calcutta," Rasheed says, giving his empty plate to a servant boy. "It is very hard to know what is going on."

"Things are getting serious for the Company," Begam Sahiba says.

"There are rumours everywhere about men who want to see the English ousted from every single town," Rasheed says.

"We don't need those kind of men," Jai Lal repeats. "I need men who will listen to me."

"Those men are just as dangerous as the English," Begam Sahiba says. "Their behaviour just as undignified."

"There are resistances all over Awadh," Akbar says again with awe. "We heard it on the train. Indians are nervous. I tell you, there are angry men who want to come here, to Lucknow. To help get the English out."

"We don't want them here," Begam Sahiba says sharply, "to help anyone. The English are in a corner. Three thousand people inside the Residency, cut off completely from the outside, and outnumbered. We can do it ourselves, but we will not behave in an unruly way. We will not behave like Englishmen who eat pigs and drink wine, who bite greased cartridges, who destroy Hindu and Muslim temples on the pretence of making roads, who wish to institute English schools, who build churches and send clergymen into the streets and alleys to preach the Christian religion, neglecting our places of worship. We will not stoop to such levels. We will ask for their surrender. Peacefully. That is the perfect symbol. Surrender at Lucknow: a symbolic act to the advantage of the whole of northern India. We do not have to indulge in misbehaviour." She turns to Jai Lal. "We don't need those foreign Indian marauders in Lucknow."

"*Huzoor,*" Jai Lal says, his eyes on the ground. "I must tell you one thing. I have recruited a skilled contingent of new-comers from outside the city. Some from far away. We had to. So many Lakhnavis have left. However, these particular newcomers are ready to serve us. I have made certain of that."

She stares at him, pulling her shawl around herself.

"I can assure you these particular men have the interests of Lucknow at heart," Jai Lal says. "We have selected carefully. They've seen what the English have done in other places. They are in disbelief and shock about what has happened to His Majesty, that the English would simply take over the Kingdom of Awadh. They want to help, *Huzoor.* They have experience, make good soldiers. They know we'll pay them well. We even have a Tamil who has come all the way from Madras to help. We have a solid Force. So tomorrow," Jai Lal raises his hands, the muscles in his arms taut as he walks to the door, "I will ask the palace advisors to compose a letter, urging Sir Henry Lawrence to surrender. We will send it after the coronation, which all of my men are waiting for."

"Everything is being packed up," Begam Sahiba says.

"*Huzoor,* the coronation must happen as soon as possible. Then we will surround the Residency." Jai Lal bows and vanishes into the night.

Amah also walks to the door, but she cannot leave. She asks, "Is there news from His Majesty?"

Begam Sahiba picks up the envelope with the letter the messengers brought. "The Queen Mother needs perfumes from Lucknow. She is keeping what fragrance she has to offer as a gift to Queen Victoria. She has an invitation for an audience with their Queen. She is sick with worry, having waited so very long to plead her son's case. And London is terribly expensive. She wants to come home."

"And my mother?" Amah asks tentatively. "Is there any news of the staff?"

"Oh, dear!" A rush of light enters Begam Sahiba's eyes and she reaches out for Amah's hands. "You didn't ask. You've been waiting all this time. There is only one letter from His Majesty's advisors, but she is well. The advisors in Calcutta pass on the news that everyone is well. Your medicines arrived, and she is well."

"She is definitely well," Rasheed says, and Akbar agrees, their faces flashing warmth upon Amah.

At the palace, Amah goes to her mother's room. There are times that her heart swells all on its own, and it doesn't let questions in her mind take over. She digs up the box, and, from the three rubies and five pearls she has left, she takes out a large ruby and goes to the kitchens to find a boy who will sell the ruby to Judea the jeweller in the morning.

The next day, Rasheed is dressed like a Hindu holy man in orange robes, and Akbar is disguised in pyjamas with very wide legs like upper-class youths like to wear. Their long faces are flushed with rest and good food. They get up quickly when Amah comes in. She gives them the small china vessel filled with rose water that she's purchased for her mother, and offers them money for the trouble of taking such a fragile package all the way to Calcutta. "No need," Rasheed says. "It's a pleasing task. Your mother will be pleased."

* * *

The Tamil who has come from Madras is a lanky, young, Hindu man named Malamud who doesn't speak to anyone. Malamud is fast with a gun, fast on foot. Some of Jai Lal's ignorant foreigners stare at Amah—they stare at Fatima, too—at any black, female guard with a rifle. But Malamud does not stare. Instead, he lowers his gaze respectfully and puts his hands together in greeting. The next day, while the palace continues to prepare for Begam Sahiba's arrival, Amah watches him perform military drills at the Chattar Manzil and then quietly joins him. They both use rifles, spurning the old-fashioned muskets that are slower to load and fire. "You are ready for much more than military ceremonies and parades," Malamud says at last, shaking his head at her accuracy.

"I'm a bodyguard. My duty is to protect, not to harm," she tells him.

He is about her age, and, after watching her practise for some time, he suddenly opens up to her, talks to her like a cousin, as if he's known her a long while. "Your name, where I come from, your name means 'mother.' *Amma*."

"Where I come from it means, 'companion.'"

"Suits you either way," Malamud says, and smiles, his gaze lowered.

"What about your own mother?" Amah asks.

"Passed away now. My father, too, a long time ago. My mother made a living as an *ayah*. Took care of English children. That, too, was a long time ago. I miss them, have sad feelings about them. You?"

"My mother is in Calcutta. I have sad feelings about her, too."

Malamud waits for some moments and then starts to practise again. She is thankful to him for understanding she doesn't want to say more. A rush of wounded anger fills her. She is pleased that her mother is well, but she is also baffled by her silence. Could she not have sent a small note to her after all of this time? She wonders if her mother is still irritated with her. But she can't know. At the best of times, her mother seems to deliberately hide away a part of herself from her daughter. A mixture of Ethiopian pride and Indian certainty in her mother's ways. These qualities are good qualities, she thinks, continuing to practise, knowing she shouldn't carry her mother like a burden in her mind.

Malamud's been in conflict with the English in other parts of India. While they practise, he tells her stories. "The English are securing loyal troops from all over the country to stamp out the revolts." He squints down the barrel of his gun, lining up the clay pots on the top of the wall. "There's this man named Neill who has come up from Madras with his battalion. Brigadier General James Neill. He's an old soldier from Scotland with white flowing hair and a moustache who believes his God has chosen him to punish any resistance he can find. Saintly Christian Crusader. More like Lucifer, or a whispering *jinni* in a smokeless fire than any saint you've heard of. He's completely crazy." Malamud picks off the clay pots and reloads his rifle.

"So," he says. "I'm in Howrah, sitting at the back of the train with some villagers, all of us trying not to attract attention. The departure time comes and goes, and there's this commotion on the platform. This man Neill wants to hold the train for his troops. The stationmaster tells him that, although he might be in charge of his battalion, he is not in charge of the railway, so Neill seizes the stationmaster, the engineer, and the stoker and arrests them—wishes out loud he could hang them—until finally his troops arrive and they get on board."

"Pompous."

"The same as ever," Malamud says. He laughs, his black eyes warm before they turn flat, like mud. "But there's more. This Brigadier General James Neill's a real sportsman. He marches to Allahabad setting up executions all the way, with makeshift gallows, calling to his men to bag *pandies* for Brigadier General James Neill's hangings. They overran villages, burned children alive, stabbed men who were planting carrots. He gets to Allahabad, and within a week he's cleared the town of anyone who might stand up to him. Thousands dead. There were fellows who simply looked the wrong way when he was passing who got lynched. He killed everyone—men, women, little children mown down, picked off one by one while they were running away. The reign of terror, everyone was calling it. Horrible."

Malamud puts down his rifle and lights one of his Madras *beedies*. He smokes for a while, the sharp, strange smell filling the air. "I skirted the area, ducked into ditches, and played dead plenty of times. I heard about it all from a mother who got away. But I saw enough. The air was thick with smoke over the fields, and wild animals ate the limbs they could reach of the hanging corpses." He takes another draw on the *beedi* and crushes it against the wall. "Who knows what his plans are now. It's important that man doesn't get into Lucknow. Communications with hunters like him need to be interrupted. I'm waiting for Jai Lal's consent to cut the telegraph wires."

Amah bows low to Malamud and does not get up. "Welcome to Lucknow," she says.

* * *

Inside Begam Sahiba's garden, the grass is littered with wood. The palace carpenters are building cages to transport Shahzadi and the black swans to Qaisarbagh Palace. In the meeting room, the royal cousins, plump Nawab Mirza and little Sharif-un-nissa, take lunch with Begam Sahiba.

"Everyone in the royal family should know what's going on—about my move, about our request for surrender," Begam Sahiba says to Amah after they greet each other.

"We have already spread the news to almost everyone at the palace that you are coming," Amah says.

"The Awadh Force is showing itself in large groups on the road below Residency Hill. Come and eat."

Amah fidgets and does not move from the doorway. "Has Jai Lal completed the arrangements for the coronation?" she asks.

"Yes, Amah. We are only waiting on the food preparations to be completed. You being hungry now is not going to solve anything. Come and eat."

Amah stares at the food. Finally, she sits down with the royal cousins to eat a little of the sweet rice dish with saffron and raisins, prepared for this special occasion of their visit. Everyone watches the carpenters finish the new cage for Shahzadi that will be carried to the palace.

A servant boy arrives. "They are hanging the soldiers who set the cantonment fire," he says.

Amah gets up at once. "I am going to the palace to make sure the food preparations are complete."

It is late in the afternoon when Sai finds Amah in Qaisarbagh's kitchens still arguing with the cooks. Alarmed at the shortage of stores fit for a ceremony, they nonetheless have started to listen as Amah insists that the stores are sufficient, even if it will make for plain fare, and that the cooks must continue to prepare immediately.

"Amah, listen," Sai interrupts and leads her away from the chefs. "Sharif-un-nissa and Nawab Mirza have been arrested," he says, "by the *Kotwal*. On orders from his English superiors. Your friend, that Red Man, was with him. The cousins were in the crowd. We were all watching the hangings. Nawab Mirza and Sharif-un-nissa were angry and shouting along with many of us. Suddenly, there were Englishmen in front of us, surrounding the cousins. We pushed forward hard, but many men came into the crowd on horseback to disperse us. The *Kotwal* made sure everyone heard that the cousins will be held inside the Residency. Held for conspiracy-mongering."

Whispers rise and fall like butterflies in gardens with broken statues. The air is stamped with hanged men, pointed guns, crumbling stucco. Dogs lie watching in the shade, adjusting their chins on their paws, their ears back, their noses dry.

"We need someone loyal inside, to find out what's happening to the cousins," Amah says to Begam Sahiba when she tells her the news. "We need to know what's happening immediately. If they come to any harm…. I'm going to Gulbadan. To find a spy."

Begam Sahiba calls after her, insistently, "It has just become more important than ever to have a peaceful surrender!"

* * *

At the *kotha*, Amah finds Gulbadan and several courtesans gathered in the courtyard. The newest resident is among them— the young woman with the long plait who no longer harbours dark shadows but has changed her fate, grown strong with training. The women have all just bathed, and Sai pours water into basins to cool their feet. Amah relays the news about the cousins and asks if Gulbadan can help find a spy. "There must be a way to get inside," she says.

"Shall I try?" Sai asks.

"Sir Henry Lawrence will hang you by the neck if you are caught trying." Amah is surprised. Her friend is too gentle for such a task.

"Yes. But I think I can do it."

"We will be involved immediately with them," Gulbadan says.

"We aren't already?" Amah asks impatiently. She watches Sai, thinks about his offer. "You could continue to milk the goats they've taken into the Residency—you could be there for the goats. There are plenty of other servants who've gone inside to make money. You could find Mrs. Gunning, milk her goats, and, when you can, look out for the cousins, see if they are safe. That is all. We could arrange to meet at specific times. You let us know how the cousins fare, and where they are being kept."

If he is careful, Amah thinks, Sai might actually be a good person to find a way to slip inside and slip back out. Sai, who slipped in and out of the cantonment, milking goats. He slipped into town to pick up mustard seed, slipped back into the cantonment to check the health of the oldest goat and contemplate the sharp verandah gossip, slipped away to the *kotha* to make ice for mango and lime drinks, and, when the end of the month came and each English woman slipped him a *rupee* for his work, he gave the money to Gulbadan, and slipped into the Gomti for a long swim followed by a full afternoon's rest, slipping under a cool sheet in his room.

"I'll do it," Sai says.

Gulbadan cocks her head, hesitant. "Perhaps it will help with your weak constitution."

Lean, Sai stretches out his arms, and then, rising on one leg, he exhales slowly while he extends one arm to the sky, curls into his chest, bows low to them all, and slips away.

* * *

At the Chattar Manzil, Jai Lal tells his men that Begam Sahiba's arrival at the palace and the coronation, too, are imminent. They wait for Sai to come out with news about where the cousins are being kept, in case there is trouble and the Awadh Force must rescue them. His letter to Sir Henry Lawrence requesting surrender is ready. His men are ready to surround the Residency.

The constant waiting hangs heavily in the air like a vendor's left-over cold kebabs sit heavily inside Amah. Finally, a boy brings word to her that Sai has come out from the Residency.

The thick sky breaks, and the first drops of monsoon rain hit Amah's hair, and run behind her ears and down her neck as she makes her way to the *kotha*. Enormous, warm drops splash her face and her shoulders, and then the water pours from the sky. The river Gomti is filled with Muslims carrying out ablutions in the pouring rain. Parsees gather water to pound with poppy seeds for their green fish curries. The river swells with Hindu ashes, *nawab* song, glittering late evening sun, and old English dreams.

In Chowk, the streets fill quickly with water, and the vegetable sellers pick up their baskets and stack them onto carts.

But the rain stops short this first day of monsoons and Amah waits only for a short time at the courtesans' shop until the water subsides and the sun comes out, the day suddenly so hot again that she forgets it's just rained. Near the *kotha's* stairs in the busy street, she spots her baby cousin Hasan. He talks to a tall, bony-faced man. The man's white, muslin clothes and cap are freshly laundered. They stand at a drink vendor's cart near some other foreign men Amah doesn't know.

"*Tasleem*. You quit your job taking care of English horses," Amah says, looking down at Hasan as she passes him. "You have a new pastime, I see."

Hasan keeps his face turned away. "*Salaam*," he says.

Abhi is among the foreign men. "Hasan, don't be a fool," Amah hisses. "That man works for the English. He is not someone you should be talking to. The English will be using their spies to divide us. He will only be trying to turn those men against us in order to try to keep the English strong—"

"A message from your master?" Abhi interrupts, pushing forward out of the crowd and flashing his red-stained smile. He holds in his hand a pair of new slippers embroidered with gold-and-silver thread. "Do you have any messages for me?"

"Not yet," Amah replies.

"No invitation to join her Awadh Force?"

"No invitation of any kind. Begam Sahiba—Begam Hazrat Mahal—is making all the preparations for the right kind of *tamasha*," Amah says.

"For Lucknow?"

"She is the city's highest patron."

He cocks his head at her, holds up a bent finger, and says, "You are not so smart, black slave, trying to frighten me by mentioning patrons."

She stands there breathing. He smiles, mocking her. His clothes smell of sandalwood and betrayal. He waves the new slippers.

"I await news of your Queen's success. Send me word through Hasan."

* * *

Gulbadan's brother steps aside so that Amah can climb the stairs to the *kotha*. "My petition against their Settlement did not ... I've lost my land," he says, shrugging in a sad sort of way. "I'll stay with my sister, become a Lakhnavi."

"Gulbadan will be glad you are staying," she calls back to him. "Find your place here."

She finds Sai in the courtyard where he's swept stray bougain-villea and the dead heads from marigolds into a large pile for some boys to take away. Freshly bathed, he hums, wearing a *lungi* and shirt, waiting for Amah under a peepul tree with its green, heart-shaped leaves that flutter in the still air. They greet each other. She kneels beside him and brings out a milksweet a Chowk vendor gave her. "We must not know each other in the streets," she says.

He takes the sweet. "Which day do you plan to attack?"

"What attack?" Amah asks.

"The Residency. I will plan my next exit from the Residency a few hours beforehand to let you know the cousins' exact whereabouts. It will be up to the Awadh Force to make sure no one mistakenly attacks their location."

"It will not be an attack on the Residency but a demand to surrender. All we want is the cousins' location in case there is trouble. How are they?"

"Everyone is on rations. A little meat. Rice. But the cousins are being treated well," Sai says.

"What about the English?"

"The men are on the first floor. I can't be seen there. I only see them going up and down the stairs."

"You don't know what they are doing then?"

"They are on the watch for spies like me. An English officer shot a *punkah-wallah* who'd been told to fetch writing utensils from a room. Someone thought he was spying. I try to keep to the same routine. I milk Mrs. Gunning's goats in the yard, then I go up to the second floor where the women and children stay. Crowded into rooms. They are desperate for lavender to bathe in, and they wish they'd brought more clothes. Some of them have larger supplies of laudanum than they do clothes. Mrs. Gunning is so happy to have me there, to bring them milk. She is paying me well. I would like to bring them lavender. I carry up milk, and then I go down the stairs and out to the yard. Mrs. Gunning arranged for some bedding for me in the yard where the other servants sleep. Enormous payments are being offered to those who are brave enough to come inside. To cook, to clean."

"They know about the Awadh Force? Have you heard anything?"

"They have seen Jai Lal's men in the streets. They realize they are outnumbered. Every moment, the ladies want to know what is happening. They are in a great state about what will happen next. They wait on their husbands, and it's clear that the word surrender is already not far from a *memsahib's* lips. They are always anxious to get news from the men downstairs. I must be careful. I tell you, everyone is on the lookout for spies."

"Abhi? Have you seen him inside?"

Sai shrugs. "There are spies slipping in and out. Both ways. The English are desperate for news. Mrs. Gunning's sweeper told me something is going on in Cawnpore. They are paying *lakhs* of *rupees* for news."

"The English have moved into some sort of makeshift entrenchment in Cawnpore, worried about violence," Amah says. "Red Man? Have you seen him?"

"I think they are all there."

Sai goes to his garden of marigolds, and Amah follows him. He smooths some of the red, sandy earth with the palm of his hand, and draws with his finger. "Second floor. This is where the women and children stay, and downstairs, here, the men's quarters. And over here on the east side of the second floor there's an inner room. The library. That is where the cousins are detained."

Amah gets up. "I'll tell Jai Lal. Let's meet again this evening. I'll find out exactly when Jai Lal's confrontation will take place."

Amah walks home. Whispers in the streets make her look up. The telegraph wires are all cut.

* * *

That evening, Amah meets Sai again at the *kotha*. A small group of Lakhnavi men sit in the courtyard waiting for a performance. There are one or two noblemen, but the rest of the men are young merchants she doesn't recognize. Sai fills their cups with water.

Amah waits in the shadows, watching the fireflies dance in the fluttering leaves of the peepul tree, and in the depths of the courtyard. They light its dark corners with continuous little fireworks.

"There must be English spies everywhere," she says when Sai has completed his work and they have greeted each other. "These people should not see you here. Begam Sahiba will move to Qaisarbagh tomorrow. We will crown Birjis the next day, before Jai Lal's Force moves to the Residency the day after that. In three days' time. If there is trouble, we may have to get the cousins out swiftly, safely. Have their captors moved them at all? I mean, do they seem to stay in the same place?"

"Yes, so far as I know they've only been in the library."

"We have to know for certain that the cousins will be in the same place. You tell me, and I'll tell Jai Lal. Jai Lal will tell the men who will be stationed outside the Residency. Can you get in and back out again in three days?"

"I think so. Usually it is quiet at midday, and I can get out," Sai says. "Meet me here in three days, in the early afternoon. But be careful with your plans ... be careful for the cousins, Amah. The English hangman is never far away."

"You be careful, too. We should not meet so obviously like this again," she says. "And you should ask Gulbadan if you can avoid the courtesans' performances."

* * *

Under the canopied trees between Qaisarbagh and Begam Sahiba's home, Amah meets Malamud who is smoking by a vendor's stand. The rich, oily smell of freshly ground coffee mixes with the aroma from his *beedi,* the smell of dry leaves burning. He greets Amah and offers her coffee.

"*Tasleem,*" she says. "I cannot stay. Coffee will make me jumpy."

"Everyone is inside the Residency now," he says. "There must be more than three thousand. Completely cut off. All the Europeans everywhere, even English refugees are coming in from surrounding areas—women and children with only the clothes on their backs. We mustn't let them come to harm. We must have a peaceful surrender."

Bougainvillea and jackfruit flowers caress Lucknow's garden walls, and water with lime loosens tight throats. The back garden at Qaisarbagh Palace is dotted with candles in red-clay dishes waiting to be set alight for the coronation. Amah stands in the garden, thinking of Sai, of the drawing he made of the English quarters, of lentils and rice rations, of bleating goats and laudanum. She thinks of a glittering *tamasha* for Birjis, the jangling of anklets, of people embracing and rebuilding, a band practising a twenty-one gun coronation salute—a reminder of a good past when that salute was a gift to His Majesty from the English Queen.

Amah relays Begam Sahiba's orders to a servant boy to watch the men Hasan is staying with in Star House—the city's royal observatory with its grand old telescope that has now fallen into disrepair.

* * *

Members of the Awadh Force walk the streets while the noblemen who have remained in the city watch them guardedly from upstairs windows. They watch the sequin-curtained palanquins fill the canopied road from Begam Sahiba's home to

Qaisarbagh Palace. The procession winds all the way around
the back of the palace to the front hall where Fatima and old
Kasim lead the Begam's servants out through the vast gardens,
under archways with stucco fish, beside marble water tanks,
through vast courtyards with Hindu umbrellas and lanterns
to Begam Sahiba's tall rooms with green shutters, orange cur-
tains, and teak ceilings deep among the palace's gardens where
His Majesty once set scenes for the performance of one of his
romantic musicals. Like other rooms at the palace, hers are
airy, with marble floors, mango-wood furniture, gilded walls,
and pottery ducts to remove the hot air. Outside, a delicate
pavilion with curtained sides, made to look like a tent, stands
in her garden—her new meeting room.

Palace residents stand in the gardens and watch. Even Aunt
Laila, apart from the others, watches. Hundreds of the pal-
ace's old animal handlers crowd the front hall—the handlers
who crave menageries of antelope and cheetahs and aviar-
ies of golden-green, silk-winged birds all eagerly surround
Shahzadi's cage when it is brought in, lifting it up, cheering
the almost-grown tiger who stands in the middle of the cage
with her diamond-shaped eyes and white whiskers, a tiger
who sneezes twice and blinks at them all. They take Shahzadi's
cage carefully past the Mermaid Gateway, through the palace
gardens, to Begam Sahiba's quarters. The handlers pluck the
black swans from their cage and put them down under a large
neem tree where the swans make bugle-like calls while they
stretch out their long, black necks. Cooks from the kitchens
bring sizzling meat for the tiger, and Amah brings breadcrumbs
soaked just this once in *ghee* for the new birds.

The black swans do not squawk like some of His Majesty's
wives squawk. "Why is she here? Why is she here with her son?"

Amah finds the wives where they wait for her at His Majes-
ty's Fairy House. They are dancers and royal princesses and
East-Africans, plump and thin, tall and short—with children of
their own who laugh and play in tapestried worlds, who don't

notice their mothers who look at Amah with hurt, questioning eyes. "She is only here to help," Amah says. "Jai Lal thinks that it is right for Birjis to stand in for his father until the King returns. It is only for the moment. Begam Sahiba has spent a lot of her time and wealth to keep Lucknow protected. It is the right thing to do." She turns and leaves their wounded eyes behind. There is nothing more to say to them.

Begam Sahiba offers a large donation to the kitchens, to keep them all going. Cooks run to purchase musk and saffron to fatten the chickens, and work speedily to make rich *pulaus*, with a broth from thirty *seers* of meat to stew the rice, for the boy Birjis who practises kite-fighting with the cooks' sons, their kite-strings coated in gum and glass. The crown set with opals, his father's favourite, is polished and waiting in the storerooms. Fifteen months since the King has left—and many more since Begam Sahiba and His Majesty divorced. All over the city, Mal-amud and the boys he hires distribute proclamations about the coronation. Thousands in the Organization of Awadh Soldiers wait for Birjis' crowning, ready for the order to surround three thousand and more cocooned in the Residency—to nudge the English to surrender, to push past false treaties, and to deliver the royal cousins like golden butterflies.

Amah is in the kitchens urging the chefs to work quickly when she hears Fatima calling for her. Her cousin stumbles in, breathing heavily. "They are taking His Majesty's possessions out of the storerooms," Fatima says.

Amah listens to Fatima as they run through the palace gardens toward the front hall. "They pushed their way in with two cannon and most of them are carrying rifles. There are too many of them. They said that Sir Henry Lawrence wants to take the King's property for safe-keeping, make sure it doesn't come to harm. They say His Majesty will be told that the English are keeping it for his own protection."

"What greedy lies. How could that man possibly expect us to believe anything anymore?"

"I was almost caught with the others," Fatima continues, "but I slipped out before they saw me."

Near the archway into the front hall, Amah and Fatima crouch, panting, behind an oval garden of tall sunflowers. Inside the hall, there must be fifty men with rifles lined up in front of twenty palace guards who are being kept to one side while Kasim is being made to stand in front of one of two cannon as a threat to everyone else. The Englishman with the parrot eyes, who months ago ordered the inventory of the King's possessions, holds a ledger as he stands near their second cannon with Red Man. Other Englishmen in blue uniforms roll barrels filled with the King's treasures toward the front doors. They carry chests of precious stones. Two men carry out the King's emerald-studded throne. Someone else carries out the Queen Mother's crystal chess set, and yet another brings out Birjis' opal crown. From their great oil paintings above, the *nawabs* have been watching the man with parrot eyes tick off ivory, gold coins, china, copper, and silver in his ledger. The front hall is full of palace guards who shout, their faces strange, unfamiliar.

Amah sees Kasim's mouth moving but she can't hear him. The hall is drowning in noise. Shouting in a large hallway is louder than thunder, rougher than stone breaking on marble; it is like warm blood filling your ears. Amah could call out anything and her voice would be lost in the noise. She could spill curses onto foreign men who ignore polite letters, let harsh words land squarely in their ears, slap their faces, leap inside them and go with them on boats across the ocean. She thinks she hears Mary, Mother of Jesus, Shiva, and Mohammed cry out, but their voices drown, too. White-haired Lal, the Queen Mother's adviser, is suddenly crouching, trembling, between Fatima and Amah. Amah presses her arm firmly against Lal's shaking arm. "I'm going to tell Jai Lal to gather the Force," Amah says to Fatima, "to halt them in the street. You go with Lal to tell Begam Sahiba that we cannot wait a moment longer.

We need to stop His Majesty's possessions from getting to the Residency. Tell her, too, to get out of the palace by the back way. We need her present when Lakhnavis will surely want to know what is going on."

Amah runs back through the palace grounds, out the back door, and onto the canopied road. At the Chattar Manzil, Jai Lal listens to Amah's story, his face grave, and immediately calls to Malamud to go with some others to ready the Force and get them to cut off the procession with the King's possessions.

Amah rides one of Jai Lal's horses out to the road between the Chattar Manzil and the Residency. She finds Begam Sahiba veiled in lace and surrounded by palace guards who stand among the crowds of people watching the listing carriages flanked by men with rifles who already are moving up Residency Hill. The brass strips around the barrels in the carriages up ahead glint in the sun. Lucknow's poetry glistens in the air, like Amah's grandmother's stories glisten and hover, like the upturned, perspiring faces of Lucknow's people shine. The Awadh Force, thousands of men, begins to emerge, moving into the road, led by Malamud and Jai Lal. The English carriages move faster, up the hill, while the Force moves steadily forward.

Begam Sahiba mounts the horse Amah has dismounted. "Our problem is that we always expect people to be good rather than to be bad," she calls to the women around her. "That has been our mistake. The Residency will be surrounded immediately to stop the theft of His Majesty's possessions and to secure a swift surrender."

Further away, Jai Lal yells something to his men. They look across the Gomti toward the burned and abandoned cantonment. The distant noise coming from across the river is confusing. Amah glances up at Begam Sahiba, her lace-covered face, and they listen carefully. Guns crack and pop—from somewhere near the silent cantonment, or from along the road to Faizabad? Lal's men listen, the palace guards listen, everyone in the road listens. Old Lal slips beside Amah and begins to stutter. A strange, noisy crowd, like a wall of water, is getting closer.

The English carriages lurch ahead and disappear behind the earthen barricades at the Residency. Jai Lal's face is mottled with rage as he yells orders for his Force to continue up the hill. As they get closer and closer to the Residency, clouds of yellow dust rise around the Baillie Guard Gate as it is barricaded and earthed up from the inside by hard-working, dust-covered labourers. The noise from the direction of Faizabad gets louder, a wall of water no one can fathom about to descend upon them all.

Women with trusting eyes come forward from the crowds and touch Begam Sahiba's feet. Others bow. Lakhnavis whisper words of hope. Lakhnavis sing prayers of mercy into Lucknow's skies, bowing again to kiss her ground, and caress with their hands the pulsing soul of home.

14.

———◦•◦———

THOUSANDS OF ANGRY Indian marauders spill into Lucknow. The dispossessed. The Company has ensured that all of these different men have been deprived one way or another—stripped of beloved Indian rulers, of fertile lands, of their chosen gods, of their dignity. None of these roaming men arrive with plans to engage in forcing a peaceful surrender. Many of them are fools, Amah sees, who came to Lucknow on a lark and get carried away with laughter over Englishmen and their servants locked up in a building. These men piss in flowering gardens, steal silks from Geeta, the courtesans' young shopkeeper, raid sweet shops, stuff perfumes into their sacks to take home to mothers and wives in villages and towns far away. They speak in gravelly voices with sharp accents, demanding that the shops in Chowk stay open, forcing vendors to sell flour and lentils at village prices. They break open Lucknow's Royal Library, and thousands of volumes of English books lie in the streets. The men rush and crowd Jai Lal and his men who have surrounded the Residency. The newcomers encourage Lakhnavi bandsmen to play "God Save the Queen" and "The Girl I Left Behind Me" outside the earthen barricades, slapping their thighs as the trumpets blast the Residency's balconies. Their musket fire and the mines they explode disrupt the bandsmen. The English shoot back from behind their earth embankments, their barricades. The marauders fire the cannon they've stolen from the English elsewhere in Awadh; they lounge against the guns when the fighting at the barricades ceases for the midday hour. A siege has started, and there is no going back.

"We need to be rid of all these terrible foreigners," Begam Sahiba says to Jai Lal. "Inside and outside the Residency."

"We have no choice but to force the surrender any way we can, *Huzoor*," he says, his voice determined. "We need to move ahead despite these men."

In the streets, Amah is Begam Sahiba's eyes on the rooftops and behind the soldiers from the Awadh Force who listen carefully to Jai Lal's orders, staying away as much as they can from any and all of the disorderly marauders at the Residency's barricades. She studies the once-handsome homes around the Residency that the English have turned into shells to avoid sniper angles and observes the dense movements of angry, marauding men who shoot arrows and bullets over the English pitched-dirt walls. She peers up at the Residency windows through the dusty haze, looking for the library where the cousins are kept, looking for Sai, scanning the broken verandahs where cannon balls burst. She listens for brave Englishmen who venture out of the Residency in the cover of darkness to spike the Awadh Force's guns, hears Malamud shout for more ammunition. She tastes the salty cartridge powder, feels the mines planted underneath Residency floors to blow more holes in the crumbling dictatorship in an effort to get the people on rations inside to listen, to admit they need to go, to stop this mad war just as it starts. But Company men fight from their rooftops, through their windows, behind their barricades. They kill plenty of men who attack their prison shell.

* * *

In the late evening, the guns at the Residency fall silent. Men's shadows move on both sides of the barricades. Amah crouches near an old home close by. She worries about Sai stuck inside. She notices Malamud further up, and she joins him.

"*Namaste*," he whispers, putting his hands together.

"*Tasleem*," Amah whispers.

They sit for a while, silent. Then he says in a low voice, "I'm sitting right here, and I see this English officer come out. He stands against a crumbling wall, like a sturdy ghost in front of a doorless door, watching. He greases his gun. He was so close I could smell the metal. He gets down on his knees and crawls away from the Residency. Then he stands up and immediately trips, falls down a well. I thought that was the end of it, but later the man makes it to the top of the well, and I see him hauling himself out. He rolls out of the well, and a gun goes off beneath him, shoots him through the chest. It must have been his gun. He must have dropped it before he fell in the well. Now. That is terrible."

Amah and Malamud sit there, staring at the ragged shapes of the barricades. Then he says, "This is the best place to watch for Englishmen creeping out to ascertain our positions. And a few of them have come out with lamp black, the soot from their oil lamps, smeared on their faces and hands, disguised as Lakhnavis, to reach the shops to purchase liquor and cigarettes. A few of those Indian foreign marauders have been good at spotting the English in disguise. They have been taking their turns sitting here, too. Some of those newcomers are working with us."

"Don't let them mistake the real Lakhnavis who are trying to get out of the Residency," Amah says, and leaves him for her rounds.

She passes Star House where Hasan is staying and watches shadows in the windows. She has seen him with his tall, bony-faced friend in the streets, but the cousins no longer greet each other. She walks on.

In one of Lucknow's furthest alleys, she meets Abhi. His silk clothes and gold-and-silver cap shine in the moonlight. He does not look like a man on Residency rations. Even at night, she can see his sarcastic smile as he wishes her a good evening.

He's recently been to the temple; his forehead and cheeks are painted with orange paste.

"Too many foreigners have come to this great city," he says. "It's hard to make you out in the black night, African foreigner."

"You sound English, talking about me like that. Your meals must be tainted. The English have eaten from your bowl with their left hands," she replies.

Abhi sucks in his breath and moves past her. She walks in pools of light, hating her words. Goddesses bow their heads, and Begam Sahiba walks beside her, telling Amah to get rid of such horridness, to touch instead the watercolour parchments in doorways, trail her fingers through clear fountain water, listen to poems in an audience sprinkled with rose water as they pass white night flowers on thick vines, curled like *chikan* embroidery, under pearl stars, pink in the sky, the colour of salve.

***

The next day, an hour's downpour leaves Lakhnavis motionless with gratitude, like Allah's order to cleanse the city, washing souls free of mud and dirty deeds. The watery sky comes down, fills Residency trenches, and sweeps the filth away. Wet air billows about, and kingfishers shake the water from the top of their heads in little sprays. The rain rinses the air of dust, and everything is suddenly vivid.

In Qaisarbagh's back garden, Amah stands beside a spiral staircase, one of the King's architectural follies that he built for the garden, while the coronation guests assemble under a sprawling tent. The bankers and noblemen who have not left are among those that fill the garden. Convinced by Begam Sahiba's newsletters not to leave, they have had to hire additional watchmen to guard their properties from angry, marauding men. From behind a screen, near the female guests, Aunt Laila wears the look of someone already departed, her thoughts constantly with His Majesty, and her sister at Matiya Burj. No one can shut out the distant sound of popping guns at the barricades, but the women nevertheless greet each other warmly, and the men greet each other warmly, and they all hover over servants who offer pearl *pulaus* with cheese covered in silver foil. Bandsmen play, warm as honey, and courtesans dance, light as pastry. Members of the Awadh Force gather near the spiral staircase, and near the pink and orange rose gardens, standing at attention away from all the guests.

Kasim, dressed in a gold tunic, calls for everyone's attention. Palace guards escort Birjis into the garden. Amah observes the boy, the soft roundness of his face, his plump lips much like his father's, his green eyes and smooth, dark-copper skin much like his mother's. Prayers for Begam Sahiba's son's good fortune escape Lakhnavi mouths. The opal crown is gone, but when a *mandeel*, a turban made of gold and silk thread, is placed on his head, Lakhnavis bow and call out, "*Huzoor.*" Amah pictures the Queen Mother in England, veiled from English crowds, nodding at her grandson who will stand in for her son until he returns. From behind the screen, Begam Sahiba bows. All the guests bow.

Jai Lal, sharply dressed in a white, braided uniform, walks over to members of the Awadh Force. He says something to them and stands there. He must be waiting for the final recitation of prayers for the boy, Amah thinks, suspecting he's also waiting for the guns at the barricades to quiet for some moments, for no one to let off a mine. He is waiting for Lakhnavi guests to fold their hands, hands that plunge into the waters of the Gomti, fill basins with clear water, wash silk clothes, place silver boxes of money in deep holes in their gardens for safe-keeping, caress young children's cheeks, and offer prayers. Hands that reach out to dance. Slender hands that play instruments and pick betel leaves. Hands that hold glass prayer beads, hold burning sticks to funeral pyres. Hands of the wealthy that sift through gold pieces and hands of the poor that salute foreign Company men.

"His Majesty Wajid 'Ali Shah's twenty-one-gun salute," Jai Lal calls.

Rifles point into the sky. The boom-boom-boom startles little pink pigeons who rise up from the trees, above Qaisarbagh's walls. The noise fills the blue sky, blows past curtains into Lucknow's living rooms, and blocks the guns at the barricades. By the orange and pink rose beds, smart men in ceremonial clothes stand in straight lines. *Boom-boom-boom,* their rifles cry.

It is a long volley of rifle fire. When the men rest their rifles in the thick grass, there are no sounds of other guns at the barricades. The guns at the barricades have stopped. And then—a faint sound of cheering, of cheering, in the distance.

When Amah leaves the *tamasha* and rides out to see what is going on, every man outside the Residency mills around in the thick dust, listening to the hooting coming from inside. Even women's gay voices can be heard. Everyone listens, peering in the direction of the Residency's broken walls, its empty verandahs and shelled doors, where unseen Company soldiers and officers, engineers, school teachers, mothers, children, librarians, bandsmen, cooks, sweepers, goat tenders, Sai, and two royal cousins dwell. Happy English voices roar through the vast rooms, the holes in the walls, the broken roof, baffling the people listening outside.

"What feels like a long time ago, Queen Victoria agreed with His Majesty that he was entitled to the twenty-one gun salute. Perhaps that is what they are remembering?" Amah finally asks no one in particular. "The good days between their Queen and our royal family?"

"His Majesty is a very important man, second only to the King of Delhi," says a member of the Awadh Force standing near Amah. The wiry man speaks with a surging pride. "The twenty-one gun salute."

"Perhaps they will surrender to it," someone else says cynically.

"Perhaps it is a good sign, whatever it is," Amah says, determined not to let the occasion of the coronation falter.

As she rides back through Lucknow, the hooting of English voices behind her, she passes an abandoned royal meadow where someone has brought their brown horses to graze. The horses chew on the wooden fence. The roses that grow wild around the fence are bright pink and orange like the ones in Qaisarbagh's gardens. Girls and boys in gold pyjamas and patterned shoes with curled up toes walk in groups down the road, holding hands. They walk away from the Residency and its noisy barricades, toward their own *tamasha* in the courtyard of a noble family's home, surrounded by watchmen and flowering plants, where minstrels play. The children skip toward the bride whose hair is oiled and braided with frangipani, whose clothes are heavily embroidered and jewelled, toward the bride and her groom who pretend to throw sparkling sweets at each other, toward the women related to the bride and groom who pelt green vegetables at each other and fight with pink flower-covered sticks, toward iced orange drinks and Arabic poems whispered by *bhang*-high poets who cherish love-bound words. The children lean on mango trees while firecrackers burst above them, making for a yellow-and-green cascading sky.

15.

————•——————

"**S**OMEONE KILLED Sir Henry Lawrence." At the *kotha*, Amah struggles to understand what Sai, who has come from the Residency, has just said.

"An eight-inch shell came through his bedroom window," Sai continues, "and it hit him where he sat in a chair. Everyone inside knows now. They've run out of coffins so they wrapped him in a blanket and put him in a pit with some others, used a broken bit of marble to mark the grave. That old English garden by the church where the rose bushes were, the statues you liked. They bury bodies there now. The chaplain says prayers lying down, amidst the booming of the cannon and the fire of the musketry. They think someone is reporting on the locations of everyone inside, that Sir Henry Lawrence was hit because the men outside knew the location of his room."

"It is surely time to surrender," Amah says quietly.

Sai chews the *paan* Amah has brought him from the palace kitchens. "Sir Henry Lawrence's last words were, 'Never surrender.' They shouted his words through the halls. But not everyone can agree with those words right now. The ladies.... The situation is so bad. And something has happened at Cawnpore. Mrs. Gunning and the ladies ... terribly upset they were."

Amah closes her eyes, feels a weight growing inside her.

"They talk fiercely. Mrs. Gunning—she's gone too now. She was always talking about razing Lucknow. She liked to tell me this when I swept her room. While the bullets whizzed past our ears, Mrs. Gunning liked to tell me that Lakhnavis will all be taxed to raise monies for a monument to be erected with the names of each of them who dies in the Residency. That is how she was thinking before she died." He spits bright red juice into a copper spittoon, wipes the corners of his mouth with his thumb, tucks the *paan* into his cheek. "Many of the servants have left since things are so bad that it is not even worth the huge payments to stay. But I sweep Mrs. Gunning's room now for the other ladies who sit there waiting and praying for all of this to end. They sleep in their clothes. There are many days they think they are going to fail. Their minds remain anxious about who will be the next victim."

He gets up, looks at Amah. Then he sits back down. "I would like to talk about it, Amah. The most frightening hours, for me, too, are the darkest hours. Mosquitoes whine in there. It's stifling hot. I hear the prayers of widows. Despair for them comes more easily than hope. They don't know if they'll see another place again. At daybreak the firing begins outside. I go to the yard to milk the goats and try to calm them. The sound of the mines is ear-splitting. The noise is terrible. The goats hate it. Everyone hates it. Out there in the yard with the goats, the smell is terrible, Amah. There are a lot of dead horses and oxen because of the English shooting and because of the men at the barricades shooting. Back inside, shells crash and burst around us in all directions. It's an amazing thing that any of us in there are still alive. The children pick up bullets hot from the guns. When I climb the stairs, they are filled with the wounded and the dead being carried down from the roof. They take the wounded and the sick to the banquet hall that is now set up like a hospital. But sometimes the attack is so bad that it sends every man, including the sick and wounded, to the walls with guns. Amah, you've finished your *paan*. Almonds?"

"No, thank you, no."

"Take some."

"Just one, thank you."

"Soldiers who just came down from the roof, who have not slept for more than an hour, have to go back up to take over from the ones that are dead or wounded. All of them have deep, long shadows on their faces. Even your favourite, that Red Man. The goats, too, have shadows."

"You do, too, my friend."

He shrugs. "Yes. But my sleeping quarters are better now. I sleep in the dining room. A Lakhnavi bearer sets the table in the early morning. He puts out silver gravy urns with coats of arms as if they will all sit down to a feast and not a bit of bone and some water, or *chapati* if they have someone to make it. There are cobwebs between the table legs and a lot of dust in the air. They are slaughtering healthy animals now to make up the half rations—a lump of boiled rice, flour for *chapati*, and lentils. Not enough to keep them away from rampant hunger pains but enough to keep them alive. It's rumoured that there are those who continue to drink Champagne daily and eat tinned meats, but not the ladies I know. They want to purchase goods from the dead. The doctor brings a little sago and arrowroot for the weakest children upstairs. Such sweet children they are, who don't know the dangers that surround them. They play, those sweet little children. I tell you, they play with bullets hot from the guns."

"Jai Lal is determined to make peaceful negotiations," Amah says. "But they refuse to respond to him. We have no choice but to keep going, to force the surrender. Everything you tell me makes me hope there's a good chance of ending this terrible thing soon. Our men are trying their best. We still outnumber the Company by far, but the Force has been joined by some untrained idiots."

"Well, when I look out from the Residency, it appears as if everyone is working together. All of the men at the barricades are dangerous. I worry the cousins will get hurt. I worry all the wrong people will get hurt. The women. The families. About twenty deaths take place every day, Amah."

"If their numbers are dwindling, surrender surely will come."

He shrugs again slowly. "Do you know, Amah…. The doctor made me fetch the ammonia. Mrs. Gunning was lying on a bed, writhing, trying to get out of her body. I'd heard a crash but there are always crashes. She had been taking a plate out of the cupboard. A nine-pounder flew through the window and shot her through the leg. The doctor gave her chloroform. Chloroform with its rotten odour—no lavender anywhere— just chloroform. He gave her chloroform and then he cut off her leg. He said she might recover and ordered many doses of ammonia to be given to her. All the ladies crouched in the corners, dazed with fright. So I said I would give her the ammonia. Her cheeks burned with heat. 'I will sleep a little,' she said to me, and then she died."

Amah studies her friend's thin face, the shadows in his eyes. Sai, standing alone in a room with a dying Englishwoman, in a room full of frightened Englishwomen, women with no mourning dresses or caps, Sai alone on the second floor of the English Residency where Englishwomen, surrounded by English china and English paintings of English hills and English dogs, try their best to care for English children who wear dusty sailors' suits and dirty dresses while downstairs their quail-eating English husbands, who smoke cheroots and drink Champagne, pant the words, "keep fighting," with their English breath.

"Have you seen the traitor Abhi yet?" she asks after a while.

"Their best spies are hidden from view. I worry, too, that he's there watching me. Someone told them about the twenty-one gun salute. Someone who came in from the city."

"You must have been deaf from all the cheering. We could not understand it. Suddenly cheering Birjis' coronation."

Sai's eyes move from confusion to clarity. He begins to laugh. "Dear Amah," he says. "They thought the salute came from an army of Englishmen who had come to save them. The rifles rattled the china and rattled our bones. I was taking a little milk to the ladies in Mrs. Gunning's room. There were shouts of joy on the rooftop at first and then shouts of joy everywhere. I could barely get through the hallways. They must have opened a hundred crates of Champagne. Instead of the *pop-pop-pop* of guns, there was the *pop-pop-pop* of Champagne bottles everywhere, even in the hospital downstairs. The officers came upstairs to toast the ladies. Some of the ladies put on the ballgowns they'd brought with them and danced in their dirty bonnets with the officers, and they did not even notice me bring in the milk and watch them. Then someone told them there was no relief, and their scene of happiness was doomed. I don't know who told them. Perhaps it was Abhi. That person told the English what was what, that the twenty-one gun salute came from Qaisarbagh ... and the reaction was terrible. They were very sad. I even felt sorry. The ladies and children were very sad ... the men in the hospital were very sad, too."

"Abhi must be in there."

"Their spies are paid handsomely. I heard from a bearer that they paid hundreds of pounds—five hundred pounds—for someone to bring back an account of what has been happening in Cawnpore."

"Your ears are very good. They haven't suffered from the sounds of musketry and cannon fire."

"That might be true."

"Who took over from Sir Henry Lawrence?"

Sai shrugs. "Hard to say. Changes all the time. Mr. Bankes, before he was shot. Then Mr. Ommaney who was killed by a cannon ball. Right now, cholera is causing them even more harm than we are. Disease kills faster than us. Anyway, they are getting wiser. After I last saw you, they realized the library had never been shelled. They moved the cousins from the library and the decision-makers have now moved their headquarters into that room, and keep the cousins next door. And any Indian found in that back passageway is suspect. They've questioned me twice."

"Maybe you shouldn't go back in."

Sai stands up and shakes out his legs. "I'll go back in. I want to help. The royal cousins need watching. Remember to tell Jai Lal they are in the corner room, beside the library. Maybe you are right, Amah, and there's still hope for surrender; we'll get us out of this thing once and for all, and I'll be flying kites at dusk again."

"If you slip back out of the Residency and meet the wrong Indian, you'll be mistaken for a traitor. You'll be killed getting out if you aren't killed by the English getting back in."

"We know little what we can bear, dear friend, till we are tried. Our strength is perhaps mercifully proportioned to our trials. That's what Mrs. Gunning liked to say. She was right, Amah. I want to bring the goats some food—they are so very hungry and can barely produce milk. The ladies need milk. The babies need milk. There is a baby who belongs to one of the soldier's wives. It is damp where they are housed, in an underground apartment. The baby is sick. Mrs. Gunning would not give such a woman and her baby any milk. The soldier's wife came upstairs to ask and Mrs. Gunning refused. The ladies live upstairs, and the soldiers' wives live in the underground apartment. They mock Lakhnavis for caste rules and yet look at that!" Sai says. "Even in the middle of such grief, they hold on to their classes. I will try to get the baby down below a little milk. Mrs. Gunning can't beat me with her walking stick now if I do."

16.

———◆·◆·◆———

THE EVENING BEFORE Amah is to accompany Sai to get back into the Residency, she walks, listening to the whispering ghosts of *nawabs* in Lucknow's alleys, and, from the city's windows, the whispering voices of sleepy children who wear cotton slips. In that sultry air, suffused with candle-lit prayers from Sikanderbagh's mosque where they once kept their blue-breasted quails, past the new post office sitting empty in the shadows, she walks the streets where Englishmen's curses have been extinguished like candles. She walks beside the city's old garden walls where jasmine blossoms; beside homes full of sweetness, wrapped in soft, green leaves; and in the narrow streets smeared with rotting tamarind—stepped on by angry marauders whose sourness they want to get rid of.

Amah is on her way to check on any news from members of the Awadh Force stationed at Alambagh Palace, His Majesty's new country house and garden enclosed by high walls just outside Lucknow. It sits on Cawnpore Road, on the other side of a canal that marks the south boundary of the city. No one knows what is happening to the English barricaded in Cawnpore, but members of the Awadh Force watch for more foreign marauders who might come down Cawnpore Road to Lucknow. In the dusk, she crosses the canal by way of Charbagh Bridge and hears a noise, a door shutting at the Yellow House, a small dwelling tucked into the trees. Abhi emerges from the house, a hunched figure, and walks into the bamboo grove behind it. When she is sure he is gone, Amah steps up to the front window of the building and peers inside. The room is all darkness.

Behind her, she hears footsteps on Charbagh Bridge. She sees the outline of two figures as she walks back and onto the bridge. In the dark, a young man's voice calls her name, and, as she reaches them, she sees that he is the tall, bony-faced man she saw with Hasan. She can make out Hasan beside him. The bony-faced man moves forward so that she has to step backward, and his fingers dig into her forearms as he pins them to the bridge's wooden railing. The man's face is right up against hers and she can smell the onion on his breath and feel the sweat on his skin and the hardness of his sword between them. She turns her face as far to the side as she can, seeing beyond him her baby cousin who leans back against the opposite railing, watching. The bony-faced man puts his weight on her hands, pushes hard, and then all of a sudden releases her. They stand face to face, and he says, "Tell your mistress to follow us if she knows what's good for Lucknow. What's good for her. Tell your mistress to step away. And you, you are entirely dispensable."

He confirms her suspicions about Abhi; she knows where the bony-faced man is getting these brave words. Amah puts her sore hands on her rifle and then takes them away. The man's sword dangles before him. Her cousin steps forward, but stays behind his friend. "You need to step aside if the English are to be defeated," her cousin's friend says, his voice cracking. That's how young he is. They push her to the end of the bridge. She feels their hands on her like rain, and they let out winning yells as she falls backwards onto sharp rocks where she lies, not daring to move. Her cousin's friend laughs, his voice cracking again, as they turn to walk down the road toward Lucknow.

She listens to their jovial voices as they retreat into the distance. Then she is up and moving like a panther; she runs with the venom of a thousand angry snakes. Stretching torn muscles and family ties, she runs. She moves into the grass, making a wide arch past them. Coming back to the road, she pulls her gun, cocks it, and stands twelve paces in front of them, concentrating on slowing her breathing. Slowing it right down. Right down. Down.

The men stop in their tracks, their hands in the air. She fires into the darkness above them and off to Hasan's side in case he stupidly goes for his musket. "Stand still," she says, and fires again. "Stand very still." She walks up to them, sees the fright on their young faces, like baby birds in front of a snake. She clenches and unclenches her sore fingers, pulls her red jacket away from a cut on her back, and tells the bony-faced man to leave. "Move fast," she says, and he is gone. She looks down on the top of her baby cousin's head, and rests the tip of her rifle on it. His head bobs up and down while he sobs loudly.

She takes his musket. "Turn around," she says and puts the rifle into his neck. As they walk back to the bridge, there is wetness around the bottoms of her rose-coloured trousers and her soft shoes, and she realizes she is walking in her cousin's piss. She makes him go down beside the bridge and stand in the canal water with her. "How many are following that deluded man?" she asks, rinsing the bottoms of her silk trousers, her shoes, her feet. "Who is he?"

"A foreigner," her cousin says.

"My little cousin knows much more than that," she says, and prods him up the bank and across the bridge and eventually they make it to her original destination, Alambagh Palace. The watchman at the gate nods at Amah, and they walk into the garden. "Sit," she says, and Hasan moves awkwardly to the ground. His silk jodhpurs are saturated in places. She calls out for the watchman to find Malamud.

"Any word on the ammunition?" Malamud asks as he comes running. "Our supply—" He falters, seeing the boy.

"I'm not going to hurt you," Amah says to Hasan. "But he might. Tell us more about that idiot man I saw you with."

Her cousin leans into himself and mumbles. Malamud squats beside him. "Tell your cousin what she wants," he says.

Hasan takes a deep breath, and the words spill out. "Omar has come from the fighting in Delhi. He was a soldier who worked for the English there. They recruited him from a village in Awadh. Lots of them were recruited from villages in Awadh. The English treated him like a dog. He's one of a group of them who fought the English in Delhi and who've come to fight the English here. For His Majesty." Hasan looks up at Amah, his face streaked with tears and dirt. "Begam Sahiba has no right to take our city. The English are listening to my new friends, to them, not her. His Majesty is coming back. The English said so. I am a royal jockey for His Majesty, Amah. "

"How many believe that lie that the English will bring His Majesty home?" she asks. "How many in your friend Omar's group believe His Majesty is coming back?"

"Hundreds," he says.

Malamud begins to laugh, and Amah can't help smiling either.

"Okay, Hasan," she says. "Let the jasmine suck up your stupidity and your odour before you return to Qaisarbagh."

She looks down at her baby cousin who is wiping his eyes with his arm, his mouth twisted in sadness. She kneels beside him. Quieter, she says, "Listen, Hasan. Don't hang around men who are only getting in the way of what we are trying to do. Those villagers don't know how to behave in a city like Lucknow. They don't know who to listen to. That man, Abhi? You are mad to trust him. He told you all that nonsense about the English listening to you, didn't he?"

Malamud leans forward to Hasan. "He is a spy who is helping to turn people against Begam Sahiba. Can't you see that he wants to control you and your volatile friends? Divide and rule. That is what he has learned from his English friends. For his English friends. And, in the end, he will make sure all of you get killed."

Amah puts her hand on Hasan's shoulder. "You sleep out here tonight and think about all of this. Malamud will watch you."

Malamud stretches out beside Hasan. "I'll sing you a lullaby."

Most of the men at Alambagh are sleeping, except those on the rooftop who watch the moonlit distance. Amah leaves and sits all night in the bamboo grove outside the Yellow House. But Abhi does not return.

Before dawn, she walks back through Lucknow's alleys listening to the distant crackling of guns starting up at the barricades. It is getting light. A man comes out from one of the doors of the homes in the alley and empties a pot into the sanitation ditch that no longer runs. The water-flowing toilets in noblemen's homes also no longer work, thanks to the broken pipes in the streets.

A new watchman carrying a set of heavy keys clinks up and down in front of the homes. He stops his pacing, and she feels his eyes on her for a long time. She keeps walking. The clinking sound starts up again.

* * *

Later that morning, Begam Sahiba takes up the hookah in her tent-like meeting room underneath her apartments deep in Qaisarbagh Palace's gardens. The water bubbles as she smokes. "News from Alambagh Palace?" she asks. Before Amah can answer, she continues. "I heard you brought them a visitor. Even one betrayal can keep us off balance. What about your cousin? He won't be welcome here anymore if he's not loyal."

Amah keeps her eyes on the hookah, on its silver bowl. Sadness burns down her throat. Pictures from her youth dance on the carpet just beyond where they sit: two girls sleeping in shady hideaways in palace gardens on hot afternoons, climbing almond trees in bare feet, thieving milk sweets from the kitchens, pleading with old Lal on their knees to give them his tangerine slices during periods of fasting, hands offering tiger cubs their water bowls, fingers pinching each other to keep awake during dawn recitals, ears listening to poets' Persian verses that swam in the air like their hot bodies swam in deep bathing pools, their peach-coloured house dresses blooming out around them. Hasan used to sit on their grandmother's lap and watch Begam Sahiba and Amah in admiration.

Begam Sahiba lifts her chin. "Why so silent? He's working with foreigners?" she asks.

"No," Amah lies.

"That's good news." Begam Sahiba puts down her pipe. "We need good news." She stares out the door at Shahzadi who's being fed by a handler and a cook in the garden. "We must push harder while we try not to run out of ammunition. Even those marauders aren't able to keep up a heavy volley at night anymore."

* * *

Before dusk, Amah meets Sai at the *kotha*. Begam Sahiba comes with her and disappears inside Gulbadan's pavilion. Indian foreigners, marauders, stretch out in the courtyard under the peepul tree watching the newcomer, the young woman with the long plait, perform one of His Majesty's Kathak dances. Amah studies the men. Perhaps they begged for an invitation to enter the *kotha* and eventually Gulbadan consented. After all, Amah thinks, her shock not quite subsiding, everyone needs money these days.

She recognizes Hasan's bony-faced friend among them. The man sits on a gilded fish pillow and laughs too loudly with a friend. They wear common pyjamas and not crimped *angarkhas*; none of them wear four-cornered caps or carry handkerchiefs, and the shoes lined up to the side are wooden, not velvet. Sun-dried opium waits on mirrored trays. Men kiss the trays and light their brains on fire. The courtyard is aflame with happy fighter visitors who've discovered Lucknow's finest performance at sale prices. The courtyard is brimming with outsiders who shake their heads in wonder and shout for more. There are *pulaus*, pink wines, hookah, opium, and dreams of love.

Amah meets Sai outside his room, near the kitchen. Confectionaries at Qaisarbagh have disappeared, but she brings two milk sweets she saved from the coronation. She ties an amulet on his arm in observation of his festival honouring brothers and sisters. "You are like a brother," she says. "Be careful." He disappears into his room to change.

Amah waits for Sai by the kitchen, talking to no one. From the courtyard, a lone sitar follows the young woman's song. Guns at the barricades in the distance *pop-pop-pop*. Relentless.

Begam Sahiba suddenly appears, angry blotches circling her green eyes. She nods in the direction of the foreign men. "Gulbadan knows the Lakhnavis who've been magnetized by these fellows. There's a fly in the water, related to you. From Qaisarbagh Palace."

"Dear friend," Amah says, and bows low to her. "Hasan has climbed out. Feebly. He will not fall in again. I will make sure of it. I will make sure that his relations with them somehow come to help us."

Begam Sahiba stares at Amah for some moments and turns around.

* * *

Amah walks with Sai in a road behind the Residency. To slip inside, he is dressed as a Hindu widow in white, wearing a *lungi* underneath. He shows Amah that her amulet is still on his arm, covered by the white robe. The road is empty except for an old bull. The ornate windows of the homes have been bricked up, the wooden doors barricaded. Yellow grass springs from a walled garden which is now occupied with sleeping mats and cooking pits. A part of the garden is portioned off where foreign men squat to defecate.

Sai adjusts his veil, hunches his shoulders. "Now I leave you for some time," he whispers. He hums for a moment, looking at Amah, his young face close enough to hers that she can smell the rose water he bathed in, his brown eyes so gentle she wants to kiss his eyelids. "Parting is such sweet sorrow," he says. He smiles briefly, then slips through the garden, out a hole in the wall on the other side, and disappears.

* * *

The next morning Amah wakes at dawn but she stays in her mother's bed. Her rifle lies beside her. Guns sound in the distance. Her mother and her aunt still smile beside the King in her mother's painting of the royal procession through Lucknow. By the window, her mother's yellow handkerchiefs gather dust. The pomegranate seeds she picked at the night before lie scattered across a plate on the floor, the red seeds all wrinkled and worried. Her red jacket and rose-coloured trousers wait for her at the end of the bed. When someone knocks, she climbs swiftly into them, slings her rifle over her shoulder, and kneels to peer through the crack beneath the door. A pair of shoes with brocade tassles. "Auntie?" she asks.

"*Tasleem*," the voice replies. "Open the door, Amah."

"*Tasleem*," Amah says, standing up to open the door.

Aunt Laila comes in, holding her prayer beads. "Why are you sleeping here? What's wrong with your own room? Make up your mother's bed, and don't treat her place like a kitchen." She indicates the plate of worried pomegranate seeds. Her thick hair is freshly washed and pulled into a coil at her neck. "Let me take that plate for you," she says.

"Please leave it. I'm going," Amah says. "I'm almost late now."

"Where is Hasan? Have you seen him?"

"A little while ago."

"He keeps disappearing. I've not seen him for days. His bed is untouched. When I do see him, he's distracted. Even Kasim says so. Fatima says so."

"Perhaps he's got a new occupation."

"Doing what?

"Defence."

"But Jai Lal.... I'd know about it. That doesn't make sense."

"Maybe what he's doing doesn't make sense."

"You mean he's up to something? What? Is he talking too much? Is he attracted to the wrong people?"

"Plenty of people are attracted to the wrong people."

"You mean those foreigners? Is he meeting with those strange men in Chowk?"

"Yes."

"What? Really, Amah?"

Amah is silent.

"I must pay him a visit. Can you help me find Hasan, Amah? You are his cousin. We need to be going."

"Don't go, Auntie," Amah says, her voice catching. "Both of you stay. You can't get through the roads. It's unsafe. Stay with me in Lucknow."

"Then find him, keep him safe here," she says. She looks down. "See the ants in the fruit. You'll cause sickness."

Amah picks up the plate. "I must go, Auntie. I'm late."

Her aunt comes forward, cups Amah's chin with both hands, letting her fingers spread out over Amah's face. "Dear Amah, you look like your mother," she says, and kisses her cheeks.

17.

———

A BREEZE BLOWS thunderclouds toward the kadam trees where dancing Krishnas play mournful flutes. Orange globes of blossom suffuse the dusk with a thick, sweet scent. The nights are cool, and dreams take the form of baffled questions.

"So," Begam Sahiba says to Jai Lal, Gulbadan, and Amah in her meeting room. "What could have seemed easier than to approach every single member of the English population locked up in one building right here in Lucknow and to have them agree to be personally and peacefully escorted out of the city? Violence was to be easily avoided. Surrender seemed utterly possible. The end of the English in Lucknow. The end of the English in the whole of the North-East. Who would believe that they would all rather die than surrender? We could not have guessed that one."

The rain buckets down, drowning flower beds and roads, pouring through holes in the Residency, where thousands of men remain tied to its earth embankments, drowning in mud that drowns the stench of dead animals, fighting for their dignity and for their land, that most ancient desire to fight, while the people inside do not surrender. Outside the muddy barricades, the men keep it up, even as they are running out of ammunition.

Outside the police station, the *Kotwal* leans against the wall, smoking. The wrecked telegraph wires hang from the sky. The Company Tax Office sits idle, its doors pushed open by marauders.

In Lucknow's homes, behind shuttered windows, women prepare *shami* kebabs with chillies and cinnamon, fill delicate hookah bowls with tobacco pounded with syrup made with spices and perfumes. In the evenings of the days that wear on and on and on, when the firing from the guns stops, fathers turn back to their Arabic and Persian literatures while the clocks on carved wooden tables tick loudly. Little girls cry from the pain of emerging teeth before they fall asleep. In Lucknow, the clocks tick and little girls snore while fathers hum songs to them. But their shutters remain tightly closed against the bright stars and the night air.

In the daytime, Amah increases her vigilance to include the Yellow House. She watches from the mango trees, makes sure the house is empty before she moves up to the front window, looks inside, spots Abhi's things. She tries the door, slips inside, walks quietly across the wooden floor. She peers at the man's bedding and opens several copper food canisters—dried figs and betel. She puts her hand into a box of bullets and takes some. A small wooden trunk lies open, the man's silk clothes, folded. Outside the back door, looking onto the bamboo grove, he's left an unclean copper spittoon. She turns away from it, and from a cooking pot filled with old chicken bones and black flies.

Malamud is a better sight in a clean shirt and white *dhoti*. She finds the young man from Madras at Alambagh with other members of the Awadh Force. They have orders from Jai Lal to continue to keep watch for anyone coming down Cawnpore Road. She stands with Malamud at the gate to the country home. "The spy Abhi is at the Yellow House," she says to him. "Don't do anything. I'm keeping watch there."

"All right," he says, looking into the distance. Amah follows his gaze, down the long, red road that disappears toward Cawnpore, that chatty place with skinny cows, English flags, and river water smelling of dead fish. The rain has stopped. The air above the red road shimmers, blurred with heat so that the lone figure advancing appears to wave about, an orange phantom. The figure is walking slowly and moves across the road as well as up it. They watch the phantom advance until the orange blur takes on shape, becomes orange robes belonging to a Hindu holy man, and then finally Amah recognizes the long, hollow face of Rasheed.

They run forward with several other men, and Kasim who has just arrived, making his own rounds, just as Rasheed is about to collapse, and they carry him into Alambagh's garden. They bring him water from the well, offer oats that some of the men are cooking on a low fire. He sits up, waves the food and everyone away from him, and pulls out the china vessel Amah gave him full of rose water for her mother, now cracked, broken, along with the letter from Begam Sahiba, torn open and smeared in dirt. He puts them on the damp grass. "I need to tell you," he says. His eyes are red and perhaps he has smoked opium or perhaps he has not slept, or both; the walk from Cawnpore would have been at least a few days in his condition. He rubs his teeth with the back of his hand, as if he wants to clean them.

When Amah brings quilts for him from inside Alambagh, he remains standing in the garden, burrowing his bare toes into the grass, staring at what he is doing, then he studies her for some time. He says, "You are my friend. We are in this together." He motions for all of them, Malamud, Amah, Kasim, and several men from the Awadh Force, to sit and not to stand. His hands are shaking—hands that have gripped medicines, letters, and payments, hands that pat the air now, telling them to please sit down.

He kneels, face to the ground, then he raises his face to the cloudy skies, wails, and he does not stop. He does not falter. He sings loudly, a prayer of thanks that belts out of him as if it's being chased. When he looks up at the skies, at times he is smiling widely, all of his teeth showing, and other times he's crying. His song is full of laughing and crying; they can't tell which. He sings his prayers until the skies shift and a little afternoon light throws itself across the garden walls and the bougainvillea. Then he gets up, and almost falls into the grass, steadying himself, coming back closer to the little group that observes him walk as if he is drunk, his heel catching the side of the broken china vessel he's left in the grass so that he pulls his foot away quickly, bends to rub his heel. He sits back down across from them. Their collective thoughts hang in the humid air.

They remain quiet, Rasheed and the little group facing each other. The letter and the broken vessel sit between them.

Rasheed starts to cry. He studies each of them, his red eyes peering into their eyes. Malamud pulls out two *beedies*, lights them both, and offers him one. Rasheed waves it away, and Malamud gives it to one of the men from the Awadh Force.

There is blood on Rasheed's orange robes; deep patches of it are almost black. He sees Amah looking at it and starts to rub his teeth again with the back of his hand.

"We ran into a lot of trouble," he finally says.

The little crowd murmurs assent.

"A lot of trouble," he says, flipping the tattered letter over and back.

The little crowd assents again.

Kasim gets up. "I must go," he whispers. Amah glances at him, and she thinks she understands her older cousin. He does not want to hear any more sounds of harsh English voices, the rushing surprise of pain, the clicking boot heels of conflict that echo on marble floors. He only wants to hear the *rat-tatting* of kites in the sky, dancing above him. He only wants to hear the patter of rain.

When Kasim leaves, Rasheed pulls out a white handkerchief, stretches it flat, and covers his whole face with it. He dries his eyes, pressing the handkerchief into his eyelids. Folding the handkerchief, he puts it away under his robes, and straightens his posture. He says, "Nine hundred of them. Nine hundred. At Cawnpore, they killed nine hundred."

"Who was killed?" Amah asks.

"English people. Women, children, before them their husbands." His voice catches and he coughs loudly.

"What happened?" Malamud says, not disguising a little impatience.

Rasheed picks up Amah's broken vessel, pushes his thumb against the sharp edge, then he shakes his hand.

"Tell us," Amah says. "You asked us to sit down here with you, so tell us."

"I will tell you," he says. "I will … I will tell you all. What we heard…. We saw…. Over a month ago the English surrendered in Cawnpore—Nana Sahib asked them to surrender. Then they killed them all."

"Why?" Amah asks.

"By the time we got there, it had all happened. Akbar and I walked right into a revenge campaign for what had happened. English Forces came into Cawnpore from Allahabad to rescue everyone a day and a half too late and found the children and women massacred. We got there at the same time. All that first week, we didn't sleep. We hid in bushes and people's yards. We would have buried ourselves alive if we could. The Englishmen screamed for revenge. 'Remember Cawnpore!' they kept yelling. A man with flowing white hair, a Brigadier General James Neill, scoured the town with his men. He said that the residents of Cawnpore had not helped the women and children to survive. He thought they should be punished for that."

Rasheed holds the broken vessel, feels the weight of the china in his hand. "Akbar got on the boat, got downstream, got out of there to Calcutta. He's a good actor. Do you remember that story, Amah, with the hero Hamlet? Akbar used to play Hamlet in Calcutta. He makes a good Hamlet—all Akbar's jolliness turns to seriousness on the stage. Akbar is my best friend. You are my friends, too. We should all be friends in this great country. Brothers and sisters."

He gets up awkwardly and pats one of the Awadh Force's men on the shoulder. The man takes Rasheed's hand, helps him to sit back down.

Rasheed continues. "Here's what we heard, the story. An old English General named Wheeler was stationed at Cawnpore. You know, he knew the language, was married to an Indian woman. He even seemed Indian himself. He trusted his local men. There were about nine hundred English—three hundred Englishmen, two hundred Englishwomen and children, the rest merchants, engineers, business owners, drummers, and so on. Servants, too, but they left. This General Wheeler, he gets worried about violence occurring in Awadh, and he decides many weeks ago now that all the English in Cawnpore should take refuge in the area around their two barracks. They had one well. Bad decision. Bad cover. It was easy for anyone to attack them. The ground was too hard for the Company men to dig trenches. Do you remember the hot spell we just had? No rain? Then this officer named Cox fired on his Indian guard when he was drunk. No one did enough about that. Cox was not really punished. And there were rumours everywhere. Rumours about the English killing people everywhere. General Wheeler's Indian troops thought there must be plans to kill them all. They saw their General's primed guns as a possible threat against them. They did not stay loyal to General Wheeler. They decided to go to Delhi to seek further orders from the King of Delhi. They took money, ammunition, arms, and left. But along the way they met Nana Sahib, a prince disenfranchised just like His Majesty, who petitioned the Queen of England like your Queen Mother is petitioning, but he got nowhere. Nana Sahib convinces General Wheeler's troops to come back with him to Cawnpore by offering them gold if they can destroy the English entrenchment. By now, in Cawnpore, the English have little water and are dying of heat stroke. One of their two barracks becomes a hospital. They are piling their bodies outside the buildings. There's no sanitation so there's disease. Nana Sahib asks them to surrender. He has thousands of soldiers. The English don't surrender, but they lose their hospital in a fire, the sick and wounded burned alive in the inferno. You know, Amah, that spy who you are always worrying about. I saw him there. He's going back and forth. They say he took messages from General Wheeler to Sir Henry Lawrence.... So then. Then there is the one-hundredth anniversary of the Battle of Plassey."

"What?" asks a member of the Awadh Force.

"The battle that got the Company more of India," Malamud says, glancing at the man in irritation. "Please keep talking, Rasheed."

"The soldiers have this prophecy that the English East India Company will fall one hundred years after Plassey, and they launch a major attack on the English. Nana Sahib sends another note about surrendering, and that is when the English finally agree. They are told they can leave, and they all get into boats bound for Allahabad. Then the men are shot down, and the women and children captured. No one knows what happened. There doesn't seem to be any evidence that it was a deliberate set up, but that is what the English are screaming—that it was a deliberate set up of innocents. So much confusion. Confusion! No one knows how the first shots happened or where they came from. But you know, those Indian soldiers must have stood there watching the English get away, thinking about all the indignities they were made to suffer. One of them, an older man who was there, and who told me all of this, said to me, 'We've waited a long time. So after the first shots happened, we moved into the water, killing those Englishmen in their boats with swords and pistols.' Nana Sahib did not allow the women and children to be killed, so they were taken to his headquarters, Savada House. Then he moves them to

The House of the Ladies. About two hundred altogether, they say. Captured women and children. They are put to work by a woman called Hussaini Khanum grinding corn for *chapatis* while Nana Sahib uses them to bargain with Company Forces coming from Allahabad, demanding that the Company Forces retreat at once. The Company Forces ignore him and continue to advance to Cawnpore. There is a man named Havelock in charge, along with that Brigadier General James Neill who had been in Allahabad a long time by then."

"Neill," Malamud says, "is an English crusader."

"More than that. More than that, friend. They advanced toward Cawnpore, and the rumour is that they are killing Indian villagers along the way. Just going into any village and setting fire to whole families while they are eating boiled rice and lentil suppers, stabbing children, slicing the clothes from mothers and fathers before piercing them through their ears, shooting grandfathers as they are running away, turning a blind eye to their soldiers who make young girls scream and scream. They execute at will, at random, sometimes shooting, sometimes stabbing, sometimes using the handles of their guns or knives. Thousands and thousands are dead on Neill's orders. So, Nana Sahib's advisors who hear all about this meet with Nana Sahib. They want to kill the female captives and the children in retaliation. The women of Nana Sahib's home oppose them, shouting at them, and go on a hunger strike against the action. The tension is so fierce that the air is crackling. I had not slept in nights, so when the old man told me this story it was just like a story; I saw fish-eyed goddesses weeping and devils laughing, their dry, long tongues hanging out," he says. "Get me water!" Rasheed is suddenly shouting. "I need water!"

Malamud gets up, leaves the garden, and brings back a pitcher of water. Rasheed drinks from it, rubbing the clay rim with his lips and letting the water spill down his chin, his neck.

He drinks, and then he talks again. "No one knows who

made the order in the end. The Indian soldiers who had rebelled against their English officers refused to do it. Nana Sahib left the building because he didn't want to witness what was going to happen. Someone ordered the Englishwomen and children to come out but they refused. The women tied the door handles with clothes and boarded up the windows. Some of the Indian soldiers were threatened with execution if they did not shoot and some of them shot through holes in the boarded windows and some of them could not, and shot into the air. They heard screams and groans from inside, and the soldiers said they would not kill any more women and children. So the woman Hussaini Khanum, who had escorted the English ladies to grind corn, yells at the soldiers that they are cowards. The old man who told me, he could hear her yelling at them. 'Cowards!' she yelled. She goes and hires butchers. I'm telling you, regular butchers who prepare meat. They went in and murdered the women with their cleavers. Women begged them, telling them they had already surrendered. The butchers grabbed them by the hair, scalped them. 'We don't want to hear your sobs now,' they told the women. Then they left, saying they'd got them all. Some of the butchers were laughing.

But several of the women and children survived, hiding under the dead bodies. The next day, when the sweepers came to put all the bodies in a dry well they found three women alive, and three naked little boys, probably about four to seven years old. The sweepers were told to strip the women and throw them into the well. Then they tossed the three little boys into the well, the youngest boy first. They were buried alive in a pile of butchered corpses. Drink!" Rasheed shouts. "All of you with your mouths hanging open, drink, drink! Then I will finish this story."

"I am not sure I want to hear more," one of the members of the Awadh Force says.

"You weren't even there when all of this happened," Amah says. "Perhaps it's not true."

"I am not a liar. I have not slept in a thousand years but I am not a liar."

"If you have not slept, your memory will be playing tricks on you," Amah says. "You might as well have been drinking wine for days."

"I saw the well," he says. "Let me finish my story. But drink!" He offers his pitcher of water. Malamud gets up again and goes out the gate. He brings back another pitcher of water and offers it around. They each drink a few drops, holding the pitcher away from their mouths.

"Akbar and I arrive and become wary right away," Rasheed continues. "There was an awful feeling in the air. We hear the whispers that new Company Forces are due to arrive. Neill and Havelock. Then there are Company men in the town square; there are Company men everywhere. No one knows where Nana Sahib went. He left. At first, the new Company men assume the ladies are still alive, but when they reach The House of the Ladies, they find it blood-soaked and empty. Blonde women's hair blows on the wind, and strands of black hair lodge in the tree branches around the house. The tree in the courtyard near the well is smeared with the brains of babies dashed head first against the trunk and then thrown down the well. They look in the well and see the dismembered bodies. And then they go mad."

Rasheed is silent. His eyelids droop, and he sits up with a jerk. He mumbles something and stares past them. He picks up the vessel and feels the sharp edge again, and draws it across his wrist. He cuts up and down his arm, making red slices. Amah leans forward and tries to pull the vessel away from him but he recoils from her, tells her to leave him alone. She leaves him alone.

"Everything is such hatred," he says. "Such horrible hatred. Cawnpore, remember!"

"Let me take you to Qaisarbagh Palace to rest," Amah says. "You need to rest."

"Not until I finish the story," he says. "Then I will never repeat this story again."

He takes a breath. "The Company men start looting and burning all of Cawnpore's houses. They yell that the towns-people did nothing to stop the massacre. They are yelling that evil, dark men dishonoured their women, that they raped them, but I tell you, nobody did that. Nobody. Those butchers had one murderous purpose and one only. Brigadier General James Neill takes full command of the men they've brought with them. They have guns and cannon, swords, pistols, bayonettes, and they go on a revengeful killing spree. Nine hundred English killed so now he is aiming for thousands of us to be killed. He makes any soldier who cannot prove he wasn't involved in the massacre lick the floor of the compound where the ladies were kept. He orders the floor to be made wet with water by low-caste Hindus and makes Indian soldiers lick the blood off the floor as they are being whipped. Akbar and I hid behind bushes, behind farm huts on the outskirts, behind piles of grain sacks near the square. Akbar made it onto the boat for Calcutta but he did not have the letter, or your rose water, Amah. We tore open the letter and he read it. It was safer that way, to carry it in his mind. It was tiredness that made me stay behind in the bushes as he got on the boat. I hate being tired. Have you ever seen me tired? I tell you it was tiredness that made me miss that boat. I watched—the Muslim soldiers disgraced by being force-fed pork and the Hindu soldiers disgraced by being force-fed beef. They sewed the Muslims into pig skins and then they hanged them. They forced Hindu street cleaners to execute high-caste Brahmins. I was alone in the bushes. They were so busy tying men across the mouths of cannon before they fired them that there was a brief time when I got out and wandered around, alone. I watched them use the butts of their rifles to kill young men; blood sprang from their temples. The houses were full of slain women whose *kurtas* had been torn off them, their men dead where they'd been propped to watch, their children decapitated. I found myself at The House of the Ladies, near the well, and I gagged, the ground littered with bits of … what can you call it? I knelt and prayed, and blood seeped from the ground right through my robes to my knees. Then I felt your vessel, dear Amah, which I'd been carrying all this time. I took the smooth china into my hand, and in the tree nearest the well I heard a crimson barbet chirp. Just as if it was another day, the bird chirped. Breaking the vessel open against the well, I watched the little bird hop from branch to branch. It chirped and sang above the dismembered bodies soaking in streams of rose water. The red bird hopped down and perched on the edge of the well. I saw the hand of a woman reach up and stroke its head with her fingers."

Rasheed is silent, thinking. He picks up Amah's vessel. "Hamlet had thoughts about killing himself." He knocks the sharp side of the vessel against his head. Amah gets up and tries to pull the vessel from his hand, cuts her finger. "Don't hurt yourself!" he reprimands her. "Take care!"

"You are the one here that should be taking care of yourself."

Rasheed ponders Amah. Then he says, "You are working hard. I see how worn your shoes are. Your face has early lines of worry. Lines at your eyes that weren't there when I first met you."

"Throw the vessel away. You are feeling shame, guilt. You are hurting yourself because you feel shame and guilt."

"We feel shame and guilt. We are hurting ourselves. The Forces at the Residency. The people inside. It is us who are doing it. Here. There. We are only hurting ourselves now."

"That's what you came back to tell us?"

"Yes. Neill is coming. They have retaken Cawnpore. We are completely cut off. His men are resting and then they will be here," Rasheed says, pointing the empty vessel at them all, and his eyes shine red like blood, hard as sun-dried earth, seeing ghosts shining in rose-water's light.

18.

—•·•·•—

OUTSIDE THE Chattar Manzil, Amah tries to picture Lucknow in its central place in the Kingdom of Awadh, but the city has been set adrift, a floating island caught in an ocean of resistances—to English waves that flog Indian men, to lavender whirlpools that threaten to suck down boats with wooden gallows built by Indian men who will hang from them, to glittering sprays of water that dampen the embers of burning villages. Lucknow, she thinks, is an Indian island sealed off by English stormy seas, but she knows the English see Lucknow as an English island sealed off by Indian stormy seas, and that Sir Henry Lawrence saw that if the English lost Lucknow, birds would carry this symbol of loss over the seas to foretell the imminent end of English rule in other lands. The Lakhnavi men and women with green and mahogany eyes, who long ago came from Persia and Afghanistan, Ethiopia and Somalia, only want to anchor Lucknow, set it down in calm waters.

Inside the Chattar Manzil, Jai Lal is giving new orders to twenty members of the Awadh Force who in turn will relay his orders to the rest of the men. Amah goes to the storeroom. There is only enough ammunition for perhaps a week. She counts the boxes herself, checks the fullness of each. A group of labourers sits in a corner fusing bullets out of broken telegraph wires. The iron pipes that held the wires are now gun barrels.

From the sound of the distant guns, the advancing Englishmen on Cawnpore Road are about fifteen miles away—a half-day's walk. They will be at Alambagh Palace by early afternoon. Amah listens to Jai Lal give the orders: some of the Force will stay in front of the Residency. Others are to fan out along the south side of the city to stop the English from finding their way into Lucknow. Some of the Force is to form a deep barricade between Alambagh and Charbagh Bridge situated over the canal that leads into the city, and station themselves at the Yellow House. Others are to go down Cawnpore Road to check the intruders. "I will go to the Yellow House," Amah says, and Jai Lal agrees.

* * *

In her meeting room at Qaisarbagh Palace, Begam Sahiba notes Amah's inventory of the ammunition stores. "Go with our Force, but stay back. I can't have you dead, Amah. I need you to be my eyes."

Amah picks up a second rifle and yam kebabs from the kitchens. Rasheed rests there, watching a cook prepare lentils; he waits for Akbar to return from Calcutta alone. The hollows in Rasheed's face look permanent, but sleep has done him good. She wishes him well and leaves him to find Kasim's grey mare.

Outside in the street, two noblemen watch workers brick up every window of their homes. Word has travelled swiftly. Teak planks have been nailed across their balcony doors and large baskets of sunflowers are put aside. The noblemen ignore Amah. She knows what they are thinking. They read Begam Sahiba's newsletters, urging them not to leave. She doesn't stop to ask after their health, and she doesn't dismount to pick up the pots of sunflowers rolling in the alley. She doesn't bestow a greeting on the black-and-white goat who nibbles yellow petals from one of the pots. She listens to the grey mare's hooves. The horse steps over the baskets, seeking bright gardens of statues and evenings of poetry.

Over the bridge and past the Yellow House, Amah reaches Alambagh Palace where men from the Awadh Force, and also plenty of the marauders from the barricades who have committed to Jai Lal, wanting to fight Neill, are stationed out on the road. Malamud is there. Amah climbs up an outside ladder to the roof of Alambagh. Fatima calls to her from where she stands with a group of palace guards. They clean their guns. "One of them coming is the man Neill," Fatima says. "He's a famous killer."

"I've heard," Amah says. "Lucifer, no less."

"Neill is here to fight all of us Satans. Thanks to the butchers in Cawnpore. How did they find such murderers? The word Cawnpore on your lips will get you killed now. Neill made Brahmins and bullock-cart drivers who had no idea about what was going on come into that terrible place and lick the floors. Women's blood. To doom their souls. Just because they lived in Cawnpore. Then he killed them."

"No more stories," Amah says.

They wait for the devil Neill to come with his little devils behind him. They can see nothing out on the road except members of the Awadh Force, and mirages.

Amah leaves for the Yellow House between Alambagh and Charbagh Bridge. In the front room, Abhi's things have not been touched. She puts them in a corner—things belonging to the man who was surely paid hundreds of pounds to bring to Lucknow the accounts of butchers in Cawnpore who have seen to it no one in their right mind will ever raise a white flag again. She picks up Abhi's box of bullets and gives it to a soldier from the Awadh Force to keep. An archer comes in, offers *salaam*, and hands Amah a bow and arrow to take up to the roof, along with her rifles.

She takes the stairs up to the roof. They need her here, among the archers, if the worst comes to the worst. She sees some of the best snipers, including Malamud, cross back over the bridge to get themselves to other rooftops in the city.

As the morning wears on, the Yellow House buzzes with members of the Awadh Force. They cannot see for all the old mango trees laden with yellow-and-red-tinged fruit that hang between them and Alambagh Palace, but they can hear men shouting beyond the trees, and behind them, too, in the bamboo grove. A barricade of men block Charbagh Bridge, the way into Lucknow.

They wait. Finally, some men burst through the trees—Indian men with muskets who run past them toward the men at the bridge. "Who are they?" Amah asks the man nearest her, who has just come up to the roof, panting loudly.

"They came running like a thousand tigers. Look at them. Not Lakhnavis. Maybe villagers who know what's coming, who've come to help."

Many of the men are archers. Some of them have muskets. "Get them back to Alambagh," Amah says to no one. "They are in our way. This is not Jai Lal's plan."

"They've come from the fighting in Delhi. Delhi fighters," someone else says on the roof. "They are the worst kind of helpers," he adds in a fatalist tone.

A glimpse of scarlet. Time moves quickly, but then it slows down, gives everyone on the roof the time to stare. A rush of frothing horses and a swathe of scarlet. White men in red coats come riding in after the Delhi fighters. They ride with anger as well as purpose—men who seem to know their way with guns that whir and rattle, rattle and whir, such odd, insistent, loud noises that at once overcome the loudest birds. Volleys pour through the old mango trees, bringing down green leaves, mangoes, branches, men. Dust kicked up from the horses' hooves coats everyone. Redcoats make their way to the bridge yelling, "Cawnpore!" There must be a thousand Englishmen in black velvet hats mowing down men. Soft velvet hats that sit on angry, relentless men.

A velvet hat lands in the canal water. Men on the bridge shoot. Everyone is shooting. There seems to be shooting and yelling and sharp musketry fire in all directions. "No one mined that bridge," Amah yells to the archers beside her. "Jai Lal should have mined the bridge."

"None of us are used to this," one of the archers says quietly.

Men lie in the water and on the bridge; wooden railings sparkle like red sun.

"Hark forward!" an Englishman yells, and a parade of Redcoats on brown Walers crosses the bridge. They do not pay attention to the paralyzed group on the roof of the Yellow House. They pay attention to a short man on a tall, Arabian horse who is giving orders. Brigadier General James Neill is just as Malamud described—unmistakable with his trailing white hair, a stocky Lucifer wearing a red coat covered in medals with a high gold collar. Lucifer pours Champagne into his glass as he gives the orders that they cannot hear. He sips from his cup of poison and rides with his thousand men into Lucknow's narrow streets where more of Jai Lal's Forces wait.

At the Yellow House and in the direction of Alambagh there is silence. "Some of you should go to Alambagh," Amah calls as she runs downstairs. She leaves the archers standing on the roof and races, not stopping to stare into the canal water or at the faces of the dead men she surely knows—who she must sidestep to get across the bridge. In Lucknow's narrow streets, Jai Lal's men are everywhere, and the men in red coats are suddenly vastly outnumbered; they do not now seem to know where they are going. The Englishmen are pulled from their horses and pinned to walls and trampled by horses and cannot get away from the thousands of Jai Lal's men who crowd around them. There are so many people that it is almost impossible to move. She sees Fatima up ahead on a rooftop and Malamud at the window of an apartment. All across the rooftops, snipers crouch behind the parapets taking slow and steady aim. Remembering Begam Sahiba's words, Amah stays back, pushing into a tall, empty gatehouse. She climbs the stairs. From its second floor window she raises her rifle, ready for any retreating man in a red coat. But the men in red coats are trying to get away from the sharp rattling volley of musketry all around them by pushing forward. A big gun somewhere booms hoarsely, smaller guns pop briskly, and bullets ping. As Amah watches, the sodden sound of cutting connects to the glint and glitter of swords and long knives. Everywhere there are deep and ghastly cuts. On the rooftops, snipers like Fatima and Malamud continue to take slow and steady aim.

Neill has somehow got ahead of his men. He has lost his glass and from his horse he is yelling at the men behind him, his white hair trailing, his small face turned shiny red. The crowd of Lakhnavis and the flashes of red coats surges forward and the wave of people threatens to overtake Lucifer while riderless English horses gallop sideways into gardens. The crowd moves up the street like water, and the flashing red becomes only a glimmer before Lakhnavis chase men in red coats right out of Amah's sight.

***

Midnight, and Amah sits under the kadam tree outside her mother's bedroom. The birds are not in their cots, gone in search of seed, and Amah's hands are outstretched on the grass.

Malamud comes out of the kitchens where he's eaten with Jai Lal and sits down with her, his hands together in greeting. He hums while he searches for a *beedi* and lights it. They listen to the guns at the Residency, the *bang-bang* of shells exploding.

"A General had a thousand men," Malamud sings. "He marched some of them up to the top of Residency Hill but he couldn't march them down again."

They listen.

"Their friends at the Residency took the risk and unearthed the gate. A few of them were lucky and made it inside. They came all this way to rescue people who refuse to surrender and now they find themselves locked up too! They lost a lot of men in the roads getting there. Jai Lal had snipers on the rooftops all the way up the streets and everywhere the English looked we were there. The English found themselves running. They had no idea where they were going. We have thousands more than the English do. Those marauders, they are with us now. We all chased the English down. Lucky, those Englishmen who made it inside."

"Alambagh Palace is occupied," Amah says. "They are sleeping in Alambagh."

"They've got two more of His Majesty's buildings along with Alambagh," Malamud says. "The royal buildings right next to the Residency. But that is all. They are contained. All of them—soldiers, sailors, rich men, thieves. Today, I saw a General with a gold-headed walking stick go inside, but I did not see Neill."

"Perhaps he got back to Alambagh."

"Perhaps he's dead."

Amah's thoughts drift in the shadows, and she thinks she sees Lucifer stalking her thoughts, sniffing like a nocturnal dog the offal from slain horses and body refuse. Her thoughts drift to the shadows of Qaisarbagh's hall, under the portraits of *nawabs*. Allah, Krishna, and Mother Mary sigh like caged tigers. They tilt their heads at her, at barrels filled with opals and rubies, at dusty, narrow roads stained with blood and perspiration, at a river carrying ghosts of old ships, and black cinders.

Dried magnolia pods skitter under the Mermaid Gateway. The night moves from slumbering darkness to slumbering darkness. The warm breeze blankets Qaisarbagh Palace, the shelled Residency, Alambagh. The warm breeze strokes birds who sleep soundly in the shadows. The dark night moves slowly into the stars.

19.

THE NEXT DAY, the dead men who littered the streets are taken away. Gone are the English soldiers lying one hundred yards from the Residency, heavy with kit. The streets have been swept clean of that misery. Amah finds Malamud swearing at a group of Indian bandsmen in the road near the Residency who never stop playing "God Save the Queen." The joke has gone on too long. None of them can stand the music any longer.

Amah walks into an old municipal office with broken walls and crumbled plaster. She climbs the stairs to the roof to find several members of the Force and two heavy-set marauders stationed behind a low wall. Jai Lal's men greet her. The marauders are quiet for some moments. Then they bow their heads. "*Salaam*," they say.

"*Tasleem*," Amah replies. She walks to the low wall and holds her rifle ready. Their guns point at the royal buildings taken over by the English reinforcements led by a General with a gold-headed walking stick, a man who apparently has razor-sharp eyes that must peer at the royal china to be had, at the royal saucers that belong to the royal cups in Englishmen's hands, teacups filled with milky tea—Chinese tea fresh out of newly-arrived English soldiers' sacks.

Suddenly, Malamud is beside Amah, telling her to come with him. "Didn't you hear? Akbar has been searching for you."

"Coming," Amah says.

She goes quickly down to the street with him. Akbar walks toward them, dressed like a pilgrim, his brow smeared with paste, his eyes distant. He remains subdued as he moves past them into the crumbling municipal office. When he comes out, he veers toward them, tells Amah to look for a small canister he's left there, his voice low and plain. She waits until he's down the street, has disappeared, then she walks alone into the building while Malamud watches out for her.

She finds the old canister among some debris by a wooden desk. Inside, one of her mother's yellow handkerchiefs hides an envelope. She takes the envelope out. An ear-splitting explosion, a mine, erupts at the Residency and she throws herself onto the ground.

"Run!" Malamud yells.

When she gets up, her hands are shaking. The envelope is torn and smeared with dust, blood, sweat.

She runs down the street and dives into an alley, beside a drain pipe. She waits but there is nothing more. She breaks the seal and opens the letter before she runs all the way to Qaisarbagh Palace to find Begam Sahiba. The bottom line, a signature, is smeared, but the first lines are clear black ink, the curl of Urdu words sharp as swords. Yet, when Begam Sahiba reads her the letter, Amah can't make sense of them. Begam Sahiba reads the words several times, slowly, quietly, before they finally come together: the words *cholera took her* push out toward Amah, blooming finally in meaning, and, breathless, she chokes out the word, *Mama*.

* * *

She doesn't touch the food that Begam Sahiba orders for her. She has slipped inside the bottom of the spiral staircase in the back garden at Qaisarbagh Palace, and she stays there for three days. For those days of mourning, Kasim and Fatima call for her, telling her that Aunt Laila is leaving at once for Calcutta to see to her mother's things, but she doesn't venture out. She does not eat, lets hunger soothe her.

When she crawls out late one evening, a light rain falls gently. *Tablas* play in the distance. A small lantern hangs on a spike in the grass beside a covered dish of *shami* kebabs left there for her by cooks who've guessed her whereabouts. Through the back door at the palace, she slips into the city and makes her way down to the river Gomti. Amah stands there listening to her mother's voice across the water, or is it the patter of rain? She listens, gazing out at the river, and her mother's eyes grow hard in front of her. "But it's me, Mama," she says. "Amah."

She drifts for hours, turning her ear toward the voices of her mother and grandmother, voices that rock and tremble between the dark shapes of His Majesty's fish-shaped boats, old ladies' voices that come loudly upriver to cut through the sounds of cracking guns, clashing swords, exploding mines, voices that hover above water that lilts against *ghats* while the sky over the Residency continues to fill with gun-firecrackers that try to overpower the sound of a grandmother's voice, light as an angel who reaches out to her granddaughter, praising her, and a mother's earthy voice telling her matter-of-factly that the best of her life was reached before Amah was old enough to know. The *pop-pop-pop* drowns out their voices.

When Amah was a child, her mother would smooth a square of silk onto Amah's lap, asking her to check the curls in her embroidery, to trace the patterns with her fingers. Her mother stayed in her cocoon, spinning her handkerchiefs with embroidery, an occupation that really belonged to her husband, until she became the talk of every palace caterpillar. Her mother spun, and the silk thread flew to her from caterpillars' hands and mouths and landed on her mother's bed. When one yellow handkerchief was finished, she spun *ghee* for breadcrumbs and she spun stories of a husband and a son who had stopped spinning love long ago. She spun until she cocooned her entire room and hid away from Amah in its sealed, suffocating folds.

Begam Sahiba is in the front hall with Birjis when she returns at dawn. Birjis, the boy King, wears his *mandeel* made of gold and silk threads. He comes to Amah, takes her by her elbows, and searches her eyes. "Amah," he says. "Come play with me. It will ease your mind."

When he tries to gently pull her, Begam Sahiba hisses at him. "Play later. She has to eat; she has to wash. Look at the scratches and blood on her bony cheeks."

20.

◆·••·◆

AT THE CHATTAR MANZIL, Amah asks the man on guard
outside the rooms reserved for members of the Awadh
Force if Malamud is there. She sits in a small room with
cane chairs waiting for him. She thinks about what Begam Sa-
hiba has told her, that Akbar returned from Calcutta with other
news—that Delhi is back in English hands, and His Majesty
has been put under house arrest. "Because of the goings-on
here at home," Begam Sahiba said, "the English are worried
about His Majesty's involvement. His Majesty simply let them
do it—extract him and some of his staff from his residence at
Matiya Burj. Really, Amah. The English have taken them to
Fort William to be watched. And there's more bad news that I
didn't want to tell you because of your own bad news, Amah.
The Queen Mother's visit with Queen Victoria. Some advisors
at Matiya Burj told Akbar about it. The Queen Mother had her
audience with Queen Victoria, who arrived with seven of her
children, including the baby just born, a girl. The two Queens
discussed one of Victoria's young sons at length. The wrong
son," Begam Sahiba added, dryly. "Queen Victoria went on to
ask about boating in India. In the end, words failed our Queen
Mother. That happens in dire circumstances. She offered the
English Queen a flask of perfume made in Lucknow and then
it was over. Just like that. Finished."

With some effort, Amah shifts her mind away from all of
this. Outside the window of the small room, some soldiers from

Delhi load ammunition into the storerooms once filled with bags of vegetables and grain. She focuses on this good news. Hasan, her cousin, along with his bony-faced Delhi friend, named Omar, is going from town to town, village to village in Awadh, organizing ammunition sales.

Malamud comes into the room, shuffling in a pair of slippers and sipping black tea. "*Namaste*," he says and exclaims softly, seeing Amah's face. He goes out and brings back black tea for her. They sit across from each other. "May Allah grant your mother peace," he says.

She does not say anything for a while, and he waits. Finally, she says, "I am looking for help."

"Yes, I was told." He sips his tea. "What are the details?"

"You will have to ask at Matiya Burj where her grave is. My aunt—her name is Laila—she will be able to tell you."

"You know Jai Lal is not happy with Begam Sahiba's request that I go. He wants a poor boy to do it. I told him, 'But Jai Lal, you know the odds of being thieved along the way, and being shot. You know I have a better chance.' And Jai Lal said, 'I know the odds.' I work for him so it's a difficult position."

He slurps his tea, then puts the cup down and lights a *beedi*. "I am fast. Begam Sahiba said that. Jai Lal was irritated when I emphasized this. And the money, well, he knows one-hundred *rupees* is a great sum for anyone. Listen, you are always working hard. If you felt you could leave now, you would be going to see to your mother's things yourself, right?"

"Yes."

"It's been doubly rough for you these past months, hasn't it?"

"Yes."

"There are some gypsies leaving in the next few days. I can travel with them." He offers her a small smile. "Leave the things with me. Go and pray. It's getting late, Amah."

Inside the box Amah has brought with her, a container holds the scented oil Begam Sahiba helped Amah to purchase. She's wrapped just a few small polished stones, some modest grave markers, in among several of her mother's yellow handkerchiefs. At the last moment, she unwraps one handkerchief and keeps it with her rifle. She hands the box to Malamud.

* * *

In the afternoon, Begam Sahiba asks Amah to go to the *kotha* to collect another sum of money to help pay for the new ammunition. "And see if Sai has come. He'd be of comfort, take your mind off your pain," she says.

The wintery-pale evening light of Lucknow fills up the narrow streets, and shines on garden walls. Jackfruit and mango trees are stripped bare by the foreign men who sleep under them. The branches over garden walls have been broken for firewood, and telegraph posts have been cut into kindling. English books taken from the Royal Library have long ago been burned. Whole gardens have become shitting grounds. The men steal water pitchers and hookahs. Amah wonders when the stars will be stolen too.

Her face and hands are cold when she gets to the *kotha*, and the bitter smell of burning wood licking the bottoms of Chowk kettles tempts her. A vendor hangs lights around his stall, getting ready for Diwali. She pulls her scarf around her head and walks up the stairs.

Gulbadan is in her pavilion talking to her brother. Her hair is more grey than black these days. She wears two pairs of pyjamas, and a Kashmir shawl. She sees Amah and breaks off. Gulbadan and her brother look at each other and then at Amah.

"We are very sorry about your mother, Amah. God rest her soul," Gulbadan says.

Amah murmurs her thanks. "Begam Sahiba sent me. She thanks you for your offer to contribute to the defence once again."

"Come with me," Gulbadan says.

They leave Gulbadan's brother and go to the courtyard to sit among the cushions embroidered with gilded fish. A boy brings them paper-thin *rotis* with *ghee,* and coffee. Around the courtyard, he lights candles. Gulbadan says, "Sai has not been back. You've not seen him?"

"I have not seen him for a long time."

"Since when?"

"Since we last met here. Before the English got in. Perhaps Sai cannot get out. There are more inside now who must be watching."

"Will they wait until the building is completely demolished?" Gulbadan presses her thumbs together, like swans.

"All we can do is hope they will have to surrender. What else can we do?"

There is no one else in the courtyard, not one *tabla* player practising, not one courtesan reciting poetry, and no one squatting outside the kitchen in his *lungi* and slippers, eating almonds, jugs brimming with water on a table beside him.

"You know, Amah, I saw Jai Lal order some men to dig up a nobleman's garden…. They were searching for boxes of savings stored there. He is paying his soldiers in Lucknow's treasure."

Amah looks swiftly at Gulbadan, thinks about this. "A short-term appalling measure," she finally says. She drinks her coffee, its rich warmth lending some comfort. "Begam Sahiba is most grateful for your continued support. She wanted me to convey to you her deepest appreciation."

"Her newsletters hearten us. Comforting us as much as they can."

Amah puts the last of the *roti* into her mouth, and lifts the cup again. From everywhere below them, the city echoes in the dusk. The sound of hammers, boards clattering, even the *pop-pop-pop* of guns at the Residency are delicate accompaniments to the women's stillness.

Gulbadan gets up and goes to her pavilion. She comes back with a heavy purse. "Five hundred," she says. "I will have it sent to Begam Sahiba tonight in a wardrobe box."

Amah thanks her one last time. On the way out of the courtyard, she steps on a stray marigold from Sai's garden. She stoops to pick it up and clutches it in her hand.

* * *

Going home, she skirts the earth embankments where the dismal fighting continues in the darkness. Nothing changes. Dark figures loosen round shots and bullets and Amah pictures a group of sad and weary watchers inside. During the day, the noise of cannon, mines, and muskets remains deafening. She pushes aside her worries about Sai's safety, the royal cousins' safety, and the violent Red Man. Her thoughts shift to the Englishwomen who made Lucknow their home, who are dazed with fright, who must call Lakhnavis the Enemy—ladies who dream of ice cream castles, who are now in deep distress when their husbands do not return from where they shoot down the Enemy from the Residency's roof top. Outside, all around the Residency, Lakhnavis, soldiers from Delhi, marauders fall. Boys run through the streets yelling for families to come, to prepare alms and perform funeral prayers. Amah listens to the shuffling noises in the darkness. Just over there, the royal cousins and Sai are listening in the darkness, too, remembering nights of lemon and coriander on the breezes, nights of Persian stories her mother will never return to, dreamy, evening silences that have turned sour. Amah moves quickly into the night.

In a lane close to Qaisarbagh Palace, something moves. She searches for the movement again and sees two shadows hugging the wall. One of them is bigger than the other, but they move together.

She follows them carefully. One figure has a slight hunch, and confidence, like Abhi. The other is just as confident but taller. Shadow after shadow, wall after wall, street after street, the figures slip over layers of broken-up brick on beaten earth; they wait in dark places for the guards hired by noblemen to pass. She has the double duty of keeping them in sight and watching out for herself; if a guard halts her, the men ahead will be alerted to her presence.

She thinks perhaps they are going to the Yellow House but they don't cross Charbagh Bridge over the canal. She follows them to a much more remote part of the canal on the southeast side of the city, opposite His Majesty's beloved Dilkusha Park with its vast grounds. She walks in the grass where she and her grandmother used to walk, her grandmother holding a silver vessel in her hands, telling Amah about the fragrant winds in African grasses, winds that blew fourteenth-century African Sufi saints to India where they camped in marble homes and primitive villages, sisters attracting followers just like their brothers attracted followers, so that Indian devotees wearing flowers and sandalwood oil perfumes kneel in soft grasses outside Sufi shrines, centuries later, remembering the African sisters and brothers who came to India to make their way—Sufi saints her grandmother pulls out of her living book for Amah like she pulls out from the silver vessel *shami* kebabs, and thin *roti* layered like handkerchiefs, all of them wrapped in gold foil.

In the darkness, Amah can just make out the men ahead. She holds up her gun, steadies it in her hands, but their figures melt into the darkness. They reappear much further away. They undress and begin to cross the canal, holding their clothes high out of the water. They easily wade a hundred yards. She is quite sure the smaller man is Abhi. They reach the opposite bank, dress silently, and disappear.

She moves into the water, up to her neck, her rifle held above her, the water freezing and muddy, dragging down her red jacket, her silk trousers. She slips getting out, and the rifle dips into the water in her efforts to balance. She crouches, panting in the puddles they've made, listening for any sign of them.

The moon rises over Dilkusha Park. Now she is certain it is Abhi. They are in the middle of the park, wading through tall, rustling grasses where the King's horses used to linger. The men are not close enough for her to shoot without a good possibility of missing them. She follows, getting closer, crouching low when they stop and change direction. The second man is tall, muscular, his jaw square. He is a Company man, she guesses, with his face and hands covered in lamp black. He is dressed in tight pyjamas, a *kurta,* and turban, and wears a sword. The disguise is barely passable. The darkness has helped him to slip out of the Residency, past Malamud and other members of the patrolling Awadh Force, and into the sleeping city with Abhi. The darkness helps them now.

They reach a swamp. Amah stays back, waiting, and then wades in after them, through the strangling weeds. She stands in the cold water, trying to free her feet of weeds, making her way slowly across the silty bottom. Frogs call to each other in low voices. The figures pause, change direction again. Abhi's friend's hands are pale, the lamp black gone. They move quietly, not one splash, and she does the same. Amah keeps to the groves of reeds. She watches the men huddle together, then move onwards, disappearing ahead, finally causing her to hurry. She almost falls, and the noise makes the men stop. She freezes, squatting in the water behind the reeds, straining to hear if they are coming back. She aims her rifle through the tall plants, urges them in her thoughts to come back toward her. She peers through the reeds in the moonlit darkness, her finger on the trigger, her rifle ready. The frogs call, like African Sufi saints call, like a grandmother calls from Dilkusha Park when she's found a crop of carrots. The figures bob ahead of her, moving away.

The crisscrossing of the swamp results in a clear road ahead, but Amah is not sure in which direction they are going. Abhi leads the way down a path, past a line of hanging, rotting corpses. Neill's work, she guesses. The bodies take her by surprise, and she forgets her purpose. She is dragging behind, too late, when she hears, "Who comes there?"

She drops to the ground.

An English voice. She listens. The man sounds as pleased as the men she's been following are to see him. Their voices fade as he tells them something in English—but she hears the word, Alambagh.

She lies on the ground for a long time thinking about the message that is getting through to Alambagh Palace. The two men are human telegraph wires bringing news from the General with the gold-headed walking stick who drinks tea from a royal china cup to the group of men at Alambagh who wait with their canvas bags. Perhaps they are sitting with Lucifer, the man named Neill. Perhaps they are telling him the best ways to get back into Lucknow.

Before dawn, Amah climbs a tree near Alambagh, checking for snakes, and rests in the thick green foliage. If she stands high enough and cranes her neck, she can glimpse a room at the end of the garden lit by candlelight. She can hear the strains of laughter—Abhi and forty English thieves drinking Scotch whisky in little glasses tinkling with ice, eating foreign tinned snails cooked in garlic and *ghee*. They are a besieged little group with a lot of Champagne, Scotch, and snails.

* * *

Early the next evening, the two men appear. They proceed down the road toward Lucknow, their gait showing signs of good rest. The night is overcast. Amah comes down from the tree, her skin a violent rash from spending the night and day in wet clothes. They walk in the shadows and Amah does the same, holding up her rifle, keeping it ready. They look behind them, slowing down, and she thinks they've seen her. But then they start walking again, a different way than the night before, and cross into the bamboo grove near the Yellow House. The small building is up ahead.

In the middle of the grove, closer to the Yellow House, she loses them momentarily. She stops to adjust her rifle, to check the cartridge, just as a fist comes down on her head. "Down on the ground," a voice says in English. "Down on the ground."

She goes down face first, one hand beneath her. She tries to pull her knife out of its sheath, but the man has her by the shoulders and rolls her over, and she lets the knife fall under her, loose. A large boot pushes against her thigh. "Following us, black devil?" the Englishman with the square jaw says in English. "Cawnpore devil?"

Abhi has pulled out a knife and bounces around beside the man. He bends down and grabs Amah by the hair. "Answer Mr. Kavanagh or I will make your ears bleed," he says in Urdu. She wonders if he knows her in the darkness or if he has sailed too far away, all the way to England.

She says nothing, and they stand above her, their chests heaving. She can smell the big, muscular man, his powerful, unwashed odour. Mr. Kavanagh takes her rifle, turns it around, and aims it at her. Mr. Kavanagh is smiling. "Get up."

Abhi pulls Amah up and slaps her with his other hand. "The good man Mr. Kavanagh said to get up."

"A good prize, this gun," Mr. Kavanagh is saying. "I'll show it to the Queen when I get my Victoria Cross. Tell her the whole story of how a *pandy* crept up on us."

A wild dog howls in the distance.

"Not a good hunting dog," the Englishman says.

"No, Sir," Abhi replies in English.

They are braver, speaking like this into the night. The wild dog howls again.

The moon comes out behind Amah, and it glows on the two men. The whites of their eyes are very, very white. The big man, Mr. Kavanagh, is still aiming at her, and he closes one of his very white eyes, and he pulls the trigger. There is a click and a peculiar noise that follows.

"Full of water," the man says. "Damp cartridge."

"The hell of this country that is India," Abhi says.

Mr. Kavanagh hits Amah with his fist cursing her for Cawnpore, and she falls to the ground again, her knife piercing her hip. Abhi kicks her and dislodges the knife. It slips away, like animals in meadows slip away, like Kings and mothers slip down rivers. The Englishman hits her with the butt of her own rifle on the back of her head, and the damp earth grips her face. Like a mother grips cold words. Amah could have loosened Begam Sahiba's grip and gone down Cawnpore Road with her mother. But she refused, and gripped onto her mother's complaints—that Amah disappointed, that Amah was not good enough, that her mother expected much more that had never arrived. Amah would not leave for His Majesty's residence at Matiya Burj because she hated to go somewhere where everything, including her mother, would be strange. She couldn't go to Matiya Burj with a stranger. Really, all Amah wanted was to be seen as she was, and loved. And in the end, Amah sees that she herself has loved her mother less. She could have loved her mother more.

The man grabs Amah by her shoulders and turns her over. Everything is black. She can feel Mr. Kavanagh's hot breath, his Scotch whisky breath, and the breathing that begins to move a little faster. He says in English, "It's a woman."

There is a long pause. Then Abhi comes forward, looks down at her. "A royal palace guard," he says acidly. "She is a she."

"Good God," Kavanagh says, sitting back on his haunches.

"We have to get rid of her. She's seen us."

"What does that matter? She can't do anything about the map. The map is in the right hands. We just need to tie her up."

Map. Amah tries to keep the English word clearly in her mind. She can't understand enough of what they are saying but Abhi's voice is nervous. She watches the spy. He has helped an Englishman communicate with Alambagh. There will be thousands after him in Lucknow once she gets back.

"The Yellow House. Remember? There are weapons ready there. Ammunition. Get a pistol," Abhi hisses. "It's getting late. Let's do away with her and go."

"Don't you be giving me orders, *cossid*. No orders. I should hand her off to the higher-ups, that's what I should do. It's their say, what to do with her, not yours. Not mine either. She's royal. The right thing to do is to take her with us. They will more than likely want her kept under lock and key in the Residency, wouldn't they? With the other royals." Mr. Kavanagh gets up, and both men stare down at her. The big man says, "She might actually be a blessing in disguise. I'm going to get a pistol to keep her quiet. I want my Victoria Cross when I get home. She can guarantee I get through the streets back to the Residency safely. If another *pandy* bothers us, I've got a hostage. A *pandy* won't care if I kill you, *cossid*, but he might if I threaten to kill a royal *pandy*. Wait here with her."

Amah hears the Englishman walking away. The back door to the Yellow House drags across the floor softly as he opens it. They can hear small noises as the man sorts through Abhi's things.

Abhi squats beside Amah. "Look," he says, his voice low. "We are both Lakhnavis. This is your chance. Get up and run. I will say that you overpowered me. Go, black slave. Go."

Amah knows the lie even before she sees her knife in one of his hands, his own knife in the other. She strikes him, and he loses one of the knives. She rolls away, gets up, stumbling, and Abhi is right behind her. As he catches up with her, she grapples with him, and the other knife falls into the darkness somewhere on the ground. She hears the big Englishman's boots coming toward the back door of the Yellow House, sees his large, dark figure loom in the doorway in the moonlight. Abhi calls to him, "She's got a gun, Sir, another gun! She is after you!" There is a series of pistol shots and both Abhi and Amah are down on the ground. Amah rolls into the cover of some bushes before she is up and running toward the deepest thickets of bamboo at the back of the grove, away from the Yellow House. The Englishman's pistol cracks again and again. She dives onto the ground, smells damp earth, feels the silence that already emanates from the dying spy she's left behind.

In the early dawn, Amah walks the whole way to Qaisar-bagh Palace. The events of the last evening lurch behind her. When she reaches the front hallway, she sees some women and she thinks for a moment that her mother and her aunt are waiting for her. Then she hears Fatima's voice come forward, and Amah drops to her knees. The palace guards' voices echo around her. They call Hasan, who helps to pick her up, and they carry her to her room.

21.

—◆◆◆—

IN LUCKNOW, the stray marigold Amah put by her mother's
window has dried pale orange like the undercoat of the tiger
Shazhadi whose abdomen grows thin. Malamud has not
returned from Calcutta. Anklets jangle as courtesans practise
His Majesty's dances to invisible audiences.

Amah is bruised with a split lip, painful lumps all over her
head, and a deep cut on her hip, but after being fed minced
meat by kitchen cooks, and bathed in perfumed water extracted
from summer flowers, she feels healthy. She has to be.

Lakhnavis whisper the news they've heard from members of
the Awadh Force. On Cawnpore Road, five thousand English
reinforcements approach Lucknow.

Members of the Awadh Force, tall, bony-faced Delhi fighters,
starving villagers, and straggling marauders spill out down
the roads. Amah climbs to the rooftop of Qaisarbagh Palace
and looks southeast. She cannot see them but Jai Lal has told
her that Englishmen in red coats crawl around Dilkusha Park.
They are eating carrots raw, pulling them up from the dirt. Big,
orange carrots that the *nawabs* of Awadh planted in the vast
fields. They are taking Lucknow's carrots. They stoop and pull,
five thousand men in the early dawn gorging themselves on
carrots. What has changed? Amah asks herself. It is a King's
picnic, and the Englishmen think they're invited.

A tide of sickness overcomes Amah. Beside her on the roof,
a small, white pigeon lands, searching for crumbs. Amah's eyes

hurt, and she rubs them. The fact that English reinforcements have already got to Dilkusha Park is not good news. They managed to avoid Charbagh Bridge altogether, and must have been informed that the canal becomes shallower at Dilkusha Park. They know how to get into Lucknow.

Lakhnavis do not stop that day for prayers at noon. They are on the rooftops in the hammering sun, all of them crawling and crouching beside empty water tanks and parapets. They are inside the gardens' gatehouses and outside in the streets, protestors fighting Englishmen who pour into the city yelping like a thousand dogs of war, clinking and cutting with their cutlasses and swords. Dressed in brass helmets and wilted feather caps, heavy kilts and short jackets, all of the foreigners seem to have forgotten the whole of the English language except for two words, "Cawnpore, remember!" Bagpipes wail and muskets rattle. Englishmen with sweating, dirt-streaked faces cry, "No Cawnpore in Lucknow!"

Amah gallops to the Yellow House on Kasim's grey mare. She tethers the horse and goes inside. African and Indian Lakhnavis, a group from the Awadh Force, are gorging themselves on the dried figs they've found in one of Abhi's copper canisters. "Look," one of the men says to her. "Look! We found more of the spy's things."

Amah moves closer. She touches the stack of rifles against one wall, examines some pistols, the boxes of bullets and cartridges. So much ammunition! There's a long knife, too, and she gives it to one of the men who carries it upstairs to the roof. "Have you got what you need?" she asks the others as she walks toward the stairs.

"Plenty," one of them replies.

On the roof, she finds men from the Awadh Force resting uncertainly where they've been told to wait for the approach of Englishmen. More of Jai Lal's men have finally cut off the canal at Dilkusha Park, and soldiers from the fighting in Delhi crowd Charbagh Bridge. Everyone else is fighting in the city's streets. She goes back downstairs. More Lakhnavis stand in front of the Yellow House, waiting. She stays at the back of the house, looking out into the bamboo grove. The lime-green leaves cool her eyes; the brimming whir of cicadas threatens to fill her ears with calm. Someone veiled in white passes Amah quickly, and then comes back. "*Adab,*" the apparition says, cupping its heart and patting its chest twice.

Sai. She takes a step toward him. "*Tasleem.* Please go home," she says.

"It's all right, Amah," he says, pulling back his veil.

"I will take you on the mare to the *kotha.*" His eyes are bloodshot, his eyelids swollen. His face is very thin. "You are not a fighter."

He shakes his head, amused. "I've been fighting at the barricades. I almost got caught inside. They shot a boy instead of me. Right beside me where I stood with the goats," he says. "Let's talk, Amah."

Maybe he's stayed awake all night at the barricades, Amah thinks, the sound of guns rattling his brain, swelling his eyes.

He takes her hand and puts it halfway up his arm. Under his robes, she feels the amulet she gave him, wrapped around his skinny arm. He takes both her hands and rubs them, searching for the knots in her palms. Then he places his hands on her shoulders and makes her sit beside him on the back step of the Yellow House. From under his robes he produces a bottle of whisky from a cloth bag, pulls on the cork, and lifts the bottle to his lips, his hands around its neck—the same hands that massaged her palms, that gently made her sit down.

He drinks fast and doesn't stop. When he sees Amah staring at him, he almost laughs and he almost cries. He doesn't say anything. He holds the bottle on his knee, bouncing it so that the dark-yellow liquid sloshes from one side to the other. Cicadas hum in the bamboo grove. Sai's elbow is cut, the skin slashed open. He sees Amah look at it, and he covers it up again with his robes. "I've been fighting," he says, and hiccups.

She puts her arm around him. "Little brother," she says.

"I wounded some English," he says. "More than three of them. Maybe even four of them." He glances at her. "I killed a guard after they killed the boy."

She holds him closer. "Sai, let me take you home. To sleep." She hears the sound of cart wheels on the road from Cawnpore, feels the heavy duffel bags, smells oily kippers, sees swords clanking against silver buttons.

Sai picks up the bottle again and puts his lips to it. He is drunk. He wipes his mouth with his hand and gazes out at the bamboo grove. "I killed the goats, Amah. Mrs. Gunning's goats. They were so very, very hungry. Then I ran."

"What happened?" she asks, giving up.

He drinks the last of the whisky and breaks the bottle against the house, bringing several men from around the front with the crash.

"Eat," Amah says. "Sit still and eat." She offers a yam kebab that she's been saving.

He pushes it away. "Inside, the ladies have flour and salt and a marrow bone between them. They are eating their artillery bullocks since there is little else. I lost my appetite a long time ago."

He stares out at the bamboo grove. "I slipped outside the barricades to be with our Lakhnavi men. The foreign soldiers were also there. Fighters from Delhi. And the landowners from outside Lucknow. Those landowners never forget the high taxes they were forced to pay, never forget their stolen land. I got a musket. I pulled it off a dead landowner outside the Residency. I wanted to get the English guards inside the Residency's yard. They are so interested in killing the men at the barricades that they take chances in order to win their bets. Everyone at the barricades was working together. But some of the foreign men were drinking, too, and shooting." Sai pauses. "Begam Sahiba would hate them drinking like that. Amah, there are no more goats in the yard.... One of those landowners took a nine-pounder through the chest. I took his musket and I fired, *boom, boom, boom, boom,* and I saw a guard peering through binoculars at me go down. The man with the hole through his chest lay dead beside me. I took his pistol, too."

"You were inside for a long time, Sai. You have been very brave. You—"

"The royal cousins are still alive," he says. "And do you know, I heard from the ladies that whoever is in charge sent a letter with a runner to Calcutta to get approval to blow up the women and children if it comes to it, while the men fight their way out. The women will not be dishonoured like they were in Cawnpore. They will be blown up if need be."

He pulls out the pistol and knocks it against the side of the house. Amah reaches over to take it from him, and he lets her. "Who was my mother, Amah?"

"I don't know."

"You know!" he shouts, and pushes her.

"She was dead before I could remember her, Sai," Amah says. "We were too little. Sai, you must go—"

"So many beautiful times at the *kotha.*" He begins to weep. "Kites, dancing. We've had good times, Amah." He puts his hand on her breast, he is that drunk.

"Come," Amah says. "We don't need you here." He lets her help him stand up. "I have a secret, Amah," he says, smiling. "Shall I tell you, dear Amah? I do not despise the English. They are dear, dear women."

"We have to go," she says.

They hear guns at Alambagh Palace. Voices. Men are coming toward them. She pushes Sai inside the house, tells him to get down behind the stairs. She goes up to the roof, takes her position in front of the others, immediately feels their low mood.

Hundreds of Englishmen burst through the mango trees. Brigadier General James Neill and some of his men come straight for the Yellow House. He must have been waiting, just as Amah suspected, at Alambagh all this time. Neill's Arabian horse is restless and frothing; the stocky man's face is red with exertion. "The *cossid's* Yellow House," Neill shouts in English to the group of men with him. "Get the ammunition."

As they come forward, one of his men shoots Kasim's tethered grey mare and she goes down. Neill's men shatter the air with gunshots, and Lakhnavis fall in front of the house and on the roof.

A big man near Amah stumbles backwards. He takes her down with him, the dead man landing on top of her, pressing her cheek, her ribs, her legs into the roof.

She can hear a big horse galloping toward the Yellow House. When the horse comes into view, she sees Red Man, too. When he dismounts, Neill's men, who've gathered in front of the Yellow House, greet him warmly. Amah can hardly breathe with the heavy man on top of her. Downstairs in the Yellow House, there is silence. Outside the front, Neill remains seated on his horse. An Englishman gives Lucifer a glass and a Champagne bottle. The medals on Lucifer's red coat shine brightly, not as if he's travelled the whole of India mowing people down. Lucifer drinks, sitting on his horse.

Downstairs, boots pound the wooden floor. There are cries for help, and pistols crack. A bullet whizzes by Neill on his horse, and he turns purple with rage. "Get the bloody whore," he says. There are more shots inside the house. Then, silence. "Bring anyone left out alive," he says.

Amah can hear someone walking, the sound of boots, to the back of the house. "The roof," a voice says in English. "They're all dead," someone else says.

She waits to hear an Englishman come up the stairs. She cannot move her arm but she can push her rifle around with her hand, flat on the roof, so that it points at the stairs, ready.

Downstairs, someone hiccups.

"Aho!" another English voice says. "Up on the roof. Check the roof."

Sai begins to hum and then to sing, a hesitant sort of wailing song. He hiccups again.

"No need," the first voice says. "There he is. The wretched fool's come out to greet us." Cloth scratches across the floor, the sound of someone being dragged, sliding, outside. Neill's horse snorts and shies.

Lucifer's men in their red coats huddle below. Neill dismounts. He pokes his empty glass into a saddle bag and stands near Red Man. Neill takes off his helmet and bats away a butterfly.

Amah feels dizzy from the weight of the dead man on top of her. The roof bites into her cheekbone. Sai is on the ground among the men in front of the Yellow House. So many men. The other two Lakhnavis that they drag out alive are stabbed through right away. The man on top of Amah has pierced her jacket with the long knife she found downstairs, and even as she tries to pull away, it keeps her pinned to him. She slowly moves the gun around so that it faces in the direction of the men in front of the house. The trigger moves out of reach, and she strains for it, tries in vain to reach it with a finger. "'Ave his nut off," someone says below. "Give him a Cawnpore dinner, like the others," someone else says, waving a knife.

Neill stands with Red Man. His white hair flows around his small face and down around the gold collar of his red coat. Sai lies on the ground in the middle of the men, face down, stripped to his *lungi*. Some of the Englishmen keep scanning the trees, the road, while others unload the ammunition from the Yellow House. Amah tries to push at the knife that pins her to the dead man, to the roof, without being noticed. Two soldiers pick Sai up by his legs and swing him, singing, "...when evil stalks upon the land ... I'll neither hold nor stay me hand ... but fight to win a better day, over the hills and far away...."

"Pull him apart," Neill orders.

Still singing, they change position and take Sai's arms. Amah grabs at the blade of the knife and cuts her hand. She chokes from the man's weight, from Sai's whimpers below. They try to tear him apart, Sai crying out, but they cannot tear him apart.

"Do something else then," Neill says to the men.

The men drag him across the ground, stabbing him in the face with their bayonets as they walk. Amah pulls against the knife, letting her jacket rip, but the man on top of her holds her fast. Sai's body is lacerated and his blood flows into the sand behind him. His upturned eyes search those men for pity. She does not need to see their eyes to know none of those men's eyes hold pity. She keeps pulling away from the knife, the smell from the dead man stifling her.

The men below are all singing as they heave Sai onto a small pile of sticks they've collected. "…over the hills and far away…." Two Redcoats put their boots on his shoulders to hold him down even though Sai's struggle is more like a bird's. But when they light the fire and step away, the whole lot of them calmly watching and not singing, Sai gets up, horribly burned, and Amah's throat is caught in wet knots. Sai flees a distance, his body in a series of dancing moves, and then he doubles up, almost as if he is laughing, and Red Man brings him back in no time and they hold him on the fire. Sai chokes up cries for mercy, but they do not heed him. Amah lunges free of the knife and the dead man, and grabs at her rifle. She tears away so violently that she falls backwards off the roof and into the bamboo grove at the back of the house. She pushes her face and her cut hand into the dry sand and she does not smell burning flesh and she does not see cracked, blackened skin. She does not see Sai die. Instead, she sees him reaching out like a yogi covered with the ashes of pearls. She gets up and runs from the back of the Yellow House to the Englishmen's horses at the side of the house. She throws herself onto a horse and wheels around, cocking her rifle, ready to kill anyone she can. The sweating will not stop; it streams down her neck like burning rain.

The men no longer need to hold Sai down but they remain where they were, crowded around the fire. There is a lone gunshot. The man with white flowing hair at the fire is down on the ground. Neill's men let out cries of horrified surprise. Near Amah, Fatima lowers her rifle from where she sits on her horse.

Amah hadn't noticed the patrolling Redcoat on a Waler who rides toward them, aiming with a rifle as good as theirs. Behind him, Neill's men rush forward, leaving their dead Brigadier General behind.

"Go, sisters!" Sai would have yelled. "Go!" Amah hears him yell.

She gallops behind Fatima across the bridge and into Lucknow's alleys. The fighting is full on; men from India and England lie dead in the narrow streets, against Lucknow's homes, and Amah loses sight of Fatima. She dismounts the horse who flies toward the sun, the bells on her hooves jingling. She scrambles up on top of the closest gatehouse and then up onto the roof of a noble family's apartment.

The Redcoat on the Waler is still after her, and she lies flat on the roof, trying to catch her breath and calm her aching throat. When the man comes upon a group of Awadh Force fighters on the ground, she goes down to the street, moving fast to get to the next walled garden with its gatehouse, to keep in front of him. She comes face to face with an Indian fellow in a red coat in the street, a man who's chosen to butter his bread with English jam instead of sticking with *naan* and *ghee*, a strange man of treachery who's chosen to serve those who train him to see her as evil. She is about to shoot the man but he raises his hands and utters a small cry of surrender. He calls her, "Brother," his mouth cracked and dry like hers, and he turns to the Englishman nearest him, stabbing the man to prove his point.

She runs, holding her breath against the salty smell of flesh. English war cries ring out against the stone walls. Lakhnavis cannot hear each other call out any kind of strategy at all. Lakhnavis are falling, and she feels as if she races with loose stirrups.

The Redcoat on the Waler is behind her. She slams the butt of her rifle against a wooden door of a home until it breaks open. She moves past the Lakhnavis inside, women and men who fall backwards in fear. She runs upstairs to the family's roof. The home is across from the English post office and from the roof she looks down at its front windows. Each window shows a Lakhnavi with a gun. A rifle cracks. It cracks again and the Lakhnavi at the window holding that gun is Fatima. Down in the street, two men lie on the ground. Other English soldiers cry out in angry curses, and then they surge inside. Fatima is gone. Amah goes down to the street again.

This time she sees Jai Lal in the road, and he is yelling for them to move to defend Sikanderbagh, at least a mile away. Lakhnavis move slowly, feeling the strength of the relentless English Force upon them.

For most of the afternoon, the Redcoat on the Waler keeps her attention, keeps her away from the ache in her mind that is Sai. She and the man are a hundred yards from each other. He keeps up with her, his small eyes piercing, his taunts of Coward and Cawnpore ongoing. He takes aim and fires again and again. Anger and hatred advance him. When he is busy defending himself from other men, she climbs the stairs to the roof of another gatehouse and takes aim. When she takes aim, the man gets free, sees her, and becomes furious. He shoots the watchman at the gatehouse opposite Amah and climbs up to its roof. Now they both have very good shots. He is young and rude. She hits his parapet and misses him. He hits her parapet. He stops to replace his plentiful cartridges, shoots again, and grazes her shoulder. She falls forward on the roof and cracks a tooth on a tile, the pain emanating through her head, down to her knees. She rolls away, his bullets pinging around her, and she is down the stairs. Once she is out in the street, he is a sniper shooting at her from above. With Sikanderbagh and its pink walls now directly in front of her, she thinks, Go to hell, foreigner. Go to hell. I will run with the speed of boats to England and I will not stop. I will run on the distant shores of ignorant people who do not know where to tread without doing harm, and I will wade through the sea of chaos that belongs to that country which insists on greed, which has refused to learn from the minds of men and women educated for centuries. I will wear my best red jacket and rose-coloured silk trousers and ride my best horse down the streets of London and I will find the Queen Mother, and I will deliver a treaty from Lucknow that puts the misguided English and their criminal activity to rest. I will kill their desire to throw centuries of good will to the wind. I will deliver that treaty once and for all. I just have to get to Sikanderbagh as fast as I can, and then that is what I will do.

But the foreign man is on the ground, too, still after her, and the thoughts that have buoyed him hour to hour come forth in stinging, ragged curses.

This is all before late afternoon, and the fight that is to come. After that, Amah thinks, not one of them will be able to stand harsh words from strangers. They, every single one, will only want the voices of parents.

She is high in a neem tree in Sikanderbagh's courtyard, her body hidden by its dense green leaves. The courtyard inside Sikanderbagh's pink walls is full of Lakhnavis and some of the men from the fighting in Delhi, all of them fighting Englishmen. The side rooms, where blue-breasted quails sang like little flutes, are also filled with fighting. Amah is crazed with thirst. How mad it all is that so many people are crazy with thirst in the enclosure of one of the most beautiful mosques there ever was, with its large, central well full of cool water.

Thousands of men in heavy kilts push Lakhnavi men across the courtyard. Those kilted dogs froth, and the fighting moves deeper into the side rooms. Tall, bony-faced Delhi fighters, members of the Awadh Force, marauders, and villagers—they all cry for help. Anyone who has not died in the courtyard is now caught in the side rooms. Amah can feel them tremble. Someone shouts orders to bayonet. Curses mingle with voices begging to be saved. She sees the big, muscular man with the square jaw, the man Kavanagh, the one who was with Abhi. He's brought out a boy on his bayonet. Men fall from the side rooms. Amah's hands grasp the branch beneath her so hard that she cuts her palms.

Fatima is in the neem tree, too, below Amah, her rifle gone, a pistol cocked. The well with its blessed cool water is out of reach beneath them. In the glimmering water, Amah thinks she sees the shifting shapes of King Wajid 'Ali Shah and his mother, the golden-green glimmerings of silk-winged pigeons.

"Over here," the women hear. "Jasus in heaven," they hear. Fatima and Amah look down onto the head of a Redcoat who is leaning over the well, his hand reaching for the bucket hanging from a rope, choking he drinks the water so fast. He pulls up the bucket again and pours water directly over his head. "Jasus Christ in heaven," he says, and Fatima shoots him dead.

Within minutes another Redcoat approaches the well. He steps over the dead man, peers into the well, and in haste he pulls up the bucket. Fatima waits until his head is tilted back, drinking noisily, and she shoots him dead. She does this three more times, looking up at Amah and smiling each time.

There are two men below them. One stands among the dead men and the other Amah can't see, just his boots, but she thinks she recognizes the voice of the angry Redcoat on the Waler with a mouth full of English curses who never caught her this afternoon. "Something's been happening here," says that man, still out of view. The man in her view glances at the five men dead around him and then looks up. Amah is lying on a branch, well-hidden by foliage, but he grabs Fatima by the boot before she can fire and pulls her down.

"It's you, rooftop *pandy*, is it?" The angry Redcoat steps into view, coming toward Fatima. He pushes her. "I've been hunting you all day."

"Okay, *pandy*," the other man says. "I see the white spittle on your lips and I would suggest you drink your last bucket of water here, like my friends before you did, before I shoot you."

All three of them vanish to the other side of the well. Amah tests her weight on the next branch below her.

"You like water, don't you, *pandy*?" the angry Redcoat asks.

Amah can hear them lower her into the well, hear her gasping as they bring her back up. "A thirsty *pandy*," the angry Redcoat says.

"Drink up," the second man says.

"Last *pandy* for the day," the angry Redcoat answers. "We are in Luck. Now."

Amah is onto the next branch. Now she can see the two men lower Fatima into the well, pull her back up, and push her down again. Fatima is throwing up like a woman with cholera, and the second man says, "The dirty devil is throwing up on my boots. Kill the dung."

The angry Redcoat pulls Fatima up, brings her back around the well, and he comes to lean against the tree. "Are you ready?" he says.

Amah vomits the heat and pain of the afternoon, a sour liquid gushing out of her and onto the head of the angry Redcoat below. Beads of sweat cool around her mouth and she aims straight down and kills that man just as he is looking up. The anger stays in his eyes even as his life shrinks away, and it frightens her. There is another crack, a pistol, and Fatima is on the ground, her jacket blasted open, her breasts bare. "Good God, a lass," the second man says. He falls to his knees and begins to cry.

* * *

Amah is hiding in the tree, a shaking quail. A thin, elderly man in a helmet with a feather plume calls to his men from where he waits on his big horse inside Sikanderbagh's gate. She has never seen him before. He tells them to rest, speaking English and Urdu. She can feel the relief of those men who seek refuge in their commander's voice.

Later, all of them leave. The sun is setting, and the foreign men hunt archers who have positioned themselves in buildings closer to the Residency. She limps down from the tree. Dead and dying men lie on the ground. Lakhnavi men. Villagers. Delhi fighters. Fatima. Amah sees Hasan under a dead man, and he is trying to move. She kneels and pushes the heavy man off him and pulls Hasan to her, but his body is shredded with cuts and his eyes roll back. His head slumps forward on her shoulder, and she hugs him to her, kissing his dusty hair while he dies. She puts him down carefully, gets up quickly, and goes to stand outside Sikanderbagh's pink walls.

The whispers of Lucknow's *nawabs* stir the air around her, and vomit lies in her belly like the cholera simmered in her mother's blood, a mother who is not there to see her daughter with a broken tooth who squints at Hasan's cuts, who squints at the memory of Sai's wondering eyes, a daughter who tries to forget she has killed. Amah is sick from the stench of flesh that sucks up the air in Sikanderbagh, and the flesh that sucks up the river, poisoning fish and birds. She is sick from the sight of Lakhnavis who've slipped on their own blood down the streets.

Kasim appears on the road, streaked with dirt, and Amah steps forward. "Go home, Amah," he says. "Go home." He motions with his chin in the direction of Qaisarbagh Palace. "You will be wanted at home. For its defence. They are going to get through to the Residency." He gazes at the scene at Sikanderbagh and wipes his eyes with his palms. "None of us can come back here to this terrible sight, do you hear? None of us."

"Did you see Malamud? Did he come back?"

He stares at her in wonder, motions with his hands that she should leave.

She does what he says and walks toward Qaisarbagh Palace. Now, she thinks, someone will shoot me. She glances back and Kasim is gone. She stops and returns to Sikanderbagh, not able to leave the dead and dying. All day, they've shared the same hammering sun.

She squats outside the pink walls, behind some bushes. She sees two Parsee men, their *lungis* tied up between their legs like fishtails. They hurry along, keeping to the grass, running in the approaching darkness along the road.

She is still there after the English come back. Well past midnight, they return to Sikanderbagh to sleep. She hears the orders to clean up the place at dawn before they move forward. In the earliest hours of the morning, someone smokes a cheroot. She smells its deep, pungent aroma. She waits, making sure no moon is about to appear, and then she leaves her spot, the cheroot, and starts back down the road to Qaisarbagh Palace. It is cold. The whimpers of the still-dying Lakhnavis, and the calls from the Englishmen who seek their mothers in their dreams—the sounds of whimpering and calling ring into the night and follow her home.

III. AFTER

22.

———•◆✦◆•———

O VER THE NEXT two days, the English in the Residency
are shielded by their relieving Forces as they all escape
Lucknow. Every single English person vanishes.

Amah is amazed. She roams Residency Hill. Barefoot little
boys follow her at a distance, eager like Amah to see the state
of things on the other side of the barricades. Outside the Res-
idency, she climbs earth embankments shored up with large
books and musical instrument cases—anything, it seems, that
the English could find. She sidesteps the old English rose gar-
den—now only a lumpy oval of earth, a common pit where,
Sai told her, the English buried Sir Henry Lawrence along with
some others. She passes under the Baillie Guard Gate and into
the empty Residency, stepping inside shattered rooms where
yellow butterflies rest, past filthy beds on floors strewn with
broken teacups, old books of English nursery rhymes, Cham-
pagne corks, and milk bottles. There's an English newspaper,
something Amah hasn't seen in a long time—dropped from
a rescuing soldier's kit? She stoops to pick it up, knocks the
soot from it, and stares at the sketch that takes up most of the
page. Dark men in turbans with ugly faces and long moustaches
lurk outside the windows of a pale lady's room while the lady
cringes inside, just out of reach of their black hands. Amah
drops the paper, steps over it.

Among the debris in the front hall is an enormous aviary
full of golden-green, silk-winged pigeons, and red pigeons with

white breasts—no doubt all of them purchased at the auction. The birds are quietly dying. Amah opens the cage door and strokes the tops of several of the birds' silky heads with her finger, stretches her hand over a green, silk wing, traces a white pattern on a red breast. Too weak, the pigeons do not startle. They do not move their black eyes. None of them try to fly.

"Go and get water," she calls to the boys who stand nearby, tentatively, in front of an enormous hole in a crumbling wall. "Someone go to Chowk and ask for *chapati*. Tell them I sent you, that we must help these royal pigeons."

While she waits for the little boys to come back, she studies some of the English trunks filled with His Majesty's china, gold utensils, silver bowls—royal goods taken from the royal buildings next to the Residency, loot left suddenly behind without a sigh. When the boys come running back with several men, their voices tumbling over each other to tell her they've brought the best pigeon trainers they could find in Chowk, plenty of old *chapati,* a whole pitcher of water, she picks out two silver bowls from one of the trunks and tells the boys and the men to come. Together they fill the bowls with water, tear the *chapati* into tiny bits and offer it to the birds. Together they kneel. They do what the learned men tell them, and they coax the birds with soft words as they dip their fingers in the water and rub it on the pigeons' beaks; when the birds open their mouths just a little, they pop in crumbled *chapati* the size of tiny diamonds. A low thrumming starts in the breasts of the birds, in the breasts of everyone kneeling there. The boys and the men and Amah pray that the pretty pigeons will grow strong, fly high over Lucknow, their silk wings glinting in the sun, their coloured breasts bursting with calm, the good birds free to find and return to old, cherished homes.

Amah leaves the boys with the men to care for the pigeons. She roams through Lucknow's streets, observing the abandoned canvas screens that shielded all those very brave people who escaped Lucknow by night, led by their General with the gold-headed walking stick, taking with them the royal cousins Nawab Mirza and Sharif-un-nissa. She studies soft roads trampled by the soft feet of starving women and their children. She puts the picture together—the darkness hiding the ladies and their children who walked in silence while, behind them, wagons rolled, crowded with seventeen barrels and eight chests of Qaisarbagh treasures, and the wounded, and the sick wincing with dysentery who left bloody waste behind them in the streets, who all rested without speaking a word at Sikanderbagh, where they were given biscuits and tea, the bodies of the dead sealed away out of sight in Sikanderbagh's side rooms. Amah follows their stunning exodus to the remains of some cold beef and chickens, of bread and butter, eaten under the trees at Dilkusha Park. Evidently they camped in the cold darkness until the cold dawn came and they all disappeared with what must have been a unified longing for basins of warm water and warm news from an English Queen, leaving behind six months of harrowing scenes and rotting bodies as they moved back down Cawnpore Road toward England.

The city slowly emerges from its alleys and bricked-up homes. Damp betel leaves are spread out to dry. Judea the Jewish jeweller opens tightly-sealed boxes of gold bangles, sets out rubies, strings his pearls like white horizons outside his shop. "Happily live the peaceful," he calls to passersby. "Those who give up victory and defeat."

Drink vendors play bottles, the colours of a rainbow, and squeeze fresh limes into sugared cups. "The English have gone!" the vendors cry. Boys in bright coats, sent to purchase tobacco, wait by the hookah shops where smoke curls through the air like sea horses. Cinnamon tobacco and honeysuckle help stamp out the smell of rot, and settle upon them all like glimmers of happiness. Meats are prepared to stew rice for *pulaus* in kitchens all over Lucknow—garden *pulaus*, jasmine *pulaus*, and white *pulaus* stained red with pomegranates. Pistachio nuts are cut to look like lentils. Lakhnavis crave jokes like they crave clean water, like they crave a *tamasha*. Lakhnavis cry, "The English have gone!"

"Weak-minded people," Begam Sahiba says to Amah, her green eyes flashing. She removes her headscarf and shakes out her dark hair. "They expect normalcy. Forgive and forget. We may be far too capable of that, but no one has ever seen in a dream Englishmen forgiving an offense. They'll be back. That General with his gold-headed walking stick is still camped with some troops at Alambagh. They'll seek revenge, send for more troops. He'll walk back in as soon as he can. We cannot let them back in. We cannot be another fallen Delhi."

Begam Sahiba announces by newsletter that the courtesans have sanctioned five *lakhs* for defence, and she adds to that a personal sale of her jewellery. Lucknow's *rupees* are fully back in circulation. Thousands of newsletters promise that thousands of broken pipes and broken archways will be repaired. The old royal post office is restored. Runners are sent out to every town and village in Awadh to purchase ammunition. Everyone needs to help. Thousands of labourers, the ones paid by Sir Henry Lawrence to fill the Residency with supplies, the same men who also built the earthen barriers and dug the trenches at the Residency, now build walls. They are immense earthen and teak walls built so high that even the green tips of Lucknow's tallest trees will not be visible from the outside. Begam Sahiba orders the construction of another wall, two miles wide, to cut Lucknow off from Cawnpore Road and Alambagh Palace where the General with the gold-headed walking stick sits. Openings in that wall are completed for guns. No foreign Englishman will ever get back in. No foreigner of any kind will ever get back in.

On the other side of Lucknow's walls, greed hovers like dragonflies where Red Man and his General stroll in Alambagh's garden surrounded by their troops. But Lucknow has become an island oasis free of the English, anchored securely by thick, royal roots that reach under the salty sea, an island where dancing mermaids and stranded Indian sailors watch, bobbing and cheering the island on, an anchored island with storm-barrier walls that will stop battering English waves.

* * *

During those first weeks, Amah visits the fish-kebab stands that have opened back up on the edge of the Gomti. She has no money to eat there but she lingers to breathe in the spiced smoke flowing from the grills. Near one of the busy stands, she sees Hasan's old friend Omar with the bony face. He eats with some other men from Delhi at a table. As far as she knows, they still live at Star House with its enormous, broken telescope. She wants to avoid them but, too late, Omar urges her to come and sit down, nodding at his plate of kebabs. "Thank you, no," she says, but he gets up, guides her to the table, and puts the plate in front of her. "For Hasan," he says. So Amah picks up a fish kebab, and she eats.

Omar asks, "Do you still walk alone at night?"

"Always," she says.

He smiles. "How is your Queen? She must be quite embarrassed about the outcome. How humiliating."

"Her interests lie in removing the group of English from Alambagh, and being prepared for another English attack."

"She's been very interested in seeking our help. Did you know that?"

"As her friend, her bodyguard, I don't know everything."

"From a family of African slaves you know nothing." He laughs.

* * *

The Yellow House is empty. Amah does not go inside. The mangoes in the trees around the building have burst like firecrackers and ooze brown juice. Ghosts hang in the bamboo grove. The Yellow House is full of *jinn* who have seen English torturers, but the sandy path in front of the house where Amah walks shows no sign now of what happened there. She made sure a palace boy told Gulbadan, but Amah could not go back to the *kotha*. She kneels and takes up handfuls of sand where Sai last lay and fills a wooden box she carries with her. The sand turns and twirls, slips through her fingers. In the bamboo grove, she sweeps away bamboo leaves, digs deep into the rich, dark soil, and makes a rectangular grave. He needs to be buried, however she can do it. For Sai. For Gulbadan. She climbs into the grave herself since there is no one else. "The angels of death will come soon now," she says. She places the box in the direction of Mecca and holds it in place with clods of earth. With all Sai's good deeds, she feels sure he will journey onwards to his mother.

Amah stands in Sai's grave and thinks of mothers. She thinks of her grandmother getting off a crowded boat—a young Muslim Ethiopian girl who will be married to an admiring Muslim Lakhnavi. She thinks of anxious English mothers in a boat on the vast ocean heading for England. She gets out and throws a handful of earth into the grave three times before she fills it in. She takes up the dried marigold she's brought with her, the stray one she found near Sai's garden at the *kotha*, along with some roses she gathered at the palace and places them all on top of the rich earth. The roses are the colour of milk sweets, and the earth is dark brown like *habshi halwa*. "Thinking of your sweet tooth," she whispers.

23.

———◆•••◆———

D RESSED IN A peach top and pyjamas, Begam Sahiba comes out of Shahzadi's cage in the garden at Qais-arbagh and joins Amah. They walk to her meeting room. She's been brushing the tiger and still holds the brush full of fur, pungent in the warm air. "Akbar and Rasheed are back from Calcutta," she says when they are inside. "This time, they only brought us a rumour. The Nepali leader Jang Bahadur Sahib has apparently accepted a bribe and may well be working with the English. He wears goggles to protect his eyes from the sun, much like he protects his country in other equally conspicuous ways. Rumour has it they are all coming here. Divide us from our neighbours and rule us. That is the English way. But listen, Amah. The ruler of Nepal is someone we can speak to. He will respect Delhi fighters. If he knows we are working with them, he will reconsider his allegiances. I've asked Rasheed and Akbar to travel into the countryside to see what they can find out, to see if he's really coming."

Amah notices a letter, a single page, tossed on the table. Blue ink is scrawled like a spider's trail across the purple-smudged sheet. She picks it up.

"From that General sitting in Alambagh with his gold-headed walking stick and his glasses of wine," Begam Sahiba says. "He offered me a pension and a treaty with Queen Victoria if we will surrender. He offered me one *lakh rupees* a year," she says.

Amah finds herself wondering loosely about this idea.

"Perhaps I will be the only one not to accept a bribe," Begam Sahiba says, shooting Amah a look.

* * *

At Alambagh Palace, Englishmen wait for the commands of a general who bears a creased face, a wooden cross, a gold-headed walking stick, and prayers for poor Indian souls.

Malamud still has not returned from Amah's mother's grave. Butterflies flutter like yellow handkerchiefs to rest on purple hibiscus. They stay away from Sikanderbagh where bones, molten flesh, and broken hearts remain sealed behind side-room doors where the English piled them.

The Englishmen came in the last time from the southeast—between Dilkusha Park and Alambagh Palace. Begam Sahiba predicts that it will be from here again that they will try to launch an attack. Amah walks the two miles of the new wall covered in rich-smelling mud. Stockades and parapets are erected everywhere. Each house in the city is loopholed. Hundreds of villagers are paid to dig a moat around Qaisarbagh Palace, filling it with water from the Gomti. Teak planks make solid barricades in front of Lucknow's prized buildings. The Gomti forms a natural northern barrier between the city and the burned-down cantonment, neglected racecourse, and empty Faizabad Road on the other side.

Early evening and Amah enters the abandoned home of a nobleman she once knew. The paned windows looking into the central courtyard are bare, the silk curtains torn from their brass hoops. In the courtyard, open to the sky, the cots belonging to the nobleman's famed red pigeons are empty. Gone are the days when her rich neighbour would show off his female flock of nine hundred pigeons, trained never to mix with his male flock. She walks back through the home's empty rooms and picks through the old books thrown on the tiled floor—mostly Persian love stories. She sits down near the doorway to the street and looks through the pages of *King Lear* and *Hamlet*.

The low sun shines dark orange, and Lucknow slides into London. The smell of tamarind bubbling somewhere fills the doorway, and the cooler the evening becomes the more Lucknow slides toward England. In the pages of the books, she knows that Ophelia grieves, and Cordelia says to her father, "My love's richer than my tongue. I cannot heave my heart into my mouth."

Lucknow's setting sun: orange-gold shafts of light send little jolts of anguish through Amah. She gazes out the doorway at the gathering darkness. There have been so many mistakes. All the wrong roads make her tired. There was a time when they had love. What happened? God showed himself as coldness, thought Lakhnavis silly for wanting to dance barefoot in the grass. The way is full of stones, sharp and grey. She pulls her rifle toward her and takes out her mother's yellow handkerchief, traces the embroidery with her fingers.

Hamlet should not worry, Amah thinks, getting up. We try and try to love in all the ways we know how. It is a good thing for Lakhnavis to want different plates on the same table.

* * *

Rasheed and Akbar, dressed as Jain scholars, arrive from their travels outside Lucknow. They confirm that the English have made an agreement with the ruler of Nepal, and that he is on his way to help the English take the city. Jang Bahadur Sahib marches toward them, six miles a day, with nine thousand Gurkha troops, their wives, and camp followers. Begam Sahiba writes a letter for the messengers to bring to him. "We have no choice but to present a bigger bribe," she says to Amah and to Jai Lal, her eyebrows raised, her lips pursed. She turns to the messengers. "In case you must destroy the letter, we offer the goggled fellow several towns in Awadh that he can govern if he will support his neighbour and restore Lucknow to its rightful place. Please get ready to go to him now. We need to get this done."

The messengers' tired faces show they understand the gravity. They change into rags, disguised as Muslim *faqirs* with clothes that appear as completely worn out from all their wandering as the messengers themselves appear worn out from all their wandering. They wear their topaz rings, payment from Begam Sahiba, low around their necks on plain strings, under their clothes. They take Begam Sahiba's sealed letter and leave.

24.

———◆◦◆◦◆◦◆———

PALACE BOYS COME back with the news. Sent out to see what has happened to Rasheed and Akbar, they discover that the messengers did not reach the ruler of Nepal. Begam Sahiba's letter was intercepted—like a Queen Mother's letter was intercepted, like a young soldier boy's letter was intercepted. Their beloved messengers do not return.

After this, Amah does not want to get out of bed at dawn but the sounds of loud shouting force her to dress. Outside the front of the palace and across the new moat, a rushing stream of men pass her in the street. Some of them are loading their guns as they walk, still groggy with sleep. Kasim is with them.

"They're coming," he says.

She goes immediately to Begam Sahiba's meeting room where her friend is talking quickly with Jai Lal and Qaisarbagh's old ministers. Amah bows her head. "*Tasleem*," she starts.

Begam Sahiba interrupts her. "Be on guard on the roof with the others."

In the garden, Amah ignores Shahzadi who wants to be fed. She walks through the gardens, past the spiral staircase, to the back wall of Qaisarbagh Palace, and climbs the ladder hidden by bougainvillea to join other guards surrounded by tall trees on the roof. She crouches down, her soft shoes curling over the plastered mud, and watches the streets below filled with men and women going to their positions at the great walls on the south side of the city.

Kitchen runners bring water and *chapatis* up to the roof and down to the defence. On the roof, they wait, listening to the muffled sounds in the distance. They spend the day standing around. They sleep on the roof and Amah stares at the stars most of the night. At dawn, they hear someone climbing the ladder from inside Qaisarbagh. In the grey light, Malamud's head, then his shoulders appear. He climbs right up, dumps his rifle, takes off his boots, and stretches out on the rooftop beside them, panting.

"Where is the attack?" someone asks him in the shadowy light.

Malamud is out of breath. "*Namaste*. Is there water?"

"*Tasleem*. Here, friend. Water," Amah says, and gives him a full pitcher. "I am so glad to see you." She whistles for a runner who comes with *chapatis* and more water. "We will listen when you are ready," she says.

Malamud sits up and holds the pitcher above his lips, pouring the water into his mouth. "Cold. Good," he says. Then he eats, his black eyes glassy, listening to the sounds of men shouting in the distance. "It's all done." He nods at Amah. "I marked your mother's grave. I had to delay coming back for a long time. I could not move fast after all. No one will trust you in the roads. Coming back, I didn't have anyone I could stay with. It all took so long." Malamud lies down. He lights a cigarette.

The smell is strange, acrid. Calcutta.

"I must go and find Jai Lal," he says.

"Rest first. Wait until there's better light."

"I talked to several men in the streets. There are Englishmen coming up behind the southeast wall, just as Begam Sahiba predicted, they say. And they're over in Dilkusha Park, eating carrots. No Nepalis yet. I heard about that agreement, too." He sits up and takes two bracelets off his wrist. "I almost forgot. Laila gave them to me to give to you."

Her mother's gold bracelets clink together in Malamud's hand. She takes them, feels their thickness with her fingers.

Malamud looks out in the direction of the river and smokes. "Do you know in Calcutta they say that the newspapers in London, and New York, too, are full of protests about what is happening here? Lots of people against the Company. But it doesn't matter. Queen Victoria sent fourteen thousand men in boats from England to come to Lucknow. Fourteen thousand crossing the ocean to come here!"

"Rest a little, Malamud."

He lies down and closes his eyes. After a while, he says, "Do you ever wish to cross the ocean, Amah? Do you ever wish to see your country again?"

She puts on the bracelets, turning them around and around on her wrist. "We made our place here a long time ago," she says.

"His Majesty's residence—at Matiya Burj. Do you know, Amah?" Malamud says, finishing his cigarette. "His Majesty has made his place there, even if he is under house arrest. Matiya Burj has become a miniature Lucknow—with dancers and poets and artists flocking to live there." He stops. "I have something more to tell you," he says. "More terrible news. They had the news in Calcutta. The Queen Mother has died."

Amah stands up. She needs to find old Lal. By the time she finds the Queen Mother's white-haired advisor in the gardens, the news has already reached him. He is staring into the mermaid fountain in the growing light, one leg up, his foot curled over the rim, throwing tangerines into the water. Amah talks to their reflections. "She was on her way home," she says, repeating what Malamud has told her. "They were in Paris. On their way home," she says. "She would have done everything you told her to do, Lal. She would have taken all of your tonics."

Lal's eyes remain fixed on the wavy water. Amah continues to gaze at the water, too, imagining holy men swimming, and soldiers washing their feet free from dirt. She imagines the weary Queen Mother standing in the fountain, gathering the billowing folds of her wet pyjamas as she watches a tiger lap the water, and a group of little English boys in sailor-suits splash, soaking the pages of her Persian poems so that the book falls apart, disintegrating the verses.

She doesn't tell Lal that the Queen Mother died on the same day that one of Queen Victoria's daughters was married. Her death found no place in the newspapers. "How hard she tried to reverse things," Amah says to him instead. "She died of a broken heart, Lal. No medicine can fix that."

* * *

Malamud leaves to join Jai Lal. Amah stays with the others on the rooftop, listening to the noise of fighting in the distance. They think they hear shots from the direction of the Gomti, as well as from the southeast, but no one is coming to tell them. The sky is a vast, hot indigo, and they keep to the shadows. Malamud comes back in the afternoon holding a flask of water. "They are firing at us from across the river," he says, drinking the water quickly. He makes a face and spits it over the rooftop. He takes off his boots and sits on the roof, his eyes shut. They squat beside him.

"Tell us," Amah says.

Someone hands Malamud a *beedi*. Finally, he opens his eyes and smokes, and they don't interrupt him. "We are fighting them off, but thousands of our men have been killed. And the English are north of us. They came around the south side and set up a bridge of casks over the Gomti further down, and they've crossed to the north side, to the Faizabad Road. Soon they could be directly across the Gomti, looking at Qaisarbagh Palace. There are no barricades there," Malamud says with awe in his voice. "Why in the name of Allah are there no barricades along the river?" He lies down, stays quiet while they watch his face, his eyes squeezed shut. "They have good fire power," he finally says, and opens his eyes. "And more imagination with tactics. They are better at war than we are."

"Yes," Amah says. "They are much, much better at war."

The second night on the roof they hear gun shots, and shouting. It is at a distance, and again it's hard to make out what is going on. Malamud leaves, promising to return with news. No one feels like talking under the black boughs of trees under the stars. But there are murmured prayers. Someone in the darkness is anxiously brushing mosquitoes away from them all, urging no one to kill them. Amah is exhausted but none of them can sleep without some sort of news. All night there are gunshots. She prays for one small piece of good news. One tiny speck of firefly light.

Malamud appears late morning, scrambling onto the roof, his face grimy. "The south wall is broken. Last night, they punched holes in the garden walls so that they could get further into Lucknow through the gardens where we couldn't see them coming.

"At dawn, we chased them through the gardens and fought them in the streets. A bullet hit a rain pipe beside me so loudly it feels like it shattered my ear drum. It still hurts," he says, rubbing his ear. "There was so much red dust in the air this morning that all of us were coughing, everyone. Still, we had to shoot and cough and cough and shoot. Your time idling on this roof is coming to an end. They are getting close."

On that roof, hearts sink. Amah is not sure when she starts yelling, but it is after a flock of gun shots rises in the air close to them. It is after she sees the men running below them. At first she pities them as villagers who are in too deep, who are running away. "The villagers are probably all dead," Malamud says beside her, as if he has read her thoughts. She realizes that it is a straggling stream of men from the Awadh Force who slip and pour like glistening honey down the canopied street. Someone in the street calls out that the Iron Bridge is red with English coats. The road along the river is soon overcome by Redcoats who pass the empty fish stalls. Along the canopied road, crowds of Englishmen pass Mohammed's abandoned newspaper stall. They skirt the high garden walls covered in yellow flowers, and glance at the bare tables set up by elderly Somalian neighbours who usually make *paan*. Everywhere there are thousands of Redcoats. Amah pictures the Redcoats crossing Qaisarbagh's new moat, crawling around the tamarind tree growing out of the palace wall by the front doors.

She yells into the air, to His Majesty's silk-winged pigeons flying toward the sun, and she is shooting in the direction of the unseen gardens where unseen Englishmen punched holes through walls and got closer, unseen. She is yelling and shooting, and Malamud tells her to shut up as he takes a sniper's position on the roof. She is not sure what prompts her to get down right then, but she walks all the way back to the ladder and she slides and falls to Qaisarbagh's gardens. It is hard to walk in the grass after being on the roof, and she falls again and gets up and walks woodenly across the lawns. She is yelling, and white-haired Lal is there holding her hand, asking her to stop, but she keeps going. She sees Begam Sahiba with Jai Lal and the palace's old advisors in her meeting room. Amah stands at attention outside the room, and it calms her. Lal is beside her, searching her eyes, and tears are in his old ones. She takes out her mother's yellow handkerchief, and she wipes his face. She runs back and climbs the ladder to the roof. She looks at the streets and watches green birds fly through the red dust and out over the Gomti. Slowly, she puts down her rifle. She strains to hear a pigeon breathe *Yahu*, or perhaps even the song from a sitar, or cooks' knives chopping ginger, anything beyond the loud voices of Englishmen, but those noisy voices bounce high into the hot air, off the city's brass domes, swirling into the pink clouds, not one note of music.

25.

I T IS LATE AT NIGHT on March fourteenth, and English soldiers are camped outside Qaisarbagh Palace. Tiny, pink-winged pigeons sleep in the trees. Amah stands with several guards, cooks, female hookah bearers, and accountants outside Begam Sahiba's meeting room. They protect the fast-talking people inside like they are topaz rings, diamond-studded thrones, and silver mermaid coins that shine in the night. Outside, English soldiers sit smoking their cheap cigarettes, smiling with their green, rotting teeth.

Jai Lal, his face dark with gravity, is telling Begam Sahiba that the ruler of Nepal and his troops have arrived in the city, that she has to go. All of the ministers in their *achkan* coats are telling her she has to go, predicting that twenty-five thousand have invaded Lucknow. Even the fighters from Delhi are making plans to leave. Jai Lal says, "*Huzoor,* I will stay closer by but you've got to get far from here. Let's move to Musabagh. From there, we will take the best route out."

Musabagh is a palace west of the city—still guarded by the Awadh Force, Jai Lal says, and the only other possible place to go. Begam Sahiba remains silent. From the meeting room's doorway, Amah watches her. Her friend's eyes meet hers and they soften; she barely smiles at Amah before she turns away. "We will all go to Musabagh," she says, "with as much as we can take with us."

Moths flutter in the lamplight, shadows bow, and the frangipani tree drops its heavy, white flowers. Cooks pack food. Staff prepare the wardrobe for Begam Sahiba and Birjis, packing their things into a waiting carriage at the back entrance to the palace. Kasim readies the palanquins sitting behind the carriage. It is after midnight. March fifteenth. The Ides of March.

At one a.m., an alert sounds, and Begam Sahiba is urged to go, even if she isn't ready. She puts on her cloak, tells Amah to wait by her palanquin, and leaves the meeting room for her own rooms. Amah joins the other palace guards lined up behind the carriage. They wait for Begam Sahiba. Jai Lal hisses, his face frantic. A white pigeon stirs in the grass. The alarm sounds again. Begam Sahiba is still missing. "I will find her," Amah says.

Begam Sahiba stands in her rooms, her cloak off, a lantern beside her on the dressing table. Behind her, Amah says gently, "Begam Sahiba, they urge you to come."

"Yes, I am coming."

"Your arm is near the lantern. Doesn't that hurt your arm?"

Begam Sahiba stares at her arm by the lantern, and then takes it away. She stands there, looking back at Amah, touching the burn.

"You go," she says. "I will stay here, Amah. With Shazhadi. You go in my place."

"That's not possible," Amah says. "You must go. Your son is waiting. Jai Lal is waiting."

"And you? Are you coming?"

"Not yet. Go, Begam Sahiba."

Begam Sahiba walks over to Amah and reaches up to kiss her. "There are three hundred *rupees* and some jewels in the wall by the bath. You'll feel the seam behind the portrait. Work fast. Don't be late."

"I won't be late," Amah says.

"Do not let failure follow you, Amah," Begam Sahiba says. She kisses her again on both cheeks.

"You must go, Begam Sahiba," Amah says.

"Give me your rifle. Can I take your rifle with us?"

"Yes. Please go now. You must go."

After she's gone, Amah goes to the bathing room and takes down the portrait of Begam Sahiba, feeling for the seam in the wall. The lantern goes out, and she returns to Begam Sahiba's rooms to find a new candle. Feeling along a low table, she finds a candle and a single ruby. She hears a rifle crack, and looks out the window at the lamplit garden below. Shahzadi could be sleeping but the rifle lies in the grass and the tiger does not move. Begam Sahiba runs into the darkness, vanishing toward the carriage and the palanquins.

* * *

In the morning, Amah is on the roof at the back of Qaisarbagh, hidden by tree branches. The kitchens are silent. She found the seam in the wall, pulling it open to reveal the hidden cavity with Begam Sahiba's money and jewels. The second candle went out and in the early dawn she heard the cheers of English soldiers breaking into Qaisarbagh Palace. She'd run to her room to find an old black robe and a veil—a black woman in black that the English wouldn't see. She put a pistol down the front of her rose-coloured silk trousers under the black robe. Her hands were shaking and she was taking too long. She dug fast for the box under the prayer mat in her mother's room but it was empty, as she'd really known, and her nails were bloody and dirty. She'd got to the ladder at the back of the palace just in time, carrying a box filled with betel leaves from the kitchen to hide Begam Sahiba's money and jewels.

Thousands of Englishmen enter their home, splitting open mermaids and pistachios, smashing glass and china on the marble terraces.

Hidden in the trees on the roof, she watches alone, the only one left to be the eyes and ears for the palace. Christian soldiers from England—milling everywhere in the bright sunshine—stuff her home into their knapsacks—Kashmir shawls and dresses, rifles and muskets, gold and silver and rubies, rolled up tapestries, silks, brocade, silver plates and gold bowls, lamps, ornate hookahs, and black swans.

Amah crouches behind a brass dome, holding her box. She leans her head against the dome's warmth. Several small, white pigeons bob toward her, across the roof, their eyes meeting hers, their heads cocked, as if she might have something for them.

A fire leaps in Shahzadi's garden. Men dump papers and newsletters into it. By late morning, many of the men are drunk, gorging on valuables and wine. Someone has pulled down the great oil paintings of the *nawabs* from the front hall and has dragged them out to the gardens. The *nawabs* silently observe the men pissing against the neem trees; they contemplate these men who have not bathed. The *nawabs* do not reprimand the drunk man in the mermaid fountain who is laughing hysterically, poisoning the water, as his friends hoist Begam Sahiba's portrait under the Mermaid Gateway. The *nawabs* silently watch the men take turns shooting the Queen.

Amah slips down the trees outside the palace wall. She moves quickly into the canopied road's yellow light.

* * *

Thousands of English soldiers are on one big Easter egg hunt in Lucknow, searching for golden egg-pearls. Round-faced, Sanskrit-loving Nepali poets in uniforms pluck vases from noblemen's homes and pluck coins from the bank. English bugles haunt every street corner where Union Jack flags are stuck into the flower beds. The men overturn stones in courtyards and gardens to unearth years of savings—dirty boxes filled with rubies, diamonds, and pearls worth thousands of English pounds. They find treasure hidden in walls and in the lips of wells. In Chowk, they steal Judea's gold bangles and rubies, his strings of pearls. They crowd around, taunting, when he begs them to let him buy them back, his hands outstretched. Judea offers *rupees* but they won't give the jewels back. Around Judea,

Chowk is full of poisoned wells, crumbling fish archways, and bandsmen with defeated, dusty trumpets.

A soldier puts his boot on Amah's shoe and grabs her box of betel leaves. Shaking it, he finds the *rupees* and jewels hidden under the layers of leaves. He takes the box and tells her to move along. After that, no one notices her in her old, black clothing. She hides in the broken gardens, hugs the walls. There are English and Nepali men shooting anyone, and she keeps her pistol hidden. She watches Indians change sides, and other men who were spies all along touch English feet.

No one swims in the Gomti. Amah sees Hasan's old friend with the bony face, Omar, squatting on a big rock at the water's edge. Dressed in a *lungi,* he smokes a *beedi.*

He glances at her. "Yes?"

"Do you know the officer with red hair? His name is John Graham. Have you seen him?"

"He is everywhere now."

"I need to find out where he is staying."

He juts his chin toward the city.

"Where?" she asks.

He keeps silent, smokes some more. After a while, he says, "What payment can you make?" and flicks the stub of the *beedi* into the water. "I am leaving today."

She scans the beach but they are alone. She pulls out the lone ruby she found on the table in Begam Sahiba's rooms. She hands it to him. He rolls Amah's ruby, the size of a pigeon's egg, between his fingers.

"In the street closest to Hazratganj," he says. "This side of it. Second to last house. He doesn't stay there much. He surely has taken over a few places." He gives the ruby back to her. "I hope that you find him."

* * *

In Chowk, Amah sees Gulbadan's brother repairing a telegraph line. She lifts her veil. "What are you doing?" she asks.

He stares at her like he's seen a *jinni,* then returns to his task. "I need to eat," he says.

"Where is Gulbadan? Is she still at the *kotha*?"

"Don't go to the *kotha*. Don't go. They told me to get out of their sight or they'd kill me. Gulbadan would not want you to take the risk." He picks up a piece of copper wire. Amah continues to stare at him. "Look, I have two choices," he says. "I can work on the telegraph or I can work on the new road they already plan to build straight through Qaisarbagh Palace. I chose this. Do you understand?"

***

At the *kotha*, a hundred Englishmen's hands have left the drawers open in Gulbadan's pavilion. A hundred Englishmen's boots have dirtied the silk pillows in the courtyard. Gulbadan is tied to the peepul tree with its heart-shaped leaves. The courtesans' teak rooms against the stony hill are silent hives of broken activity. Curtains flung against windows hang there embarrassed. She unties Gulbadan, stands near the marigolds, listens to Gulbadan's story, and sweats in her *burqa*.

Those soldiers and Red Man stood in a line to inspect the Indian and African women who gave lessons in etiquette and social graces, who taught Lakhnavi children how to put other people first. The women sat together, Gulbadan says, their hands quietly clasped, women with kohl-lined eyes who made nonsense of all the inspecting.

The prize of all of Lucknow's prizes. The loot of all loot. The extra Easter eggs found in a basket of marigolds. An accordion squeezes in and out. Like history. Amah listens to Gulbadan's words. She hears Red Man say, "Finders, keepers." She sees him take the young woman with the plait by the arm. "Finders, keepers," he says again to the young woman who'd worked so hard to find her voice here.

Gulbadan continues. Responsibility has come to rest on Englishmen's thin shoulders for the needs of two thousand soldiers who will stay to do the dirty work and resettle Lucknow. The dirty soldiers in dirty clothes will have their needs. Men who have never been to India before, who do not know Urdu or Persian. Men whose needs need to be contained. Two hundred men to one woman. "We need to keep things clean," Gulbadan says they will say. "Contain disease. Clean up the city, limit effluence."

For their part in helping to defend Lucknow, this outrageous insolence, the courtesans have paid and will pay some more. Not like their patrons who paid in *rupees* and ruby bracelets. They won't pay in dance or poems. Nor in late-evening songs. Oh no. The soldiers pulled the women into the teak rooms, and closed the doors. Amah can hear the shouts of women surprised by pinched arms and dirty names.

Thuds on wood. Muffled grunts. Screams die against silk pillows embroidered with gilded fish, gurgling underwater, silent pockets of poems wriggling to the surface, causing quiet bubbles in a strong swell, underwater sea horses galloping. Silk sheets bunched up to hide history's stains. Mutinous courtesans rendered silent.

Amah helps the older woman down the stairs. They walk past Chowk's shops that are being sacked, toward the courtesans' empty shop. "Young Geeta left for Faizabad," Gulbadan says.

"Rest in her shop," Amah says. "I have something to do."

"Life suddenly deals sadness. Such sadness. Just like that."

Amah says, "Rest. I have something to do."

Further on, an old vendor's eyes light up when he sees Amah. He says nothing, but he holds out a *chapati* as she passes. On the street near Hazratganj, the main road, where Red Man lives, she crouches beside a rain pipe and eats the *chapati*. She waits all night, but no one goes in or comes out of the house where he supposedly stays. But at dawn, she sees him come down the street, leader of English thieves, his red hair made darker in the low light. He moves from one side of the road to the other like a wandering minstrel-thief in the *chikan*-embroidered shawl that is draped over his shoulders. His gaze, soft from wine, slides over Amah and to the rain pipe, to the wall beside her. He swoons away to the other side of the road, and then he starts back toward her. She waits until he comes abreast of her, and she lifts her veil.

She gets up, and, when he sees her gun, he bows and pats his legs as if he's searching for a cheroot or a match, but she knows he is looking for his own gun. He wears topaz rings on the index and third fingers of one hand. She stares at his laughing face, sees Pavan try to get up on his sick pony, hears the scream of an elephant like wild pigs, smells the stench in a jail cell, feels the acceptance of death in blue-breasted quails and a soldier boy with gold earrings, tastes ashes in the sand where Sai died. The sweat starts in her scalp, like burning rain, and her mouth is full of ashes and hot sand. She thinks she can hear a mournful song on a courtesan's lips, but then she hears bagpipes, and butterflies caress her hand, bringing the pistol forth, and the butterflies caress her sweating fingers, and she shoots him. Her pistol cracks against the morning air, the sound bouncing off brass domes and *nawabs*' tombs, and it settles down upon them. Her bullet reaches Red Man's stolen shawl and closes his wine-drenched mouth, and his hand paws the air as he falls.

Amah goes straight to the Gomti and takes off her black clothing. In her trousers and red jacket, she kneels in the water, turns her back for good on death-dealing violence, and prays alone in the dawn. Her heavy head falls down in the water like it is made of stone.

* * *

She crosses the Iron Bridge and walks past the charred cantonment and the racecourse on the other side of the river. On the Faizabad Road, a man driving a bullock cart slows, a stranger to town trying to make fares. Vendors selling *paan* pass her on their way to Chowk.

It's always dawn and the heat is always about to burn the sky. It's the day her mother leaves. It's the day that Sai is dying. It's the day Begam Sahiba is gone. Old trees bend with baby mangoes. The sky is indigo blue; a flock of golden-green, silk-winged pigeons fills it. She walks onwards, down Faizabad Road.

The heat gathers, the air like hammers now. It breaks over her, cloaks her in perspiration. She glimpses a kadam tree with orange blossoms, a tamarind tree laden with rubies as big as a child's hands, a red sun setting over Lucknow.

It is getting late.

And then she sees them. Malamud is wearing rags. He walks beside a cart that carries Gulbadan, the tall driver on a donkey out in front. The driver turns a little, and Amah recognizes Omar's bony face. Gulbadan is stooped and frail and they move slowly, the cart kicking up a little dust, and Amah sees how hard Omar is working to soften the ride. Amah can call out, but they are up ahead. A shout would startle the sky; all the heat would muffle her words.

They do not look back but keep their pace. No one says to Amah, Come with me. No one tells her to stay. No one says, Turn around now. She feels the pulsing heat and her own body's pulses.

She catches up to them, lets the perspiration drip off her face. She smells Malamud's *beedi,* like burning leaves, and feels silk when she puts her hand on Gulbadan's shoulder. Gulbadan reaches for Amah's hand, holds it tight. "Like a daughter," she says.

Amah turns to Malamud. "Where are you going?" she asks.

A white pigeon circles the bright, blue sky, follows them, calling *Yahu.* "To change our kismet," he says, and smiles sadly. He touches her bangles, looks up at the bird in the sky. "Let's mould our fate, Amah. Let's find our place."

POSTSCRIPT

IT IS NOT POSSIBLE to know the number of Indians who died in Lucknow during the uprising against the English but most certainly the number is in the many thousands. After 1858, British investigations verified that no Englishwomen had been raped in the Cawnpore massacre, although that myth circulated in England for many years, and is still mistakenly reported today.

The Indo-African population (or *sheedis*, as they are called in India) dwindled significantly after the uprising against English rule in 1857. British "forgiveness policies" that followed the sacking of Lucknow were never granted to Indo-Africans, and, for decades, they continued to be economically punished for their part in the resistance in Lucknow. Much of the community remains destitute today.

The courtesan profession, so highly regarded for centuries in Lucknow, was gradually debased into common prostitution under British law.

Begam Hazrat Mahal (Begam Sahiba) died in Kathmandu, Nepal, in 1879 where she was granted refuge by the ruler of Nepal, Jang Bahadur Sahib, after fleeing from Lucknow in 1858.

His Majesty, Wajid 'Ali Shah, was offered a pension by the English in November, 1858, and he accepted it. He spent the rest of his days at the "Lucknow" he created in Calcutta.

The Queen Mother died in Paris on her way back to India. Her unmarked grave was identified in 2000 but, according to the historian, Rosie Llewellyn-Jones, the short notice posted about her at the grave is full of mistakes.

The royal cousins, held prisoners in the Residency, were released in Calcutta in 1859.

Brigadier General James Neill was actually killed as he approached the Residency on September 25, 1857. Memorials to him were erected in Lucknow and Madras, as well as in Scotland. Neill was commemorated in Lucknow by the British who named an area in the city after him, called "Neill Lines." An island in the Andamans was also named after him, to honour him, and is still called Neill Island today.

Jai Lal Singh was hanged in 1859 by the English in front of Star House for his involvement in the uprising.

Thomas Kavanagh, who took a message from the Residency to the relieving Forces at Alambagh Palace, was awarded the Victoria Cross and 20,000 pounds that he reportedly drank away.

Of the royal goods taken from Qaisarbagh's storerooms, only the jewellery was returned to Wajid 'Ali Shah sometime in or before 1860.

Four black swans were taken from Qaisarbagh Palace and given to Lady Charlotte Canning, the wife of Governor General Lord Charles Canning, in Calcutta. The city was severely looted in March 1858 when Lucknow was recaptured. Many treasures travelled to Britain from Lucknow. It is more than likely that the sale of prize items taken from Lucknow directly benefited Queen Victoria. The *Ishqnama* manuscript, the King's illustrated autobiography with the portrait of Begam Hazrat Mahal, was presented to Queen Victoria in 1859. It languished at Windsor Castle until it was properly identified by the historian, Rosie Llewellyn-Jones, very recently. It remains in the British royal family's possession today.

A British fear of Islamic activism was initiated in large part by the uprising against the English East India Company in Lucknow when Muslims were disproportionately blamed. The misrepresentation of Indians in general as evil, a stereotype that stemmed from the uprising, has never entirely disappeared in Britain.

The English East India Company had already been criticized for its policies in British Parliament and also in editorials in London's newspapers prior to the uprising but in 1858, due perhaps especially to the difficulties the English East India Company experienced in Lucknow, the British Government under Queen Victoria dissolved the Company and took direct control of all English-ruled land in India. Their control continued until Gandhi's national polices of nonviolence gained ground, and the British finally were forced to leave India in 1947, ninety years after the failed resistance in Lucknow.

Lucknow never recovered its former glory as an internationally recognized cultural centre with its diverse world outlooks and its wealth of art and music. Thousands of Indians were buried in the demolition and renewed English construction. They remain nameless, unlike the tributes to the English on statues in India that still can be found in rather amazing numbers today.

Acknowledgements

———•◆••◆•———

MY GREAT-GREAT-GREAT AUNT, Ellen Huxham, whose diary was the inspiration for this work, and also a source, was the last English survivor of the group held in the Residency during the siege. She died in Boxhill, England, aged 96.

This book would never have been possible without the incredible work that has been accomplished by the historian Rosie Llewellyn-Jones on the Indian uprising, the city of Lucknow, the virtual discovery of Afro-Indian resistances during the uprising, and on the actions of the English in Lucknow and elsewhere in India. I deeply thank her for a first reading of the manuscript (although all factual and other errors that remain are mine), and for her excellent suggestions over many drafts that helped to create this fiction.

Saleem Kidwai graciously completed a final reading of the manuscript, and I am indebted to him for his corrections.

I am also grateful to other vital readers and those who very much helped this novel along its way: the All India Democratic Women's Association (AIDWA), Julianna Baggott, Wynna Brown, Roger N. Buckley, Janet Burroway, Heather and Maurice Cullity, Mark Eagles, Mary Ferguson, Demira Handzic, Cathy Hird, Miriam Hird-Younger, Nathan Hird-Younger, Kay Irvine, Milton Israel, Royce Kallerud, Brinda Karat, Catharine Leggett, James Alan McPherson, Karen McElmurray, Chinna Oommen, Prajwal Parajuly, Jay Parini, Judy Polumbaum, Palagummi Sainath, the Progressive Women's Spiritual Council,

Gerry Shikatani, Jael Silliman, Lee Smith, Janet Sylvester, Joe Visconti, Adelaide Whitaker, Heather Whitaker, Mark Wine-gardner, and Paul Younger.

I am sincerely grateful to Luciana Ricciutelli, Editor-in-Chief, for her faith and for her great commitment to Inanna writers, and also to Inanna's publicist, Renée Knapp, for all her terrific energy. A big thank you to Jocelyn Sealy who produced the map with her usual flare and fine spirit.

A Writer's Reserve Grant from Insomniac Press through the Ontario Arts Council in Toronto, Ontario, Canada got the project started. A New England Writer's Scholarship from A Room of Her Own Foundation allowed me time to explore the story with other women during the writing of the manuscript. Trinity College in Hartford, Connecticut generously granted me funding to travel to India, research assistants, Greg Leitao and Caroline Healy, and access to a fine librarian, Katherine Hart. Thank you to the School of Arts and Letters, and the Department of English and Linguistics, at Truman State University for travel grants to produce final revisions and first public readings of the work, and to my student at Truman, Jessica Howard, who launched the online material. This novel was written with enormous affection for Sister Jo-Ann Iannotti at Wisdom House as well as for Preston Browning at Wellspring House who warmly facilitated so many writing retreats.

Certainly not least, this book would never have been without my parents and especially my mother and her family's generations of stories about India that were passed on to me, and for a family donation that allowed me time. Thank you.

And finally, this is for Prakash, Leela, and Meenakshi—whose love, patience, humour, and support have been invaluable.

* * *

The looting and deliberate destruction of property in Lucknow in 1858 mean that many vital sources of Indian perspectives on the uprising in Lucknow have been lost forever. The following primary and secondary sources were instrumental to this work of fiction and would be of great use to anyone further interested in the subject.

Begum of Oudh, Counter-Proclamation by the Begum of Oudh in reply to Proclamation of Queen Victoria November 1, 1858. Available at: http://oudh.tripod.com/bhm/bhmproc.htm.

Edwardes, Herbert Benjamin, Sir, and Herman Merivale. *Life of Sir Henry Lawrence, Volume II*. London: Smith, Elder & Co., 1872.

Ghose, Indira, ed. *Memsahibs Abroad*. Delhi: Oxford University Press, 1998.

Ghose, Indira. *Women Travellers in Colonial India: The Power of the Female Gaze*. Delhi: Oxford University Press, 1998.

Hibbert, Christopher. *The Great Mutiny*. London: Penguin Books Ltd., 1978.

Humphries, James, ed. *Mutiny: 1857*. Leonaur Ltd., 2007.

Knighton, William. *Elihu Jan's Story or The Private Life of an Eastern Queen*. London: Longman, Green, Longman, Roberts, & Green, 1865.

Llewellyn-Jones, Rosie. "Africans in the Indian Mutiny." *History Today*, Volume 59, Issue 12, December 2009.

Llewellyn-Jones, Rosie. *Engaging Scoundrels: True Tales of Old Lucknow*. New Delhi: Oxford University Press, 2000.

Llewellyn-Jones, Rosie. *Lucknow: Then and Now*. Mumbai: Marg Publications, 2003.

Llewellyn-Jones, Rosie. *Lucknow: City of Illusion*. Munich: Prestel, 2006.

Llewellyn-Jones, Rosie. *The Great Uprising in India 1857-58*. Woodbridge, Suffolk: The Boydell Press, 2007.

Llewellyn-Jones, Rosie. *Portraits in Princely India 1700-1947*. Mumbai: Marg Publications, 2008.

Llewellyn-Jones, Rosie. *The Last King in India: Wajid 'Ali Shah*. London: C. Hurst & Co. (Publishers) Ltd., 2014.

MacMillan, Margaret. *Women of the Raj*. New York: Random House Trade Paperbacks, 2007 (originally published by Thames and Hudson Ltd., London, 1988).

Majendie, Vivian Dering. *Up Among the Pandies*. Forgotten Books, 2012.

Oldenburg, Veena Talwar. "Lifestyle as Resistance: The Case of the Courtesans of Lucknow." *Lucknow: Memories of a City*. Ed. Violette Graff. New Delhi: Oxford University, 1997.

Rees, L.E. Ruutz. *A Personal Narrative of the Siege of Lucknow From Its Commencement to Its Relief by Sir Colin Campbell*. Elibron Classics, 2005.

Ruswa, Mirza Muhammad Hadi. *Umrao Jan Ada*. New Delhi: Rupa Publications India Pvt. Ltd., 1996.

The Lucknow Omnibus—a compilation of three essential works: Abdul Halim Sharar's *Lucknow: The Last Phase of an Oriental Culture*, Rosie Llewellyn-Jones' *A Fatal Friendship: The Nawabs, the British and the City of Lucknow*, and Veena Talwar Oldenburg's *The Making of Colonial Lucknow: 1856-1877*. New Delhi: Oxford University Press, 2001.

***

The author and publisher would like to thank the following for permission to use details:

Oxford University Press:

Ghose, Indira, ed. *Memsahibs Abroad*. Delhi: Oxford University Press, 1998.

Ghose, Indira. *Women Travellers in Colonial India: The Power of the Female Gaze*. Delhi: Oxford University Press, 1998.

Graff, Violette, ed. *Lucknow: Memories of a City*. New Delhi: Oxford University Press, 1997.

The Lucknow Omnibus. New Delhi: Oxford University Press, 2001.

Photo: Taisia Gordon

Jocelyn Cullity's English family lived in India for five generations. Her short stories and essays have been published in American, Canadian, and Indian journals and anthologies; her award-winning documentary film about women and social change in China, *Going to the Sea*, aired on television and in festivals in Canada, the United States, and in Europe. She is currently completing a second novel. Cullity has a Ph.D. in Creative Writing from Florida State University and is currently the Director of the BFA in Creative Writing program at Truman State University. She lives in Columbia, Missouri, with her husband, the film scholar Prakash Younger, and their two daughters. Visit her website at: www.jocelyncullity.com.